Edited By Susannah Carlson & Shelley Valdez

What We Talk About When We Talk About It

Variations on the Theme of Love

VOLUME 1

What We Talk About
When We Talk About It

Edited by
Susannah Carlson and Shelley Valdez

Copyrights

TABLE OF CONTENTS

TABLE OF CONTENTS

The Origin
by Kelly Magee

Once, a girl found a stray tornado. She lured it inside with a dog biscuit. It was a juvenile, so she kept it in a box beside her bed. Sort of brindle, like her second dog. But blurrier. Twice a day, she fed it dry leaves in a stainless bowl. It preferred saltwater to fresh. She named it Tor because she was not particularly creative and liked to call things what they were.

Training left her bruised. The tornado pulled on the leash, gagged over the collar. Once it bit her, and she had to get six stitches in her palm. The Urgent Care doctor made a joke about fashioning her a new lifeline.

"A prosthetic future," he called it.

"My life will be different now," she told him, thinking of the tornado. "That's for sure."

When asked about the origin of the wound, she blamed it on a vicious, unidentifiable dog, then regretted her choice when the doctor brought up rabies. She didn't know if tornadoes could carry rabies or not, and it wasn't the kind of thing she could easily find out. She didn't know anyone else to whom this had happened, and internet searches proved useless, so she went ahead and got the shots.

At home, the tornado sniffed the raw gridwork of her hand and spun placidly on the floor all night, as sorry-seeming as a tornado could be.

—————————·••·—————————

In two weeks, it reached shoulder height; in a month, it outgrew her. She wasn't sure if she should keep it, but she didn't like goodbyes. The tornado filled the house in a way that seemed familiar, all clamor and bustle. Anything not secured blew around wildly, so she boxed up most of her things. The wind made the faucet spray her right in the face if she forgot to shut the bathroom door. The windows rattled; her hair tangled. When the tornado got excited, the ceiling fans spun in reverse. When she spoke gibberish into its funnel, the words came back in order.

Everything happens for a reason, it said.

Take all the time you need, it said.

Don't flip out on me, Susan, it said.

She didn't know who Susan was, but of course the house was haunted. Anyone could've told her that. It'd been fully furnished when she moved in. She'd brought some clothes and books, hung and stacked them next to the existing ones, and now she couldn't remember which were legitimately hers. The handwriting in the books was so similar, and the clothes fit so well, that they might as well have been her own.

The yards in this part of town were built to prevent neighborliness, with aggressive layers of hedges and fences and underbrush, so no one need know the new pet/roommate she'd acquired. She had one neighbor whom she saw exactly twice a year, when he asked permission to collect blackberries from her yard in the summer and when he reminded her to top her trees in the fall, which she never did. He lived with a wife the girl had not met or even seen. She only knew the wife existed because her neighbor referred to himself in the plural, the way married couples do. For all she knew, when he said 'we,' he could've meant himself and his tornado.

"We were wondering if you're going to use all those blackberries," he'd said this past spring, as he did every year.

"Help yourself," the girl said, as she always did. "We won't be using them."

When he came by in the fall, she hadn't answered the door. Her neighbor must've heard the breaking glass, the pounding and yelling, and assumed what he assumed. He didn't return.

<hr>

Her second dog ran away, so she taught the tornado to fetch. It was easy to teach when it wanted to learn, which made her suspect it was older than she'd initially thought. Maybe tornadoes didn't have ages, or maybe, for them, size wasn't proportionate to age. It grew and shrank with its moods, if you could call them moods, though not in any predictable way. Its happiness posed as much of a danger as its anger, the way both generated mid-sized ball lightning that left scorch marks on the wood floors and burned holes in the walls. She cleaned up or repaired its messes, and coached the tornado to contain itself as best it could. Her favorite times were when, in sleep, its wall clouds relaxed and covered the room in soft, gray fog. Some nights the girl climbed inside the funnel and slept suspended two feet off the ground in a white-noise wind-hive where she could not hear her dreams.

Other nights, she dreamt that the trees she'd neglected to top as advised fell and crushed her in her sleep.

To teach it how to fetch, she had to take the tornado outside. They started in the backyard. Once, she threw a stick, and the tornado brought back an apple tree. She quickly harvested the carefully tended fruit and shoved the tree husk into a ditch where the previous occupants had discarded their Christmas trees. She'd stumbled on the Christmas tree graveyard while searching for a suitable graveyard-graveyard for her first dog, who'd died right after she'd moved in. At the time, she thought the dog must've gotten into something poisonous in the overgrown yard—mushrooms, perhaps, or bella donna—but after a thorough search, she'd found nothing. She buried him by the woodshed, nervous over every shovelful. The house was haunted, after all; who knew what she might dig up? She found nothing but rocks, so many big rocks that it took her all day to dig deep enough, which was okay because she wasn't looking forward to the next step, which was dragging the dog into it. She didn't call anyone because, in that part of town, there was no one to call. She'd gone over to her neighbor's house, but no one was home.

The largest rock, she'd used as a headstone. The rest she piled into a decorative firepit. She didn't intend to ever build a fire.

She tried again. She threw the ball, and the tornado brought back a tire.

She threw the ball, and the tornado brought back a cracked windshield.

She threw the ball, and the tornado brought back the rest of the wrecked car, which she pushed into the street in front of her neighbor's house.

She didn't like where this was headed, so she tried throwing a stuffed toy instead. The tornado brought back her second dog.

She buried him by the woodshed with the first. The tornado spun the hole in five minutes flat. It seemed a little too happy to help. This was how the girl came to understand that the tornado needed to go. She suspected that living with a tornado would mean having to regularly bury things, and she wanted to be done with burying things now.

She put its bowl outside and shut the door. What was she supposed to do? There wasn't a shelter she could call, and she certainly wasn't turning it over to a meteorologist or a storm chaser. It was a stout and ferocious tornado, but also, in its way, a little naïve about the outside world. A little sheltered. Stuck outside, it pawed at the door with mid-level winds, whirled in a slumped way. The girl tried to feel good about being able to brush her hair for the first time in months, to read a book. But even with her bedroom door closed, she could hear its sad scraping out front. Her bed felt muggy and stagnant, her body feverish. She'd become accustomed to the noise of the wind, and now understood what people meant when they called silence deafening.

The tornado stayed on the stoop the whole first night. In the morning, she filled its bowl and sat in the yard, throwing balls that it brought back exactly as they were, as if obedience was the solution.

After a while, she went back inside. She left the tornado out, and again, it stayed on the stoop all night.

The third night, it left. She listened to it go, holding her breath. It was back by morning, sleeping heavily, its wall clouds wispy and discolored.

The fourth night, it didn't come back.

The girl tried to read but couldn't concentrate. She walked around her neighborhood, telling herself she wasn't listening for the tornado, looking into the dark windows of the houses around her. The wrecked car was where she'd left it. The trees tossed ominously overhead.

She considered leaving town but didn't like to drive. Anyway, there was nowhere else to go. She could always change her mind, she thought, leave another night, or come back, or do something altogether different. It was important to remember, during hard times, that you could always do something altogether different.

When she got home, she turned on the TV, something she hadn't done in all the time she'd lived here. The first station was network news, so she watched that. She watched it night after night while waiting to see if the tornado would return. People went missing during this time because people were always going missing one way or another, so the girl didn't think anything of the reports she saw. Except for one. The one was her own. The reporters seemed to have confused her with someone else. It was her face on the screen, but they called her a wife and mother. They showed a picture of her street with the wrecked car in front of her neighbor's house. The car must've belonged to the missing woman, she thought, which sort of explained the confusion. And sort of did not. Then a cop with streaming blue eyes said her name into the camera. His pronunciation was off, but it was definitely her name. He looked like a fountain, like not really crying. It would be unusual for a cop to cry like that. The tears disappeared under his chin.

The girl went to the police department with a case of mistaken identity.

"That poor woman deserves to be found, whoever she is," she told the front desk. "She has a husband and children."

She was given a can of soda and told to wait right there.

She waited for a long time, long enough for the soda to give her a stomachache and then for the stomachache to subside. Long enough to wonder if she should leave, to give it five more minutes, and to think at the end of the five minutes, What if I leave and they come right now? Long enough to wonder what if she did have a husband and children that she'd somehow managed to forget, and was that even possible, and if it was, how, and did it even matter if it was possible or not if it happened to you, and hasn't the whole idea of impossibility gone stale in this world of medical miracles and technological marvels, and isn't the real impossibility life itself, like how does anyone survive infancy let alone childhood, with so many dangers stacked against them, a list of dangers so long you could start now and never reach the end? Long enough to wonder how much of one's future could be sewn into the skin by a qualified doctor.

Eventually, a uniformed officer emerged from behind a partition and lumbered toward her. His body puffed out, like it wanted to burst from its clothes. At first, she thought he must be a superhero. A breeze blew back her bangs as he approached. Her ears popped. He moved his jaw like it was a new appendage, then said her name with the same incorrect pronunciation, but also like a question.

"Do I know you?" she said.

"You must," he said.

She rose, cupped her hands around her mouth, and blew speech sounds into his ear.

"Time heals all wounds," he said.

She understood, and was both afraid and intrigued. She was a mixed-up mess of many things, which was why people always trusted her.

They walked to a private room, him leaning heavily on her arm, nearly pulling her down. His skin vibrated, vented from every pore. She figured he couldn't be too dangerous in a public place, which was the logic for strangers but not storms. He was both and neither. As so often happened to her, she had no idea how to protect herself. She was charmed by the lengths he'd gone to for her, and she wanted to believe that a man was somehow safer than a tornado.

This is called magical thinking.

"What should I call you?" she asked him.

"Whatever you want to," he said.

She called him Tor. He gave her bold coffee, which made her rattle on about her life, all the things he didn't know, which was mostly a catalog of news stories. She thought of the tornado as he now because of the human form. He kept forgetting to blink, then scrubbing with fists at his eyes when they blurred over. She realized that a body must be a lot to keep track of.

Finally, he shoved back his chair, stood, and said abruptly, "Maybe I could visit you sometime."

She put down her cup. "Yes. Yes, I think so."

"Maybe that time is right now."

"Oh," she said. "Okay."

Sometimes the girl did things without questioning why she was doing them, even though she knew the thing she was doing was exactly the kind of thing she should question. This was one of those times.

As she led him down the hall, down the elevator, and out into the day, she thought instead about how many of the people they passed might be inhabited by storms. It would explain a lot, she thought. It might even provide some comfort, letting humanity off the hook as it did.

On the train home, she thought it again. Suddenly people seemed so much more understandable to her.

The cop was not just any storm; she hadn't forgotten that he'd killed her dog. But it was kind of like when your cat brought home a dead bunny. You could keep the cat inside or get rid of the cat, but you didn't get mad at it for being a cat.

So, she took the tornado into her home again, this time as a cop in a uniform he wouldn't take off. He sat unevenly on a stool at her counter, working at good posture and polite behavior, and attempted to drink a glass of water by pouring it in his mouth and jerking his head back. When she told him to make himself at home, he collapsed on the floor. She lay beside him for a while, unsure what was possible or appropriate.

"I missed you," she said.

He took her hand, but while she waited for what would come next, he began to snore. The snoring sounded like a waterfall and smelled like cut grass. When it was clear he was not going to wake anytime soon, she turned on the TV news, but someone else had gone missing, a man, so she quickly changed the station. Landed on a show called How Are We All Not Dead? that investigated the lethal potential embedded in everyday objects as evidenced in actual police and autopsy reports, narrated intermittently by a cartoon pirate. Number 42: stapler. Number 43: vacuum. The show was too aware of its attempts to be funny to be funny. It couldn't figure out its genre. The girl had too much time to think about it while the cop's snores spun in eddies around the room.

At some point, she slept, trying not to sleep. She didn't want him to wake without her. She dreamed she was a wife and mother, but her husband was a tornado and her children were dogs.

She woke feeling grateful, and almost without thinking, laid her body on top of the cop's. He stirred, the tornado already pacing inside, the human skin like a gate from which it longed to burst.

"Are you able to come out?" she whispered in his ear.

"If you want me to," he whispered back.

She didn't. She blew gibberish into the cop's ear and he said, "We need to talk" and "It's nobody's fault" and "Don't leave like this, Susan."

"Who is Susan?" she said, and he said, "I thought you knew."

The tornado pressed on her through the cop's body, and she pressed back in a familiar way. She still didn't know what was appropriate, but now she knew what was possible. They both unzipped but stayed mostly clothed. The tornado didn't know what it was doing, but the girl did. During, she thought they might be in love. After, she thought not.

"You can't stay in there forever," she told him, but she was also fishing for information.

"No," he said. "But if I could?"

She felt terrible. Her heart kept jumping out of windows before she could talk it down.

"I can't stay here either," she told him. "This house is extremely haunted."

"I never noticed," he said.

She left barefoot. The trees were swaying as they always were. Someone, maybe her neighbor, had pushed the wrecked car farther down the street. The houses were all unlit, though she could see those peripheral movements that disappeared when you looked at them directly.

Once again, something was happening to her that she could not explain or even tell anyone about. But everyone walked around with impossible things lodged in them like splinters. They had survived what they could not have survived. They loved what they should not. They lost what they could not bear to lose.

The Alchemyst
by Sage

The alchemyst pulls astrolabe after
astrolabe out of his seamed chest.

They pile up like tiny microbes on the table
then spill over as giant organisms on the floor.

It's all very interesting, but not as promised
by his billboard on the side of I-80

where that Coca Cola truck tipped over
and wiped out a whole family of deer

grazing on a patch of heather near the curb.
When my mother calls and asks

"How's life on the West Coast?" I like to tell her
the deer here are just as timid as back home.

I'm lying, of course—I've been close enough
to some to touch their noses with my hand.

Once, on the drive home from school at night,
my high beams caught a young buck on the road.

He stood there in the middle of the pavement
staring me down through the windshield

and I realized every metaphor of deer and headlights
was wrong. There was no fear in his eyes.

Only teenage rebellion, young-adult-invincibility.
"Strike me down and the sky will weep

but it won't weep for you." I have crying trouble.
What I mean is, I have trouble crying.

Every three months I tell my body "Let it out"
but my body is still fighting every war declared on it

since last Tuesday. There is still a part of me that knows
we all have a last Tuesday, a final straw.

A prophet and his boys sat on some straw
when they had their last supper together

before the night was ruined by a kiss.
That's how it is between boys.

Close enough to know a kiss means nothing,
afraid enough to know nothing can mean everything.

"You're more timid out here," I say
to the young stag standing silent

and pale in my headlights. I say this
to convince myself. It's not me, it's the deer

who doesn't want to make the first move.
A sound from the bushes, some doe

or another buck come to see the ruckus.
That's what we're doing out here, right?

We make a ruckus, we make a scene.
We make ourselves seen.

It's a transformation, like blood into wine,
like boy into boy. I've drawn the circles

and systems to my center of mass.
The rest is a waiting game with gravity.

The thing about alchemy is you never get gold
on the first try. The thing about patience is

it has to last a lifetime. And even then there's no telling
if the one holding you at night has dreams of you

the way you dream of them. There's no telling
when the axe will fall, unseam your chest,

and spill a world out into the world.

WHAT SHE TOLD ME WAS THIS
by MeeRee Orlandini

If I were to describe you I would just describe all the things that aren't you.

Healthy eater, honey dipper, heartless or toothless, owns a Maserati, takes me to Taco Bell.

In a hundred years you're going to be dead and you know what you're going to be thinking? You're going to wish you came out with me tonight.

And you can tell him that I don't care if he hasn't slept for 10 years. If a beautiful woman asks you to go to a bar, you go.

And you can tell him that I would like the Christina Satin Bodysuit with his discount at Urban Outfitters.

You aren't ugly. You aren't crazy. You aren't sad. I've gotta be honest with you, though, you are way out of their league.

I told everyone at the party, "You know I love you, baby, but I gotta go," then, I came and found you.

Will you move to Japan with me? Join a Zen Buddhist monastery and become enlightened? I want to become enlightened. Why don't you want to be enlightened?

You shouldn't eat so much butter. Butter is bad for you. Butter is the leading cause of death.

Ramen, Bukowski, shrimp tempura, make a list of the definites, here is mine:

No one younger than 21, no past allegations of abuse or assault, no drug addiction, no children, no fraternities, no serious belief in zodiac signs,

Passionate about human rights, loves animals, little to no interest in sports, no firefighters, police officers, politicians, models, DJs, lawyers.

I have my reasons.

Just don't have sex without me.

Keep my plant alive.

I'd like to straddle Tom Brady's big Italian sausage while his Italian meatballs slapped my thighs.

I'm kidding, don't tell him I said that.

On Either Side of Jonah
by Erika Rasmussen

Today, the fish I swallowed whole as a child stands still, fins paused for dramatic effect in my pancreas. That's where good things go to die. Limp and loaded, filtering oxygen and poetry through washboard gills, he settles, burbling like a baby would. The end is so like the beginning. Fragile. He rises from death on the fourth day. Thought about the third, but it was Sabbath. Back to the throat he swims, beast saddling my water, catfish snout breaking bread with the dark. Glides sweet, guzzling the chocolate silt. Now watch that thing swallow my body whole. All this running from destiny sets you right in the fish's mouth. Sour. But I welcome it, welcome the specks of light inside him, the dawn upon his whiskers. Get that out of here, that lack of imagination. Twist that unbelief until the bubbles speak, and your mother comes to ring the bell for supper. But she won't mind if you're still swimming. She never does.

Daddy's Girl
by Anonymous

I know where I belong. How could I not?
In the house where I was born, my father showed me what my life would be like. He put his hands around my little neck, and he locked his ankles around my little hips, and he told me, over and over again, that this is all I will ever be good for.

Some things you know way down deep. Some things you learn, and they go even further, they penetrate so far beneath the surface of your skin that their poison takes hold and grows and grows. Until all that you know how to sow is misery like the kind that you grew up with, misery like you think you know that's all that you will ever, ever get.

I'm not sure she had a name. I'm not sure what she looked like or what her voice sounded like because when I reach to that place where my memories of her lie, all I get is a hazy white fog. All I see is his face, hovering above me on my bed, telling me what I am worth. What I will always always be worth.

She was worth everything to me, that woman. Did I tell you that already? I want to push my face into her lap like a cat, I want to let her gold rub off on me. She is coated in a fine dust of perfect and that perfect looks gold and that is what I want, is to be perfect. Is to take on a little bit of her perfect until she can stand to look at me, the image I see in the mirror can look back at the person I am now, without seeing this. This thing I am monster and woman. The monster and the beauty. Some things work best in fairy tales. Some things should stay there.

I am that disgusting thing, now. Doesn't matter if I was originally. Some things change you and there is no going back, no matter how long you slog and I have been trying, I have read all the books on trauma, I have fought my way out of hell after hell but here I am. Ugly and all elbows. Hardly able to talk when it comes to those I love. Lonely, with eyes too big and a cunt too small.

When I think about sex, I think about my father. I think about burly men with too much hair, and I think about that hair scratching me, I think about the cheeks of a man who needs a shave. I think about what it means to be fucked like how fucking someone over and fucking them sometimes happen at the exact same time. I think about how if I ever want to be touched between my legs again then I had better resign myself to being laid out underneath some other man's body who is my man in another form but really the same. Always the same.

I think about how I will never escape my father. How being fat on me looks different from fat on other people, how other fat women get fucked or fuck and they wake up the next day next to partners who will be there the next day and the next. I think about how even love looks different on me, panicky, like need. Like desperation to be touched so when I get too desperate I stop eating. Or I find a way to get my body beneath some man's body who is my father with another face. I think about how if I want sex then I have to accommodate the pain and the tearing and the despair. How if I want to be normal, I have to lie and say I like it like this, I like the pain. If I am not a thing that someone hurts, fucks, tears open, then I will never be a thing that someone touches. Because I cannot be a thing someone uses I do not want to be a thing someone lays hold of just for fun then lets go of and. My father told me I will never be a thing that anyone loves.

I have to believe him. He's here, he's always here, in the corner of my mind where I have him penned up but not yet dead, no. Not yet.

If you help me kill my father in my mind, maybe I can save some part of myself that she can love. So I do not have to watch her from the corners and hate everyone else she dances with who is not me. I am really a very good dancer, it's just dancing is something I do not do, like laughing too loud or flirting with someone I would actually really really like to see naked or. Loving is something I am learning how to do but I am convinced I am doing it incorrectly. Even if no one else knows I know.

I know there is something wrong with me that pervades everything I do. I do. I know that.

I know I belong in the corner watching, and this woman who is me in another version of my life belongs in the center doing, and I cannot touch her, she whirls away and I want to follow and maybe she would have asked me to follow if I had told her I wanted to. There are so many maybes in this world in this life they pile on top of my chest I am the Wicked Witch of the East the maybes are the bricks of a house that belongs to some little girl who is not me. A little girl with a home to go back to.

It has taken me this long to learn that sexuality is not my enemy even though. Because I am touchable and it is not my fault the men who are my father in different forms do not ask first, it is not my fault they think that I want them or they think they can get away with touching me anyway. I want to be touched I want to be touched by her I want. To be touchable to the people that I love.

It has taken me this long to learn that sexuality is not my enemy even though. Because I am touchable and it is not my fault the men who are my father in different forms do not ask first, it is not my fault they think that I want them or they think they can get away with touching me anyway. I want to be touched

I want to be touched by her and loved I want. To be touchable to the people that I love.

I want to be touched by he/the person that I love.

I don't want to start a goddam revolution I just want her.

I don't want to start a goddam revolution but to let her love me back, I will. I will.

In My Movie, Everybody Dies:
An Open Letter to My Uncle
by Woody Woodger

Kent, how many years ago did we start letting so many puddles bloom between us? At what age do any men? We've run out of jackets to lay across the dirty water, to walk across in our lizard-lipped dudeness. I remember sitting in your living room every weekend. We'd watch a shitty Blockbuster, put some paper towels in the popcorn bowl just so we wouldn't have to wash it later. Our motto: minimal effort. You helped foster my love of not reading. Dyslexia made books so exhausting and you showed me how to just sit back, open my mouth, let the TV flick some reduced-fat truth straight at me, cheer when a single kernel went in. Easy was how we wanted our relationship to be. No, what's new at school, no political talk at the coffee table, Woody. Movies make it all look so easy, don't they, Kent? Heists, car crashes, seduction, acne, orca rearing, tuition—everything manageable, like origami backward, every conundrum slung over the hero's shoulder like a drag queen over a chaise longue. I'll tell you this much: without you and our marathons, Shia LeBeouf's stringy abs would never have snipped the flint of my back-alley gay. Perky pecs, the white meat. Same as our KFC order. You taught me a proper goatee should be as natural as a mother's shaved legs. Three bags of popcorn in, and you called it your rodeo-clown-gut. The way you laughed—it was like joy broke into you for the first time each time. A foreign tremor you fumbled with but never learned the steps to. When you were on your last bender, splayed out on your living room floor, covered in blood and vomit, it was Grandma who found you. Not like the movies. Not some Noir detectives in trench coats talking wise over your body. You were lucky, Kent. It could have been them. You died so soon after, it might as well have been. But Kent, this isn't us. You'd want another joke right? You were the "K-man", always buy-a-round-for-the-bar, still-saying-"bro"-at-55 kinda guy. But you probably don't want another joke about me and gay sex in an alley, right? Fine. You liked golf puns, right? I remember local newspaper comics clipped out and taped to your fridge--yellow, peeling. Ok, so: what do a dyslexic and an amateur golfer have in common?: A handicap. We liked our humor a little dark, didn't we? Another: what do you call sneaking a gin and tonic every time we drove?: training. How was your mutation from human to my material? I ended up there with you, fumbling with something dark, nervous as a movie screen right before it opens on the freckle-faced hero we've watched a thousand times before. I'm disappointed. I know how this is supposed to end.

Sixth Grade
by Lisa Dordal

Under a warm June sun during the break
between Social Studies and Language Arts,

they married us off. Our bodies surrounded
on the cracked pavement of our schoolyard

by friends, classmates, then
by something larger, sovereign and invisible.

Bruce in wide jeans, a pink Oxford button-down,
and brown tie-ups so shiny you could see birds

in the patches of sky they reflected. Everything
about him beautiful. Me, in a short purple dress

and soda-orange sneakers that the older sister
of my best friend told me had to go.

A boy named Peter officiated, spoke the words
that blended us together. The same boy

who told me there were two types
of women: that I was the kind men married,

not the kind men used for practicing
(what they never wanted to perfect).

Even in the race-sore seventies
on Chicago's South Side, no one minded

this one rupture, this one tear in the
taut dictates of order: that he was black

and I was white. But they wouldn't tolerate
our queerness. The clang of missed baskets—

other kids shooting hoops—was our music.
That, and the cursing that always followed.

Little Things

for Ira

by Lawdenmarc Decamora

A couple of weeks back everyone
was chanting ¡Habemus Papam! in the garden,
on chimney tops, on the floor of the plaza smitten
by bird beaks, but not in the libraries of philandering
codeheads and newly circumcised trapeze swingers.
On that special day no one wanted to hear something
like a "freelance boner." I'm sure you too didn't throw
an ear for words like papal shit or quantum Christology.
You know, I'd like to brush your hair when things go
ugly, as in when a tsunami hits the seawall and there's
no one to fix your hair out of fear. I will celebrate
your eyes' uncalculated blink as it might change
the season from tinder-parched mornings to being 68
and still writing you poems. You know, I'd like
to see you cry, laugh at people off to work, because
you're edged to clear the skies of jinx and throat-clogged
pretensions. The paddling mallards, oh, I want to count
them out for you and give you my monthly salary
lest I fail to do the maths. I want to carry your bag
when you leave home, check your stuff, and remind
you of the bills to cut soon after the afternoon
glows upon our shoulders. I want to see
you wear that big hair the next time you take a swim.
Last thing, please let's do it in church. It's not
what you think, no. I mean let's do it, the laundry.

film reel
by Lisa López Smith

Mom gifts me a copy of the disc,
newly digitalized, and casually
         I slip it into the laptop.
We laugh,   each reel spliced together awkwardly,
a precious three hundred sixty seconds—
fragments of a kindly childhood
I had mostly forgotten
or tried to—
The handheld mic catches
every sideways breeze and
constant clack of the flapping filmstrip:

infant eddie almost rolls over   and mom is smiling and
         /scene change/ we play on the swings and /scene change/
                  my grandmother flicks a cigarette ash
on the porch of the old kitsilano house with those vintage vinyl
chairs and my uncles were still slim in polyester trousers and
/scene change/ i dig in the sand at the beach
         the ducks are swimming and /scene change/
relatives i don't know from the old country wave at the camera and
         /scene change/ i toddle around the playground equipment
    with no modern safety nets   for those unexpected falls

and you ask me
         What are you doing Lisa?

         I hadn't heard your voice in   twenty-five   years.

and three year old me grins at the camera and says
         i'm looking at you

Theory
by Richard Weems

Three months into my thing with Karin, she asked about my previous girlfriends. "Tell me about your prior conquests," she said, her arms and legs splayed along the length of my futon. "I have an hypothesis in development."

"Right now?" I asked from the bathroom. After disposing of the condom, I started to wash up. Karin responded, but I didn't hear her over the running water. I asked again after I turned the water off, and she said, "As good a time as any." When I came back to bed, she skootched to make room and grabbed my arm as though ready to swing over a chasm.

"A hypothesis," I offered by way of correction. I surrendered to her grip, my wrist at rest on a swatch of her pubic hair. "An apple. An eerie sound. A banana. A hypothesis." Karin was the one with the recent BA, but my seniority gave me the right to lecture.

Karin wiggled her lip ring with her tongue. "An hypothesis," she said. "If it is proper to say, 'an historical event,' logic dictates that one develops an hypothesis." An early evening screw like this, though we had reservations at a Chinese restaurant with an impressive dim sum selection, applied to Karin's Ass-Backward Theory of Dating: Karin found that men tended to be more relaxed and pleasant on a date when they'd already gotten laid and had nothing left to maneuver the evening toward.

"Would you say, 'I am going to have an hissy-fit,' Karin with an i?" I rushed through the last part as though it were a Welsh surname. I drummed my fingers on the damp, slick surface of her inner thigh as she sneered at me, Elvis-style.

Karin pulled her superior glare. "That's an hysterical thought," she countered. I conceded.

Karin had a host of theories about men—that men were more likely to turn women on to new music than vice versa because men depended on music to express their feelings. That the amount of space two men kept between them in a movie theatre represented their level of sexual insecurity. The subject area of Karin's current hypothesis was obvious: Though I was eleven years older than her, my apartment reeked of relentless bachelorhood. My only wall decoration was a museum print, "Flaming June," thumb-tacked above the computer. My DVD player and TV rested atop a pair of orange milk crates. With my cache of condiments, I could reconstruct barbecue beef into something resembling mango chicken. My history of relationships mimicked life expectancy before modern medicine—most died in their infancy. I could find something fatally wrong with a woman once I was determined to do so. I hadn't yet subjected Karin to this tendency since she was generally easy to be with, even though she was now digging into the roots of my romantically nomadic nature.

Karin tended coffee bar at the Hill of Beans, where I stopped en route to the sneaker shop I managed. Karin was a pleasure to watch as she poured and buttered—short, neon hair stylishly mussed, her jeans faded and torn in enticing places. One day, I came by for lunch and found her on break with a cranberry muffin. I asked her name, which was when she said, "Karin. With an i." I asked her where she got her first piercing: the standard lobe-punch, or did she start somewhere more daring? She suggested the latter, though it took some effort to find out where. I promised her a discount on some new Vans when a toxic-green toenail poked out of her present pair. She fingered the sleeve of my work shirt, which had referee's stripes, and said, "It's a date, zebra-man."

Now, "This hypothesis," I said. "About my bachelorhood, I presume?"

"You're way ahead of me, buckaroo." Karin put on a scientific expression, as though she were looking at me over the rims of glasses perched on her nose.

"Just don't try to convince me that I'm repressing a desire for men," I said.

"I've got too much evidence to the contrary." Karin slid her tongue along her lips. "So, let us find the cause of this effect. Or rather say, the cause of this defect." She pulled my arm toward her body until a breast spread across my bicep. "If clothes make the man, so may his string of prior triumphs. Tell me about as many of them as you can remember. Associate freely—let one inspire you to the next. And please keep your responses to five-hundred words or less."

"If you're collecting data," I said, "don't you need a clipboard or something?" I swirled my fingertips against her, and Karin pulled the sheet up to her waist. The paltry central air suddenly became quite noticeable.

"Just get rhapsodizing," she said. "I'll be the expert here."

Karin let go of my arm as I sat up and slid on a pair of gym shorts. Instead of getting dressed herself, Karin rolled to her back and picked up the book I kept next to the bed, a collection of short stories that would rock my world, according to a cashier at my store. So far, the stories were about men who behaved badly because they had nothing in their lives but shit jobs and crummy apartments or trailers. Sometimes, mean dogs dwelt under their porches. They drank and shot roman candles at cattle. They threw cans of Aqua Net into bonfires, or they plowed down corn stalks and mailboxes with their trucks. Amy, the cashier who gave me the book, got it from an English teacher who wanted to bone her. Those were Amy's words—'to bone.' One story was about a guy in his thirties banging a high schooler on her bedroom floor while her parents watched Wheel of Fortune down the hall. He kept his eye on the light from under the door. He wanted the parents to discover him on top of their little girl. He wanted that image to stay with them for the rest of their lives. Amy the cashier wore sweatpants with print across the rear—"Pink," "Aeropostale" or "What boyfriend?" Whenever I texted her about coming in to cover for a sick call, she responded with smirking emojis. When she told me how the horny English teacher talked to her cleavage, I took an involuntary peek myself, and she smiled. She had dotted the i's in the aforementioned story with tight little hearts.

And now my naked girlfriend, still pungent with the smell of our fluids, stood the same book on her breasts. She flipped some pages about and read aloud a passage about a man's guts burning with the need for recognition. Evidently, another lonely man was getting ready to spray paint a police car or feed Alka-Seltzer to seagulls. Karin said, "Do you find your guts burning with the need for recognition? Or do you want to start telling me about your old flames now?"

I lay on my back and folded my hands over my chest as though ready to have my blood extracted with a trocar. Karin lay the book face down between her nipples and turned her face in my direction.

"Where to begin?" I said. I chose my words carefully around women, especially those I was attracted to. I could drum up a streak of witty banter easily enough, but I generally avoided un-rehearsed material. Karin stared, unwilling to let me out of this testimonial.

"I made it through middle school and a year of high school without a single date," I offered as a start. "I never asked girls out because I was afraid that they would say something far more harsh than no. At my eighth-grade dance, I sat by the speakers and sucked down enough half-pints of orange drink to dye my guts. High school was worse, because the other boys had PhD's in picking up girls while I was still studying for my GED, so I just pretended that I wasn't interested. When my friend Sanford's girlfriend insisted on a double date with her friend Madge, he brought me along."

Sanford's girl turned out to be a cute Asian, Madge of course the plain-looking friend. We went to a movie together (a comedy, thoroughly unmemorable) and split off into pairs afterwards. Madge and I necked by a heating unit behind the theatre that made us laugh into each other's mouths when it snapped on and off at random. At one point, when my tongue was tired from all that flopping about, I hugged Madge and said, "I think I love you," while she bit my ear.

The next day, we talked on the phone, a two-hour conversation I didn't know I had in me. She never brought up my awkward profession of love, but I could already feel it weighting the air between us. A week later, we met at the same theatre for another date. My plan was a repeat performance—movie, then another smooch-fest by the heating unit. But this movie had a scene where an old woman snuck through a bedroom window and fell onto a couple having acrobatic sex under the covers. The little old woman wobbled around on top of them as though on a sand dune in the middle of an earthquake.

I slid the book off Karin's chest. "I can say now that the sex was unrealistic," I said, "all that reeling and moaning and legs flailing, but I had no idea at the time that people did it any other way." I could still remember the way Madge held my hand and stared at the screen with a slight grin.

Karin said, "So the roly-poly sex bothered you?"

"It wasn't the roly-poly so much," I said. Madge had me hungry for some necking, but that exorbitant fucking up on the screen made me nervous. Could Madge have picked this movie because she wanted to have sex with me? I had no idea how we were going to roll around like that behind a theatre and finish up before my mom came to get me. "Does that make any sense?"

Karin looked as though mine were a rhetorical question. "How did she taste?" she said after another long pause.

"When?"

"That first kiss. How did she taste?"

"That was an entire date ago. Have I spoken for naught about witnessing an accidental ménage a trois while sitting next to my very first girl?"

"One question at a time," Karin said. "This is scientific, after all. I just need to follow up on some possibly revealing information. What did this Madge taste like?"

"I don't know," I said. "Metallic. I didn't like how she tasted, but it was my first kiss and I knew I had to get used to the flavor if I ever wanted to make out again."

Karin took Amy's book back and flipped through it as though she were looking for an answer key. "And during date the second, you weren't sure how you were going to manage some nookie with this Madge and keep to your curfew?"

"This Madge," I said. "Are you expecting others?"

"If you like, we can call all of your old girlfriends Madge. This one can be Madge$_1$, if you want to preserve some anonymity." Karin smirked, but had I decided to revise all the names on my romantic credit history, she would have gone along. People told Karin intimate details about themselves because she carried an air of humble omniscience—she never looked surprised or shocked at any revelation. Her boss at the Hill of Beans revealed to her that he embezzled a hundred pounds of coffee beans a month and sold them on eBay. The pale, flat barista with a purple streak in her jet-black hair fantasized about being a gay boy and had once paid five-hundred dollars for a seminar on anal masturbation. Karin's roommate, Devin, a thoroughly unwashed guy who had long ago given his life up to watching television, was a secret fan of Hanson, a briefly popular teeny-bopper band of blond brothers, and had a slew of fan blogs and interviews from teen-beat magazines bookmarked in his browser.

"There was only one Madge," I said, "but I'm not sure that I'm always going to be able to give names." For some, I remembered only what turned them on the most, whether they preferred to sit on my left or right, how they were lousy kissers or didn't know what to do with their hands. Some threatened to have major breakdowns if I didn't call them again, so of course I didn't. Bland, scared women who worried aloud about their attractiveness and asked for progress reports mid-date, women who handed out roadmaps to their insufficiencies and the shortcuts to breaking their hearts. For some, I remembered their kids more easily than I remembered them. But what could Karin learn from all of those lost causes?

"There are just a lot of them," I said. "It's going to be hard to sort some of them out."

"Then we'd better finish up with your first girl so that we can get moving," Karin said. "You're way over your word limit, but I'll consider this a warm-up."

The evening was temperate enough to keep the heating unit quiet, but Madge and I still broke out laughing every now and then because there was nothing else to interrupt neck session #2. Even worse, she said nothing about the boff-fest we had just witnessed onscreen, so I had to guess whether she was looking to get it on out here, or if she was planning our life together now that I loved her, even though I had only ever kissed or held hands with this one girl. I dared to bring my hand down low enough to finger a loop in Madge's waistband. She hummed into my mouth, a hum that could have been a warning as much as encouragement, so I backed off. Then she brushed up against my erection and put her hand on it. I snapped back as though she had aimed a fist at my balls.

"She had clearly made out with boys before," I said. "If she was a virgin, it was only by technicality. I was in far too unfamiliar territory to risk taking the plunge."

"So, you sucked out each other's esophagi until your mom picked you up," Karin said. "Did you ever get comfortable with a Madge crotch-grab?"

I didn't. Just two days after the second date, I wrote her a Dear Madge email. "The embarrassment," I explained to Karin, "was that I had told her that I loved her on the first date, but of course I gave every reason I could think of except that one." In the letter, I predicted that she would consider my letter a chicken-shit way of breaking up with her, and I told her I wouldn't call her again. I wrote other things too, about four pages' worth, but I couldn't remember any of it now.

"Damage done," Karin said.

"And so ends the saga of Madge." I put out my hand as though signaling for applause to the orange-decked woman in the Leighton print push-pinned to the wall. That, or the first volley of eggs. "So does this explain why I'm a little shit who avoids commitment?"

But instead of taking the bait for a compliment, some assurance that I wasn't so bad, Karin stared at the ceiling as though she were ordering bubbles of information up there. "One example does not a pattern make," she said. "Especially when it comes to starter-relationships. How often do you tell girlfriends that you love them?"

"There was one other," I said, but I wasn't ready to talk about her yet. "She didn't come right after Madge, though. This was much later." After Madge, I learned how to talk to girls, how to get them to want what I wanted from the start. Before Karin, I was wondering if I had the stuff of long-term commitment in me, or if I was the type who would end up buying a wife from Guam.

"Men," Karin said, and she snapped shut Amy's book as though she meant all of us, living and literary alike. "I don't need chronological narrative. Hell, I don't need narrative. Let's do it this way." She sat up and put her hand on my chest. "This is very important. Think in blurbs. The key here is not so much covering the whole story with adequate closure, but honing each relationship down to the details you find most important or memorable, as well as how you move from one to the other, what inspires you to your next item. Keep moving. Keep a broad perspective. Don't burden me with all the snitty particulars."

I cupped one of her breasts to let her know where I expected this interview to go. She didn't respond to my touch, but she didn't ward me off, either.

"All right, then," I said. "Do you mean something like, 'I dated a marathon runner who talked only about what she didn't want in a relationship'?"

She leaned forward and kissed me. It was a wet kiss, a reward. "You got it now, bub. Short and to the point."

"The runner," I said. "She had amassed a litany of details she didn't like about her past boyfriends and thought that reviewing this shopping list on the first date would make all of her future relationships start off on the right foot. She didn't think watching porn was sexy, nor did she want a boyfriend to ever refer to her butt in public. She told me how much she hated it when a guy pushed her head down into his lap. We dated for two months. She used her hand on me, and we dry-humped a couple of times, but she freaked out when she realized that she wanted to go all the way with me. That was supposed to explain why she didn't want to see me again. How about that?"

"Not bad," Karin said. "Was this still in high school?"

"This was two girlfriends ago," I said. "She worried about how I was going to describe her after we'd broken up. She brought this up on our second date. She said, 'I'm going to sound so awful when you say, "You won't believe this one girl I used to date."'"

"That's funny," Karin said. "You said that she said what you were going to say. You must be disappointed to realize that she had reason to worry." Karin gave me another wet kiss, this time a little longer, and she put my hand on her ass. "Now you're getting the hang of it." Karin had a calm, reassuring tone that could have talked down a jumper. "Keep them coming. Who does the neurotic hand-job runner bring to mind?"

I told Karin about an older woman who dated me because I reminded her of a boyfriend she regretted breaking up with. This mytho-historical ex had taken her to premieres and galleries in Greenwich Village, but she couldn't attend such things anymore because she didn't want to bump into him, so before me she dated rednecks who fucked around on her.

"She wanted to be with someone who had at least read a book or two, could watch a movie and understand the plot, even when there wasn't much of one." When we had sex, she refused to look at me. I found out later that she was still doinking some married rig-driver.

Then I told Karin about a divorcee who couldn't bring herself to have sex with other men yet. Our dates would end on a rather lukewarm note, with some kissing until she couldn't go any further, but as soon as I got home, she would call and ask me if she should spank herself. I'd tell her yes, she should. Then she'd tell me how she was pulling down her panties and bending over the arm of the sofa, and I'd tell her to smack herself harder, harder. She'd ask me if I was playing with myself. I always told her yes, even if I wasn't, and she'd tell me how one day we would do this in person. One night, after dropping her home, I went to a local bar and took home a sagging, lonely woman who let me do all the things I was only allowed to imagine with the divorcee. The divorcee's messages piled up, and I erased them. Every now and then, usually after some drinking, I would call and maybe get things started over the phone again, but then I would avoid her for months again.

I paused. "What a story to tell the woman you're sleeping with, eh?" I said.

Karin played with the ties on my gym shorts. "Don't think," she said. "You'll throw off your momentum. I'll make the conclusions here, if you don't mind."

Karin had lured me into stark, raving honesty. Details came to mind, and I handed them over without a moment's editing. Karin listened to them without a hint of disgust or disappointment. I wanted to hear Karin's conclusion for my regular bouts of loneliness, my spans between girlfriends that, whether momentary or prolonged, made me wonder why I couldn't find any sane women in the world.

So, I told Karin about the woman I once proposed to. I had no particular reason for wanting to get married—maybe because she was from Alabama and had an accent as smooth as yogurt. Maybe because I was still in college and hadn't yet grown tired of working long hours only to write checks to pay off my tuition bills. Maybe because everyone else thought her name was Lindsay, but that she had confided to me that her name was Linseed, as in the oil. Linseed and I were hanging out in someone's dorm room, and I dared her to go to City Hall with me. She thanked me with all her powers of Southern charm, though I insisted that I was serious. Because she turned me down, I cheated on her the very next weekend at another party. In plain sight, I made out with a redhead who had dared me to guess what color underwear she was wearing. I grabbed at the redhead while Linseed, the woman I had proposed to a kegger ago, yelled, "That's my man," to no avail.

I stopped as though someone had just given me a well-deserved shake. I had always considered myself the scorned lover seeking comfort, Linseed aware of her mistake only too late. This was the version I had convinced myself was the most accurate, but with Karin the word "cheat" slipped out of me as easily as if it had been dipped in a slick coating of truth.

"So, I'm a cheater," I said in summation. "I cheated on the woman I proposed to."

Karin leaned over my chest and glowered. "What did I tell you about making conclusions? We're looking for patterns here, correlations that lead to causality. You can't be a cheater if you only did it once."

Karin statement was like a challenge to my honor, so I had to prove to her that I was, in fact, a cheater. Thus, I told her about cheating on a girlfriend I had just moved in with, the only other woman to whom I had said, "I love you," even after having cheated on her. Two days after we moved her stuff into my place, I met up with Ellen, an old friend from high school, and Ellen and I made out in front of a pizzeria across the street from my sneaker shop. She was in a relationship too, a guy she would end up marrying. Ellen and I agreed to keep that night a secret, and I went home to my freshly moved-in girlfriend. I made vague overtures about how boring it was to meet up with high school friends and continued living with her for eight months until she realized that I had no intention of marrying her.

"I'm still not sure how it happened," I said to Karin. "Ellen wasn't an old girlfriend. I knew her through a friend of mine, a guy she dated my senior year, when a bunch of us would drink in the woods together. Ellen and I ate pizza and talked about old times. Then we hugged out front and started kissing."

"Funny how stuff like that just happens," Karin said. She rested her cheek by my right nipple. How could someone look so dispassionate while her boyfriend told her about his adventures in philandering? I wanted her to be angry with me, or at least proud that I could be so forthcoming. I wanted some sign that what I was saying was revelatory. I was tempted to tell Karin about a fantasy of mine: I walk into the back room of the sneaker shop while Amy is stocking shelves, and we have sex on one of those shitty folding chairs—quiet, quick and painless—with the other clerks and customers talking size and width and pricing on the other side of the flimsy black curtain. Then we go back to work as though nothing happened. We still flirt with each other, make suggestive remarks—every now and then I bend her over in the back room—but everything else in my life remains exactly as it was before I started boning my seventeen-year-old clerk.

But I kept this to myself. Karin leaned her elbows into my chest and propped up her chin with her hands. "And did you have sex with your high school friend that night?"

"No," I said, and I was embarrassed to admit it. I tried. I told Ellen that this was our one and only shot, and shouldn't we go ahead and go somewhere together (motel room, car seat)? But Ellen only pushed my hands away when I ran them down her back or reached for her breasts. We made out for an hour or so. She told me how much she loved me, and I told her that maybe we could reunite some other time. My live-in girlfriend texted me eight times during the whole incident, each one adding to the number of question marks in the previous.

Karin shook her head and ground her elbows alternately into my ribs. She even chuckled.

"I'm glad you're amused," I said.

She smiled, as though she had a follow-up that would put everything in perspective. "You haven't told me anything about the girlfriend you lived with," she said. "Except for cheating on her, of course."

That was when I understood: I had lost Karin. She had come over tonight not for dim sum, but to say goodbye—but not before she seduced me into explaining for her all the reasons she needed to leave me.

"I came home and had sex with my live-in girlfriend," I said, my voice quiet and strained. I took Karin's hand and spoke as though fessing up to some great, unsolved crime that I couldn't bear living with anymore. "Leigh. Her name was Leigh, and I turned her around, so I didn't have to look at her face. I came and I came, and every time it was for Ellen. I had sex with the girlfriend that I was in love with, but I was really having sex with another woman, and it was probably the best sex ever, because I was having sex with both of them." All of this rolled out of me as though telling Karin every ounce of truth I could muster would somehow negate it all and prove that I was no longer that kind of person. I even told Karin about how I fantasized about Amy, and Karin scrunched up her face as though annoyed that I had repeated myself.

"And how did it end with the woman you lived with?" Karin said as though she had led me through a lesson that we were now wrapping up. Like a good teacher, she was letting me connect the dots myself. As I talked, I swear that she moved her lips along with my words as though she already knew everything that was going to come out of my mouth.

"She moved out," I said. "She said that living separately would bring us closer, but as soon as she had her own place, she came over and said I was a wonderful man. She kissed me and said she loved me and sat on my lap. She kissed me with her eyes open." This was in the very living room down the hall from my bed. After two months of staring at blank walls, I bought the print of "Flaming June" and tacked it up, as though the woman in the print could offer any kind of company. "She never once said that it was over, but I cried anyway."

"You cried?" Karin squinted with doubt.

"You're right," I said. "I was upset, but I didn't cry. I just felt lonely. Again."

"You never had sex with two women." Karin crept out from under the sheet. "You didn't have sex with either of them, and that was what made it the best sex ever… for you."

I still haven't figured out that sentiment. Karin had, by this time, climbed on top of me. She took my hands and placed one on her breast, the other on her hip. She reached back to ease down my gym shorts.

"One more time," she said.

Out of loneliness, I made every move that she wanted me to.

Second Honeymoon
by Lorna Wood

Helen felt The Hague was right for her and Paul. Whereas Amsterdam was a hive of youth, the people they saw walking around their hotel seemed to be mostly middle-aged lawyers like Paul. The hotel, too, was comfortably old-fashioned, with marble pillars and grand, carpeted staircases.

But they arrived before their room was ready, so they followed the suave young clerk's directions to the Mauritshuis Museum. It was raining, so Paul put up his black umbrella and Helen leaned on his arm.

It was pleasant to walk the few blocks to the museum close together, with the rain thrumming impotently on the umbrella. They both stopped to admire the large floating Mondrian squares in the pool next to the palatial Binnenhof, and Helen thought how good it was to be with someone quiet, who didn't whip out his cellphone to document every passing instant. They no longer had to prove anything.

At the museum, Paul checked the umbrella, and they went quietly from room to room. Paul went at her pace, and they remarked occasionally in low tones on the paintings. Paul wondered aloud whether Banksy would think he could learn anything from the Dutch masters. He didn't expect a response to this. It was just his way of reminding Helen how they had both disliked the exhibit of the graffiti artist's work that they'd seen in Amsterdam. Helen smiled politely, but at the same time she remembered that little girl reaching for the heart balloon and teared up a little.

They were about to pass under a grand doorway with six portraits set above it, a youngish father with his five children arranged around him. Helen's eye was caught, especially by the cherubic little girl at the top of the grouping. While Paul went on to the next room, Helen hung back, thinking how happy and intelligent the children looked, and how satisfied the father seemed. She tried to imagine what a different person Paul would have been with five children hanging on him—probably irritable and harassed, not at all his calm, good-humored self.

She wondered, too, why the mother wasn't in the group. It was so dangerous to have children back then, and so many mothers and children died.

"Excuse me," said a woman wanting to get into the next room.

"Oh! I'm so sorry," Helen said. As she moved to one side, she saw Paul sitting on a bench. He saw her too and patted the space next to him, so she hurried to him and sat down.

For a minute he looked straight ahead as if he were drawn in by the art, but the pictures on the opposite wall were too small to be appreciated from the bench. Helen scrutinized his profile. She could see the muscle working in his jaw, the way it always did when he was tense.

"You're still thinking about it, aren't you?" he asked, without turning his head.

"Sometimes," she admitted.

He got up abstractedly. Helen followed him, reached out for his hand, thought better of it. They both looked at a Rembrandt self-portrait.

It was from the last year of the artist's life. Unsparingly, he had detailed his puffy skin, the deep lines around his eyes. Helen thought he looked sad yet defiant. "Here I am: this is what life has brought me to," his eyes seemed to say.

But there was mystery as well. A shadow on the right side of the painting concealed half his face. His left shoulder seemed to dissolve into it. His eyes were black pools.

"It's hard to get old," Paul said, sympathetically.

They went on silently for a long time.

In front of Anatomy Lesson of Dr. Nicholas Tulp, Paul stopped for a while, even though he had to dodge around other tourists taking pictures. Helen did not like the stringy muscles and tendons in the corpse's flayed, incised arm, or the way Dr. Tulp was pulling them open with what looked like scissors to demonstrate his lesson. She tried to concentrate on the faces of the doctors looking on.

Paul said, "What an exciting time. Even the bodies we'd been walking around in for thousands of years suddenly became amazing worlds to explore."

"But his face is so cold and closed," Helen said, thinking of the dead man.

"Whose? Oh, the cadaver. Well it would be, wouldn't it?"

Eventually they arrived at the room where View of Delft and Girl with a Pearl Earring hung. Helen remembered them from their first honeymoon, so many years ago. She remembered how the bright bits of paint in the bricks of the Delft buildings seemed to hint at busy lives behind the dark openings of windows and archways, the receding buildings of the city promising a thriving community.

Now she saw how much smaller the city was than the great, cloudy sky, and how the people on the shore were even smaller. And it seemed to her that even though the spires of the city strove upwards, the dark arches and the cloudy reflections of the massive buildings in the water dragged the eye back down, and though there were no doubt many lives in the receding vistas between the massive buildings along the shore, nothing was promised to them except insignificance and uncertainty.

The famous girl looked different, too. Seeing her suddenly as the crowd in front of the protective railing shifted, Helen was struck by how young she looked. The sensuality she remembered was still there—the slightly open mouth, the glistening lower lip, the wide eyes. But whereas before Helen had seen seduction, now she saw vulnerability, innocence, startled surprise. The girl seemed caught on the point of fleeing, as if in the next moment she would be gone with a flip of her turban headdress.

Paul remembered to pick up the umbrella, though it had stopped raining. They strolled back to the hotel, careful where they put their shoes on the wet gravel. Somewhere a lovesick pigeon called desperately.

Their room was on the top floor, what must have been the servants' quarters, back in the day. It was cozy and crammed with Victorian charm and modern comforts. There was only a single window, like a porthole. The blind was drawn almost all the way over it, but when she pushed it aside, Helen could see a fragment of the balustrade running around the top of the hotel and beyond that a glimpse of the city.

She was reminded of her favorite childhood book, A Little Princess, and how Miss Minchin made Sara Crewe live in a barren garret, but one night the Indian servant from the house next door crept in through the window and transformed it into a comfortable haven while Sara slept. Helen remembered how, wriggling with delight, she had read Sara's awakening over and over, savoring the magical change.

She enjoyed the comfort of the room, the luxuries of her life with Paul, while the two of them unpacked just what they would need until they checked out and went to the airport the next morning. By the time they were finished, she felt almost hopeful. Maybe if they had a nice dinner somewhere quiet and then walked together along the canals for as long as it took, all their emptiness and resentment would dissolve, and their love would rise, phoenix-like, from its old husk.

Paul sat on the bed and patted the space next to him. Helen sat down, and he took her hand. In the dim, soft light coming in under the blind, his face looked younger, less hard.

"Look," he said. "I know you've been—second-guessing our choices—since… the change."

Helen looked away from him. She didn't like to discuss menopause.

He squeezed her hand painfully. "What I don't understand is how this is my fault. Damn it. We agreed!"

She took a deep breath. "It just seems—like a cocoon, sometimes." Her pale arms waved through the underwater murk of the room like the wings of a luna moth. "So selfish."

Paul stood and began to pace. "Selfish!" he said. "What's more selfish than having kids? Replicating yourself, inflicting more humans on the earth. Not to mention, you know how my parents were. Never home. I'd be a crappy father."

He had raised his voice. In the pause after his words there was a soft knock at the door. "Evening service," said a voice. The English was accented, but not in the Dutch way.

Paul opened the door with a courtly flourish, covering his embarrassment. "Please. Come in."

The man was tall and thin, with big white teeth. He looked as if he might be Indonesian. His head was shaved, so it was hard to tell his age. Unfolding two white cloths, he spread them on the carpet on either side of the bed. Then he went outside for a moment and came back holding two pairs of white slippers in crackling plastic. "These were the last two pairs of slippers in the whole hotel," he said, crouching down to lay one pair next to the white cloth on Helen's side of the bed. "But I got them for you." He came around to Paul's side, where Helen was still sitting. Crouching down again, he smoothed the white cloth and laid the second pair of slippers next to it.

"Will there be anything else? Sir? Madam?" he asked, rising and looking from one to the other of them. "Shall I draw the blind all the way down?"

"No thank you," Helen said.

"Thanks." Paul tipped him.

"Thank you, sir," he said, smiling even more broadly and bowing himself out.

They looked blankly at one another. Nothing was resolved, but it seemed impossible to vivisect their marriage after the low comedy of the slippers. "What are you going to do now?" Paul asked kindly.

"I think I'll take a nap," Helen said. She got up and kissed him on the cheek.

"I'm going down to the lounge then," Paul said, pointing down toward it apologetically. "See what the Frankfurter Allgemeine has to say for itself."

He was reminding her of how good his German was. "Okay," Helen said, stifling a yawn. "I'll come down later and you can tell me all about it."

"Okay." The door closed behind him with a hushed click.

Helen hung up her dress and got into bed. She thought of the hotel servant, so proud of his slippers, and the similarly white-clad Indian servant who delighted in the happiness of Sara Crewe. Now, of course, Helen was aware of the racist, classist imperialism of Sara and her creator, and how the diamond mines that made Sara rich again enslaved countless workers in a living hell off-page. Not only was there no magic, Helen thought, but everything keeping her own luxurious little world afloat was just as rotten with exploitation and pretense as in Sara's Victorian times.

Yet it was so hard to know where to begin. She couldn't have refused the slippers without offending the man, nor could Paul have invited him to join his law firm. Helen doubted she could even fix her own marriage. If she and Paul lifted the veil of everyday politeness and consideration, what diseased inner workings might be exposed?

She could not sleep. She felt a great pity for Paul, with his lonely childhood, his careful plans, his ungrateful wife. She owed it to him to make an effort.

Feeling as if she were pushing a great weight off herself, Helen got up, showered, and put on a fresh dress and a little makeup. She went downstairs and gave her name and room number to the clerk at the lounge desk, who informed her that her husband was in the little glass-enclosed cigar lounge. She grabbed a New York Times from the rack as she went in and peered at the cigar lounge from afar. She hated cigars but would not disturb him if he was indulging a whim. The thought that Paul liked an occasional cigar and she had never known this even gave her a little flicker of hope. Later on, he could tell her how he developed a taste for them, or perhaps they would laugh about how he turned to cigars in his moment of desolation.

The main lounge area was not very busy yet, and through the glass walls of the cigar lounge Helen could glimpse only a few patrons, floating in the fug of smoke like fish in an aquarium. She saw two other men and Paul, who was leaning toward the lone woman, a plump lady in her late thirties (Helen guessed). Her dress was intricately draped and looked expensive, but it fell awkwardly over her ample bust.

Helen could tell immediately that Paul was drunk. She had not seen him that way often, but she recognized it by the exaggerated angle at which he was leaning toward the woman and the fact that he was touching her, and she was laughing and holding a match to his cigar.

Helen felt faint. She thought she would just sit down for a few minutes, out of his line of sight. If he came out, she could always throw her paper over her face. Then she would go up and end it. She would even try not to be bitter. It could all be very civilized.

She retreated to the recess next to the grand staircase dominating the side of the main lounge farthest from the cigar lounge. Here she sipped a glass of wine and pretended to read while thinking of how invisible a middle-aged woman alone could be. Through the clinking of glasses and the indistinct surf of voices, piped-in music penetrated, music that seemed too young for the hotel's over-thirty clientele, and Helen wondered why young people preferred needy moaning to melody.

She was only keeping her mind busy, but it was pointless to dwell on Paul's misbehavior. She couldn't even blame him, if she were fair. She should have hashed it out with him before the trip and all this—she looked around at the marble pillars, the grand staircase ascending into obscurity—this big show.

A sudden burst of German and female laughter made her look up. The dumpy woman was holding Paul by the wrist and towing him unsteadily toward the staircase. Helen threw the paper up in front of her face, and in a moment, they were gone.

It was one thing to fantasize about freedom, but quite another to flee alone into uncertainty, darkness, and eventual death. The cozy room evoking childhood memories of days spent enchanted by a book seemed as close to a refuge as Helen was likely to get. Helen got ready for bed mechanically but remembered to wear the slippers the man had gone to so much trouble to get.

Lying down at last, she let scenes from her life with Paul drift through her mind. She recalled walking down the street in New Haven when their love was still young. Paul Simon's voice from the CD he'd put on the night before mingled in her memory with her Paul's gentle coaxing. She remembered how the wind softly lifted her skirt as if it were his desire, unable to leave off touching her. Then there was a blur of years, dinner parties, visits to both sets of parents that fell off as that generation aged and died, and the proud moment when she was elected to the town council that first time, and Paul had swooped her up and carried her over their threshold as if she were a new bride, never mind her sensible shoes.

Now it all seemed like pictures in a story of someone else's life. Helen felt empty and useless, like something left in the freezer too long. "The only real magic is time," she thought. "And it only makes good things disappear."

She was still lying there when she heard a fumbling and scrabbling at the door, and some sotto voce swearing. Paul felt his way in on a wave of boozy cigar fumes. He made his way clumsily around to her side of the bed and knelt down. "Helen!" he stage-whispered. "Are you awake?"

She shrank inwardly from him. His head dropped down next to her stomach, and she could hear him breathing heavily. After a while, he gave up and came around to his side of the bed. He threw his clothes onto a chair and sat bent over on the edge of the bed in the hotel robe and his underwear.

It was well into the evening, but still the light of the long northern European day streamed under the blind from the porthole. Helen saw Paul start to jerk, first silently, then with strange gasps and whimpers, and finally, throwing himself at full length on the bed, with sharp barking sobs and agonized animal howls.

She was shocked. Paul was always so verbal, so self-contained. She got up on her elbow, but though he noticed, he only coiled away from her and beat the bed with his fist. She had never seen him like this, not even when his father died.

Now was the time, she thought, seeing it in her mind's eye. She could pack and leave with dignity, and later they would agree it was for the best. But even while she saw herself reaching into the dark armoire, she reached out instead and touched his neck.

The warmth of his damp skin was like a spark, lighting a way forward, out of the darkness. Just here, in the connection between her hand and his ropy tendons, his throbbing pulse, a new, unexplored world was opening. As he gradually grew quiet and still at her touch, she quickened with awed wonder at the intricate mazes of the human heart.

Another Fire
by Sharon L. Charde

Since I've seen my friend Tessa, she's learned
to swallow fire. Well, not swallow, but stop it
in her throat. Don't inhale, she says, when I
question her, incredulous, unsure why anyone
would want this skill. What if you do? I ask.
Not good she says, you have to study, practice.
Otherwise you die, though most people don't. She
tells me the oxygen's cut off when you close
your mouth, so the fire goes out. Just some blisters.
She's taken a course, swallows swords too, says
it feels good to put the blade down her throat.
Tessa's a beauty, blonde hair, long legs, black
framed glasses, PhD. I love her. A sideshow freak?
Toured with the circus while her mother was dying,
flying back and forth between two kinds of swallowing.
I understand one, I've just lost mine. She was 100,
Tessa's mother only 69. Swallowing fire, swallowing
grief, swallowing how life usually doesn't give
what you need. My son's wife is too busy to love me.
Tessa's mother-in-law has a house full of guns
and Republicans. We decide to trade in the real
relatives, become a new match of surrogates.
We've got oxygen for it, why not another fire?

White Flag

by Alexis Rhone Fancher

On Edward Hopper's painting, "Morning Sun," 1952

No one paints loneliness like he does. Those half-clad women by the bed, on the floor, hunched over, staring out the window, in profile or from behind, always clean lines, such worshipful light. The gas station in the middle of nowhere, estranged couples on the bright-lit porch after dark. Even the boats sail alone. And the diners. The hatted strangers, coming on to a redhead, a moody blonde, all of them losers, all of them desperate for a second chance. This morning the sunlight pried open my eyes, flooded our bedroom walls. I sat alone, in profile on our bed in a pink chemise, knees drawn up, arms crossed over my calves, staring out the window. Desperate for you. No one paints loneliness like Edward Hopper paints me, missing you, apologies on my lips. Come back. Stand below my window. Watch me beg for a second chance. Downturned mouth, sad eyes, parted knees, open thighs, that famous shaft of Hopper light a white flag, if only you could see.

Siam
by Kacie Berghoef

Many people dream of adopting a dog or cat, but when it came
to my pet preferences, I was always a little bit offbeat. Ever since
a friend introduced me to her rat pack, I'd dreamed of having my
own. When my partner and I moved into an apartment that only
allowed caged pets, I jumped at the chance to get my first pair
and experienced a type of love I haven't yet felt from a human.

Life with pet rats was full of unexpected pleasures, but no one
warned me about the most painful challenge of being adopted by
them: their little lives are very short. Rats rarely live more than
three years, but with their loving, intelligent personalities, losing
each one is as difficult as saying goodbye to a beloved family dog.
Rats are social creatures by nature, so each time one of my rats
died, I'd sadly go get another one, to keep the living one from
being lonely. I felt trapped in a cycle of constant grief from these
losses—until I adopted Siam, who was to be my final rat.

Originally found in a garbage can and brought to the rescue
where I found him, Siam's story both charmed and horrified me.
At middle age, he was cage aggressive, not suitable for families
with children, and unlikely to get adopted. I stroked his creamy

fur and he nuzzled in response. We took him home on the spot, to be our other rat's friend. Initially there were a few bumps as he bit me hard enough to draw blood, but soon we became as close as a rat and human can be. My other rats had always been more active, but Siam's large size and older age made him my perfect little study buddy. Soon, he was my constant companion, content to hang out next to me or on my shoulder as I churned out school papers.

Several months after I adopted Siam, I noticed his breathing growing labored and noisy. The veterinarian prescribed medications for his respiratory infection, at the same time warning us that rats with this condition didn't usually live much longer. But Siam was a tough old guy who took his daily medications like a champ, easily outliving the once healthier rat we'd adopted him to befriend, growing even closer to me after her death. Unlike most rats, he preferred the company of humans, so we never got him another rat friend.

It was easy to ignore Siam's slowly worsening condition, imagining him remaining suspended in this state forever, until one day he started panting and gasping for breath. My partner and I rushed him to the emergency veterinarian, and almost like magic, she revived him in an oxygen tank, but warned us that his illness was end-stage. He'd lived eight months with the infection at that point, longer than she'd ever seen before. The vet, my partner, and I agreed on the spot that we'd humanely euthanize Siam if he started struggling to breathe again.

Three weeks later, I returned home after a weekend away, happy after graduating and spending some quality time relaxing with my parents. I walked back in the front door, waved at Siam in his cage, and started unpacking my overnight bag. Not five minutes later, I walked out of the bedroom, excited to take Siam out of his cage for a more proper hello cuddle. To my horror, he was once again gasping and panting for breath. He had waited for me to come home, and now I had to take him to die.

I abandoned unpacking and rushed Siam to the vet, knowing it would be the last time we'd make that trip together. Our veterinarian was extremely gentle and compassionate. Once again, she put Siam in a cage filled with oxygen, temporarily perking him up and allowing him to feel a little bit normal. I gave him a grape she had on hand, and I scratched his back while he enthusiastically peeled and devoured it. My heart sank as he looked so happy, knowing what was to come.

As the medicine was prepared, Siam ran up on my shoulder one last time. During the procedure I stayed calm, wanting to be strong for Siam, but my insides were bursting with pain. When the initial injection didn't work, the vet had to use a different procedure, one that put him in an enclosed box and meant I could no longer hold him. It was as if the plastic that blocked me from Siam was severing the loving connection I felt, and I felt myself detaching from what was happening and starting to get numb.

I came home face to face with an empty cage, with no rats. Somewhat lost, I cleaned out his cage for the last time. It was so heavy, and I felt so weak, that I didn't have the energy to do anything but sit on the couch and stare at it for the rest of the day. My partner and I now had a cat, and instead of having Siam by my side, my cat came over periodically, also confused. Siam's scent was gone, and he seemed just as lost as me without the familiar smell. I tried to pet him, but compared to Siam, he was haughty and distant.

The next day, I mustered the muscle power to haul Siam's cage into the storage shed. Two days later, I ran off on a welcome post-graduation trip to Ecuador, delighted to postpone post-graduate life a bit and get some major distance from the loss I'd experienced. The following month, I moved 20 minutes away, dutifully bringing Siam's cage just in case, and then promptly ran off on two more solo trips. Each one cut me off further from Siam's death, but also removed me from the love we'd once shared. My partner reminded me more than once that we could always adopt rats again, but I was tired, severely emotionally worn out from managing their short lifespans, their health challenges, and the dry emptiness that just seemed to increase every time another one left.

One year after Siam's death, my partner and I ended our relationship for reasons unrelated to our pets, and I moved out of town, amicably agreeing to leave our cats behind. The question of the rat cages was a massive, cube-like block in my memory, so by default I left without them too. A few years later, my former partner, in the process of moving, contacted me and asked if I wanted the cage. I declined. At that point, I lived in a small San Francisco apartment that didn't allow pets, and the pet-loving part of my life seemed like a distant memory.

It was about five years after he died that the memory of Siam turned from distant and fuzzy into the full color remembrances of his bright red eyes, brown nose, and creamy fur softly brushing against my hand. For years, I'd told people about Siam without much emotion, but then the emotion started to come back through my dreams. Repeatedly, I dreamt that he was still alive, sitting on my shoulder, defying the odds, the miracle rat who'd lived almost a decade. He was alive in those dreams, but sluggishly, moving at the pace of a snail and sometimes bloating, almost as if he was on the edge of not existing.

As I started to dream, visions of Siam's final moments came back to my waking life, too. Every few months I had new pangs of guilt for choosing to euthanize Siam, intensely remembering how he seemed fine being put in the oxygen tank, knowing that I could've taken him home that day. I remembered how the veterinarian had to take him out of my hands and put him in a plastic box to euthanize him, feeling repeated horror in assuming that he felt terror alone in there, without a reassuring hand on his fur while he took his final breaths.

Weeks or even stretches of months went by between the episodes of guilty tears, and each time I dreamed about him and sobbed through my horror and guilt, he came back a little bit more to me. I started to see times that he was my healthy, playful snuggle buddy, holding me together as I put the finishing touches on my research project. The tears finally dried up—I had cried all of them out that I possibly could—and there he was, my sweet little rat, vibrantly in Technicolor. He was sitting on my shoulder, sniffing at my ear and grooming my hair, never leaving when I went through relationships, when I started and then quit new jobs, when I moved apartments and then abroad. Siam had been with me all that time, and now I could finally feel him there.

The Strike
by Mel Carlson

Crazy Bob was feeling high glory that July evening when he marched out ahead of the striking miners, down the middle of Main Street. His shoes were cracked and broken, his ragged pants too short, and his bare ankles were dirt gray but he stepped high like the leader of the American Legion Drum and Bugle Corps, pumping a filthy baseball up and down as if it were a baton.

He stopped at the corner of Second Street, tugged at the bill of the red baseball cap he'd stolen from me, licked his fingers, wound up, and pretended to throw a fastball. When the crowd on the sidewalk cheered, he strutted to the center of the intersection and waved his arms, directing traffic. Irritated drivers honked, then in frustration, backed up, and turned onto side streets.

It was not a proper parade. No drums or bugles, just a flood of silent, angry men dressed in bib overalls and denim shirts, over five hundred miners down Main in slow, frightening cadence. Members of the International Union of Mine, Mill, and Smelter Workers, each shouldered the handle of a pickaxe as if it were a rifle or shotgun. Carbide lights on their hard hats glowed. Behind the miners, the lights on the helmets of a disorderly mob of company strikebreakers wobbled and bobbed and blinked as they swung mock blows at the miners.

Four unmarked police cars terminated the parade. Packed with vigilantes armed with pistols and shotguns, the cars drove two abreast, protecting the rowdy strikebreakers from any counter attack at the rear. Deputized in Kansas to terrorize miners in Missouri, they had dragged strikers from their cars and beat them; pulled strikers from their houses and beat them; hauled men to the headquarters of the company union for interrogation; spent the night parked in front of strikers' homes, headlights trained on the window, implying threat to the miners' families.

This night crowds pushed along the sidewalks, keeping pace with the parade, anxious to see the drama unfold. No policeman appeared. Bicycle Willie, the generic name for whichever policeman was riding the city's only motorcycle that night, was holed up at the police station with his fellow officers. Probably they had unlocked the tear gas cabinet; probably they had unlocked the shotgun rack, no use taking chances with an angry mob. Hole up. Shut up and stand by to repel boarders.

As they clowned their way down Main Street, many strikebreakers stared intently at Carlson's Feed, Seed & Hardware Store, and I thought, at me. When you are twelve years old and several people look in your general direction, all at the same time, you tend to feel that they are looking at you in particular. I felt like that British general in the Lives of a Bengal Lancer, on a reviewing stand watching my soldiers ride past, doing an eyes right to look at my family—tall Grandpa Carlson, round Grandma Carlson, my medium sized father, and admirable me—under the street light. If I had held a swagger stick, I would have tapped the bill of my pith helmet with it. Jolly good, I thought out loud.

Grandpa, understanding the Blue Carders' intense stares, muttered to himself in Swedish. Unfortunately, the family hardware store owned the largest stock of ammunition in the Tri-state area, a whole railroad carload of shells and cartridges, purchased cheap from a Depression-failed supplier. It was stored in Grandpa's locked garage.

The tons of firepower slammed down on Grandpa's conscience. "Tam," he said. "Oh Got Tam fools. Oh Yeesus, yeesus, yeesus."

Grandma turned, stepped off the sidewalk, and joined the crowd.

"Wait Bessie," Grandpa shouted. "Where are you going?"

She forced her way back out of the crowd, squared her shoulders, and stared up into his face. "Home." she said. "I won't stay here with a blasphemer." Again, she walked away.

"Yeesus, Bessie." He raised his voice. "They are going to come for our ammunition. They will kill each other with our ammunition. Don't that bother you?"

She turned again. "I told you, Charlie, not to buy it. You bought it." She turned and muscled her angry way through the crowd.

Grandma hated guns. Her younger brother had shot himself while crawling through a fence with his shotgun. They brought him home on a door for a stretcher. He bled to death on the family dining table. She hated guns as much as she hated liquor, and she was an agitating member of the Women's Christian Temperance Union. If there had been a Women' Christian Anti-Gun Union, she would have been an agitating member of that too.

When he got home, Grandpa went straight to his bedroom and fished a pint bottle of local white mule out of his dresser drawer. He held the bottle, then shaking his head, put it back in the drawer and dejectedly walked into the living room.

"Bessie," he called. "Are we having supper tonight?"

"No, Charlie. No supper."

"Thank you, Bessie."

"You're welcome, Charlie."

The exchange was sweetly voiced and without irony or sarcasm. He was asking if her anger occupied the kitchen. She said it did and he best not come in. He thanked her for being so honest about her state of mind. She thanked him for being so nice about it.

"Would you turn on the garage light? Please, Bessie. I'm going to guard our ammunition."

"Your ammunition, Charlie. Not mine. Be careful of the black widow spiders out there."

The direct route to the garage lay through Bessie territory, her kitchen and the screened porch where she preferred to sleep. Charlie went back to his room, had a long pull at the bottle, dragged a straight-backed chair from under the dining table, and carried it on the detour route to the garage—out the front door, down the porch steps, and around the house. Because of his arthritic back, he carried the chair high, held tight against his chest. The maneuver made it hard to see, forcing him to probe with his feet for the porch steps and the high place where the roots of his sweet gum tree had lifted the sidewalk.

After placing the chair in front of the ammunition room door, he rigged a bare 100-watt lightbulb over the chair, stepped back to check the effect, clutched his lower back and groaned. He filled his pockets with fat, home-grown pecans from the cache he maintained in his workshop, took a long drink from the garden hose outside, then sat under the light to wait. Charlie Carlson looked like an elderly suspect in a movie, waiting to be interrogated under the dangling bright light in a dingy Chicago police station basement.

There he waited for angry men to burst into the garage. He held no weapon, had little strength in his arms, knew no convincing argument, but he calmly awaited a confrontation. He had bought the ammunition to sell to men living in the Ozark hollers to kill rabbits and deer to feed their families. He could not allow men to kill each other with it. His duty was clear. He would block their way. They would have to go over his body to get the ammunition. He would act on the highest moral principles. He would practice nonviolence. He was doing the noble thing. Once again, he had been given an opportunity to put his balls on the line for a high moral cause, a thing he lived to do. Twice before in his long life, he had been called to a man's accounting, and had stepped forward to be severely beaten.

Charlie was pleased with himself but growing nervous. The Blue Carders who had stared at the store with such fascination would be in Carlson's Seed, Feed & Hardware Store the next day, for ammunition.

Late at night, Grandma arrived with a plate of corned beef sandwiches and a glass of milk. She held the food out at arm's length, like she didn't want to get too close to the place that held so many instruments of death and violence.

"Thank you, my Bessie."

"Not your Bessie, Charlie. Not this night."

The night held no event more exciting than sandwiches and milk and three trips to the dark side of the backyard pecan tree for relief from an irritable prostate, a poor reward for high resolve. Nothing in life can be more demoralizing than to commit oneself to high moral purpose, prepare to man the barricades, and then find that no one has even noticed that the barricades are there. Charlie returned to the house by the direct route, leaving his chair behind, feeling depressed, pondering the frivolity of the master of a universe who organized great events then neglected to have them occur.

Inside he didn't speak, but sat at his place at the table, tucked his napkin under his chin, and waited for the habitual breakfast that must have also nourished the prostate cancer that killed him: two sausages and two eggs fried in their grease, plus several slices of heavily buttered toast, a cup of coffee, half of which was cream. He placed his elbows on the table, held the saucer delicately on each side with thumbs and middle fingers, and blew until is was cool enough to drink.

Grandma looked away, always, when Grandpa saucered his coffee.

That day must have been Saturday because I was at the store, working, when the strikebreakers arrived. Twelve cars, bumper to bumper, parked in the middle of Main Street. A delegation of men organized itself out there, then marched, single file into the store. They looked like the walking wounded in a World War I movie, complete with bloody bandages, clothes, and boots. Grim, shocked. Their leader had lost most of an ear, his face had been peppered with fragments of some kind, or perhaps bird shot. He looked like he suffered from a thousand bloody pimples.

My father, who had watched the convoy arrive, busied himself at his desk. Clerks and customers clustered at points of good observation. Grandpa took my shoulders and pointed me toward the door. Go look at the cars, he said. Get out of here. Then he pushed me. I slipped down the narrow aisle with my head down, looking at blood-spattered boots, smelling sweat and tobacco.

Outside, I gawked at the cars, their windows cracked, the doors and hoods stippled with birdshot. The men proudly showed me their pathetic armor; magazines stuffed into the spaces once occupied by window glass. I understand now that it was significant that no one had fired at them with 00 buckshot, which would have killed them all.

When I looked back, Grandpa was standing stiff and haughty in front of the cash register, an elderly Horatio guarding the bridge. I knew about Horatio from reading my 1911 British edition of the Book of Knowledge, which minus the volume for G for gold, was my reference library. I also knew about the Pipes at Lucknow and the British square at Waterloo.

I marched back around the paint and putty counter and stood at attention beside my Grandfather, while Grandma came in the back door and settled behind the cash register.

"I'm here, Charlie," she said.

"Thank you, Bessie."

After a conference with his troops who were gathered at the cash register, the strikebreaker—the leader who had lost an ear—pulled a piece of paper from a shirt pocket, handed it to Grandpa, and said, "This is what we need." It was a formal presentation. Grandpa accepted the paper with equal formality, looked at it and noted it was a list of shotgun shells, and pistol and rifle cartridges. "I won't sell ammunition to you because you plan to shoot people."

"We are your customers." The strikebreaker's hand shook. "We have to fight our way to work tomorrow, Charlie. God damn it, Charlie."

"No, I will not."

"For Christ's sake, Charlie," the strikebreaker said. "We will take it from you. You old fool."

Bessie came around the counter and stood beside Grandpa.

The strikebreaker kept his eyes on Grandpa. "Move," he shouted.

Grandpa pulled himself up to his tallest.

"No, we will not let you pass. By Gar."

In the next frozen moment, my father, his back turned to the tableau, tapped a key on his adding machine and pulled the handle. Eight dollars and eighty-four cents. Crack clunk. Twenty-seven dollars and eighteen cents, crack clunk.

Sensing the dramatic moment, I stepped in front of my grandfather and said, "They shall not pass." It was a phrase adopted by the French Army on the Marne in 1914, when it stopped the Germans from reaching Paris. It was a grand phrase that echoed through the times. Small boys used it in their war games. I wanted to repeat it with additional grandeur but someone at the edge of the strikebreakers snickered. Witnesses began to laugh. Grandpa put his hand on my head.

The strikebreaker held his hand out and Grandpa shook it.

"We'll will go someplace else," the Blue Carder said. "No hard feelings Charlie."

"None taken," Grandpa said. "Please don't shoot anybody."

"I hope not," the strikebreaker said.

My father's adding machine stopped.

Customers looked at each other in a baffled way. No one spoke. No one blew a bugle. No one banged a drum.

Indication of Love
by Amanda Moore

When I dropped her off at camp last week
she said, "Mom, just go," and wouldn't
kiss me. I didn't think much of it
until later when I sat to work

and found her awkward 8-year-old scrawl
on the last pages of my notebook,
some school assignment, a description
of a painting in our home:

> The way the feet are
> is the indication of love
> because the woman and the girl are holding hands
> but the woman is mostly behind.

Newly born, she slept between us, fluttering
and sucking like a disembodied heart.
While she slept we crept downstairs
to make love. She will never know

all the forms her life embodies:
crucial as lung, breath; more than limb,
not the same as brain. Before
she split my body in two,

sloughed off my skin like a callous,
before she stood or spoke or even wrote,
she was already leaving.
And then her own room, her own bed,

the first day of school when she flung herself from the car
and didn't look back. Every day I learn
to function with less. Every day
I am mostly behind.

Last Words from a Pillar of Salt
by Shelley Valdez

"But she did look back, and I love her for that,
because it was so human."
- Kurt Vonnegut

to fall in love with a prophet
is to fall in love with a poet

      i knew this   from the way he talked of ghosts

      how everything illuminated
      began in the bloom of his throat

for decades he lived in my city,
      my streets, made of thunder and flesh

but the God of Fire does not stand   for storms and skin
not even ten of us would settle   from his smoke

      this   he tells us
      is how time
      will test
      its teeth

when the winged men come to bring slaughter

      my prophet houses heaven in our walls
      gives them our best bread   offers
      our daughters to the wolves that lick our doors

in return, our glowing guests send us far
from the lightning   warning
to keep our backs to the flame

but what did i know
of the God of Light
and Destruction   what did i know
          of redemption and dust?

when i move to gaze at glory
when i move to salt from skin

my poet does not turn

and this   is how to bear witness
        to the nameless

     how to stand vigil
     for the damned   how

     you can still have ordinary
     devotion but only
        with your eyes closed

this   is how
you learn   to burn

     into something
     close to nothing

     and then burn some more

Sisyphus in Love
by Jenn Richter

The Bengal cat hisses and howls
at the confines of the crate,
braces her back legs against the bucking
of the truck as it bumps along the mountain tracks.

When the afternoon gets hot,
he will stop the merciless
movement, open the metal grate, and reach
inside, crooning his affection for his pretty girl.

She will launch herself at him, all teeth
and claws and bitter
yowls, attach herself briefly to the crown
of his head before vanishing
into the woods

only to come crawling back after dark,
to slip into the tent he set up in her absence,
to rest against the small of his back
before tomorrow's journey home.

Different Ways to Say the Same Thing
by J. White

It's hesitating at the moment of orgasm. It's seeing the numbers on the alarm clock—4:00—and seeing your legs tangled around his, in a languid, glistening heap like the roots of trees. It's realizing you don't know his name. It's knowing he looks more beautiful than you thought was possible—not beautiful like a painting, or a butterfly resting against an old building, but beautiful like seeing your own mother being saved from a sinking boat by Jesus himself or beautiful in the way that cools your eyes and makes you smile without wanting to. It's understanding what he's doing to you, biting your lip, and letting him do it harder. It's saying no and saying yes at the same time.

It's a sharp intake of breath. It's his lips. It's this night. It's the smell of the bar and the smell of his skin and the sterile smell of a hotel bed made twice today and three times the day before and two times tomorrow. It's grabbing his fingertips and pulling his palm over your chest and pressing down and squeezing. It's the little cries you didn't know you were making. It's the sound of the bed and the sound of his voice and the sound of his skin meeting yours. It's the dumb thoughts you know better now than to say out loud: "I love you," "I haven't done this in a while," "what was your name again?"

It's being scared and nervous and excited and foolish too and it's giving up your pride. It's being strong and confident and stoic and foolish too and it's holding something back. It's reaching up to put your hand on his chest, now, and seeing the color in his eyes, and only then remembering that you too have a body and a heart and a face; you'd forgotten all about it; it's losing all involvement with yourself when you start fucking him like you love him. It's coming back to your senses and assuring yourself that you don't. It's lifting yourself up to kiss him anyway.

It's not about the connection, or anything as rudimentary as that. It's about entering his life as a star, a sun, a golden blip against the dull background colors of real life. It's about wanting to be remembered. It's about twisting your hips just so, and tucking your bellybutton down to your spine, and wondering if he can feel it. It's lying on your back to come out on top. It's never letting anyone take advantage of you, even when they are. It's about adding a notch to your belt, a feather to your cap, a check on your list (you've always wanted to do this with a redhead) and steeling yourself—no, it's about the melting, the giving, not the taking— no, it's about the moment when it ends and the world seems to pause! flash! explode! celebrate! congratulate! console! and you realize you're gripping him pretty tight. It's about letting go.

It's the aftermath. It's his eyes and the world that swims behind them, the world you're swimming in, the white-blue ocean of serenity. It's the laugh that breaks the silence, the smile that won't fade, not yet; it's the glistening radiance of labor-induced love. It's flexing your abs. It's biting your lip and twisting your hips again just so. It's the collapse of a thousand civilizations; it's the collapse of your head against a pillow. It's the rise and fall of your chest as your reality reunites with your body. It's the little voices, the questions, the rationale, the flood and the drain of emotions as your world struggles to find equilibrium after the big bang.

———•••———

He doesn't know anything about me. I'm everything and I'm anything, right now. I'm in the bathroom. I'm in the mirror. If I pout my lips like this, I look like the girls in the magazines. If I paint my eyes black, I look like the girls in the photos. My skin is glowing. I'm smiling. I don't want to keep him waiting, but—

I don't know anything about him. He's everything and he's anything, right now. He's in the bedroom. I'm in the mirror. If I flex my abs like this, I look like the boys from the videos. If I shave my head into a Mohawk, I look like someone he'd know. My skin is taut. I'm unsure. I shouldn't be here, but—

I move like a fairy from the bath to the bed. When it's just him, when it's just me, I can be whatever I want. I can move my hips like the girls and I can flex my abs like the boys and I can show him my eyes and not be ashamed of anything. I can hide me and offer all of me by colliding into his chest, not stopping when I get to him, but pressing forward until we're two substances mixing together. I want to kiss him, but—

It's the aftermath. It's the subtlest, most dangerous dance of the night.

It's knowing it's going to end, that it's already over, and planning your next move. Extricate, extricate, untangle your legs from his and your fingers from his and your hair from his and your words from his and your plans from his. Abort, abort, leave while you're still flawless! Leave him remembering you as a poster of a boy, a one-dimensional perfect fuck, a body and not a mind. Don't let him see you think! Don't let him see your nervous smile, your uncertain eyes, your slow thoughts. Keep your poses strong! Tilt your chin this way, pout your lips like that, speak in small and mysterious words only when prompted. Hide yourself, lose yourself, and remain perfect. Light a cigarette at the edge of the bed: your shoulders are raised like the walls of a castle and you let him see your spine, let him see the constellation of freckles on your back. When did posing become truth? Take a drag, take a drag, let him watch you withdraw, make him wonder.

It's the war between transience and permanence—between right now and always—between drinking and remembering every detail—between sleeping together and waking up together—between being sweet and being genuine—between leaving now and getting brunch—between kissing with tongue and a kiss on the cheek—between being another one and being the only one—between dirty talk and small talk—between freedom and monogamy—between adventure and comfort—between what you know and what you don't know—between what you want and what you think he wants—that prompts you to get up, and smile, truly, stubbing your cigarette in an ashtray, saying naked and proud:

"Do you want to come to a party with me?"

…and then kissing him everywhere to end all wars.

Tina

by Claire Hawkins

Once you hit his pen, you knew he was the one. He was that cute guy, Rodney, with studs in his cheeks and dimples that made them twinkle. The two of you meandered away from the group to sit on the steps of your high school and watch the flow of students pour out of the doors of the classrooms. You leaned against the glow of him and he feather-brushed your cheek with the tips of his fingers. You knew then that all the sappy romantic songs were written from truth.

You and Rodney became an item. Through the halls you'd walk as if each was an appendage of the other. You were voted "Cutest Couple" in the yearbook even though you weren't part of the popular crowd. You took each other's virginity and when the two of you marched, hand in hand, in cap and gown, you were four months pregnant.

But you and Rodney did okay. You rented a three-bedroom house in a neighborhood that was mostly safe. Rodney had a stable job with a construction company, and you were the weekend manager at the minimart of a gas station. Two of your boys were diagnosed with ADHD but they were sweet kids, not oppositional or defiant. The family went on regular camping trips and one year you saved enough money for a trip to Disneyland.

You hadn't planned on going to the party, an impromptu reunion with old classmates just days after your youngest started kindergarten, but Rodney was out of town, working, and his mother had uncharacteristically offered to babysit. So, you found yourself in the backyard of a friend, drinking warm rum and coke. Metallica wafted from a dented boombox, and you were commiserating with the other women about the toll motherhood takes on one's looks. You were having fun but there was a tickle in your chest and head saying that you wanted something MORE, though you would not have been able to articulate what that was.

In a corner of the yard, in a patch of high weeds next to the remnants of a fence was a small group of women you'd vaguely known in high school. They had always seemed fun, so when they motioned for you to come over, you went. Up close, they were a little more ragged than you remembered. One had coarse, pock-marked skin, and another was missing a tooth. But you didn't judge. After all, you and Robbie had often skated on the brink of hard times. You could probably use some dental work yourself, had you better insurance.

After a few minutes of small talk, they introduced you to Tina, and you fell hard for her. Tina had a presence that allowed you to forget yourself. You had been feeling low lately, thinking that you weren't successful, that you had lost your looks, and that you weren't providing a good enough home for your kids. But after a short time with Tina you realized that you were stupendous—smart, sexy, and loved by everyone! What you had not yet accomplished, she told you, you easily could. You stayed with Tina for the entire party, and it didn't take much convincing to take her home with you.

The next three days alone with Tina were so passionate and exciting that at times you were certain you had transcended your body. Tina kept reinforcing your brilliance and creativity. You were going to take over the world! You would be rich and buy a house where each boy could have his own bedroom. You would go on vacations to Europe and Hawaii. How this would happen was a detail that you would think about later. In the meantime, you would landscape your yard. You were certain that you could make it look like something from Sunset magazine.

When it was dark and you had to go indoors, you and Tina painted the interior of the house in maroon and gold, the colors of your and Rodney's high school football team.

When Rodney returned, he came home to a yard filled with haphazard piles of dirt, half-painted rooms, and three filthy, hungry children (it turned out that childcare was not Tina's forte and that the children had spent the previous days eating dry Captain Crunch and hacking into porn). He was furious. He bathed the boys and fed them spaghetti and even made them eat broccoli. After he put them to bed, he was ready to have it out with you but, before he could, you introduced him to Tina, and he, too, was instantly head over heels.

Your shared devotion to Tina brought you and Rodney closer. The three of you would stay up all night laughing and talking, playing video games and rearranging furniture. You also started to spend more time with Tina's friends. Your bond was so close that they came in and out of the house unannounced. If Tina was there, then the whole "gang" would be. In the bedroom, Tina became a welcome third party. While your boys fended for themselves in the rest of the house, the three of you would go at it, non-stop, for over twenty-four hours, sometimes.

As much as all your passions were enflamed beyond anything imaginable, there were downsides to Tina's presence. You had always kept a clean house, but soon after Tina's arrival, all housecleaning fell by the wayside. The kitchen counters were strewn with moldy food and greasy fast food wrappers. You would forget to take out the trash to the point that it was difficult to walk into the kitchen without stepping on wads of squishy paper towels, moldy food, and crusted silverware. Tina also told you it was okay to let the dogs do their business in the living room and hallway.

A few months later, when Rodney was working, he was distracted by Tina and caused an accident that cost the company thousands of dollars and seriously injured a co-worker. After a decade with the company, he was fired. Two weeks later Tina convinced you to steal from the minimart, and you were caught and subsequently let go. Rodney worked some odd jobs, but it wasn't enough for living expenses and for Tina, who was getting more demanding. Not only were you evicted, you were fined for the condition of the house. Tina had caused fist holes in the walls, missing appliances, broken windows, and an illegal firepit in the backyard. You were forced to move into a rundown studio with a shared bathroom down the hall. The neighborhood was dangerous, but closer to Tina.

You didn't know that Benny, your youngest, had all those burns on his back until his shirt stuck to them. You took him to the hospital, as a good mother should, but the hospital called Social Services, and in a blink of an eye, all four of your boys were in foster care. You were allowed to visit for one supervised hour once a week, and this hour was more important than anything, but somehow Tina got in the way. You were told that you had to be on time, but it was difficult with Tina around. And you especially could not visit, they told you, if Tina was with you. After you had missed too many visits, they told you that if you wanted to see your boys, you had to attend a program where you could learn to live without Tina.

The anxiety of ending your relationship with Tina kept you from committing, but you did go to a few of those meetings. You sat on a folding chair in a church basement where the walls were festooned with postered slogans. You listened to people talk about their own relationships with Tina or with Blow or Smack or Oxy. You ached for your children and for Rodney, who was incarcerated for possession of firearms. At the end of each meeting, they told you to come back because "it" worked. But you couldn't see how it worked if you'd always go home to your tent by the creek, and by the light of a flashlight in your mouth, you'd wrap a cord around your arm and shoot Tina's love into your veins.

The Book of Condolence
By Ali Abbas

You didn't know her, not the way I did. The newspapers focus on the blood and scars, the dead stare and the rucked-up dress. I loved her when her eyes were sapphires. Before she lit up the world.

She knew she was beautiful, bought and bribed her way through life with it. Always with a smile, never malice. Generous with her gifts, the notoriety of her orbit. Once, in the time before fame, when she was just someone who caught and held the eye, there was a splinter in her cycling shorts, just below the crease of her right buttock. She stopped in the middle of the market square, a hundred eyes looking on with hunger and envy as she asked me to remove it.

I still remember the warm promise of the bread we had bought for lunch, and the stretch of the gray and pink fabric. A rare moment my skin was intimate with her skin, unhooking a splinter more precious to me than a piece of the true cross. A moment that made me visible. Her generosity, her orbit.

My hand hesitates above the book of condolence. This is not the story to write here. The memory warms my nights. I leaf through the pages. Platitudes of candles that burned too bright and worlds that are darker. I wonder how many of them have known the candles and the darkness, if someone who has signed this book brought them into her life.

In bold strokes the famous ex-lovers have left their marks. Crafted lines from PR firms copied from scraps of paper. I need to believe them inane. There are truths about her that should be mine alone. Let their words share the veneer of stardom you all saw. The shell above the grime, the grime above the girl. The girl who once lay with me on a bed.

We met at university. She had the key to my room. Coffee, paper, condoms all went missing with her breezing in and out. She took my copy of Jude the Obscure. Months later it turned up, misplaced on my shelf. Dogeared and ring stained. I riffled the pages with my thumb. Arabella loath to miss out on The Bumps, Jude dying in despair.

"I do love you, you know that right?" scrawled in the margin, in her trademark rounded script.

I have come prepared with Shelley's words to a married woman, but now I want to write her words back to her. I can't. I left her for the last time with candles and darkness. My last act was abandonment when she was in despair. Her eyes dim and desperate. I walked out as demon shadows crawled up the walls. Her last words to me were "Fuck you." Not said but screeched. "Fuck you." And the clatter of a plastic cup against the wall. Not even the satisfaction of shattering glass. Sobbing. "Fuck you," echoing behind the closed door.

I didn't leave for an hour. The marble porch, cold seeping into me. I waited until I thought I too had become stone. I could have taken keys for any one of her three cars, knowing she would never hold that against me. I walked. Away from her quiet house with the long gravel drive, pre-dawn too early for the paparazzi. Sobbing from inside. Outside the first chirps of birds.

Should I write how I lost her? Somewhere in that lightening chill and the gentle rain. The three-mile walk to the station, the waiting for the train. Fifty yards down the track, out of sight of her house, I took off all my clothes, held my arms up to the sky. As if washing her off my skin would be enough. As if she was not lichen, bound through skin to bone. I took away her keys to my life and said goodbye. Holding only the market square and the minutes we lay together on a narrow bed.

Those minutes had come in a student high summer. Sticky, a room designed to keep out the chill. She burst in, a Catherine wheel of excitement. Incandescent. She leapt upon my prone form, threw aside my book. Careless of the thin sheet between her and my nakedness. Our bones touching through cotton and skin.

"I got the part." Breathlessly between kisses. It would be her breakthrough, a platform that propelled her to awards and riches; that opened the door to the darkness. I don't know which agent or co-star brought the needles and the candles into her life. Perhaps I set her on that path, when she won the part to my play, to say my words. My gentle suggestion to the director had been unnecessary, I had written her, he had seen it at once.

I think if I had put my arms around her then I could have made love to her, the door to my room still gaping open. Instead, I returned her sexless kisses with a congratulatory one of my own. What if I had asked for her not to be cast? What if I had pulled away that thin sheet? What if I had said, "Stay Charlotte Emily Greenberg, don't be Lotte Green on the playbill."

She shone that season, inhabiting the mortal form I had wrought for her on the page. Her performance made my reputation. My play made her a star. I orbited her for years thereafter, sometimes arm in arm on the red carpet, between the lovers and the breakups. Periodic perigees between flashes of flirtations with other stellar bodies, as predictable as the long vacancies in between. She would call, I would answer. Until I couldn't bear her weight loss and her spiral, her skeletal feet and the dark shadows under her eyes, the dark shadows that danced on the walls.

I lost my words. Playwrights are more easily forgotten, but she was a point of deeper contrasts for the lenses and the columnists. Her decay was documented, the absence beside her ignored.

An object cannot change its orbit of its own free will. I lacked the power to cast myself into a void, outside her radiance and her shadow. It was inevitable that we would at some point collide in the atrophy of separation. I went back, to hold, to heal, to remonstrate. To see if the piece of her I held inside me could find some resonance in what remained. And I left her in the debris of her impending extinction. A star burning out to the sounds of sobbing, screaming, and the false promise of a new dawn.

I washed her off my skin in the cool of that arriving morning. I scrubbed rain through my hair, clothes strewn across guardian granite boulders, faces scarred by the elements. I wanted to be something new, freshly cut from the quarry like Seferis. I failed to detach the part of her that was imprinted on my bones the one time our bodies had lain together. I still have that copy of Jude. It falls open at the page of Arabella and The Bumps.

I don't know what to write. Shelley is insufficient. It's not enough for her to be a seraph, it's not enough to remember her as youth's vision, gentle and betrayed.

I think I might be crying, there's a blot on the page, a shuffle in the queue behind me. I don't sign my name. I write what she was to me. Emily.

A Graveside Nuptial
By Sean Finucane Toner

I wonder what Robin sees as she ushers me through the jewelry shops, the Irish shop, the store with its '60s paraphernalia. The streets in New Hope, Pennsylvania, are tree lined. The restaurants have charm. The engagement rings we finally choose are hand-crafted. But how closely does what I feel match what she sees?

She guides me down to the canal. Today, on this rare day, I am in the lead, her arm hooked around mine, as if we were any other strolling couple. No walking with her in front, me off to her flank with my left hand on her shoulder. The white cane is still in my right hand, but this is our betrothal day, a day for traditional roles of man and woman, as well as we can portray them.

As we walk, she describes sundry forms of spring verdancy—swatches of lawn, ivied trees, jaybirds and cardinals in flight. We walk along the waterway, approach the place where it enters the Delaware, and I picture the reflection of life on its face.

"How wide is the canal?" I ask.

"You could throw a ball across it. Easily."

And now I've got scale and color to add to the memory—images of canals and wide-porched homes from my three decades with sight, which preceded this one without.

"Let's step aside," she says as a beleaguered tow horse or mule draws a tourist sight-seeing skiff toward us. There's a respectful "hello" from Robin to the animal, and then we walk on until she pauses, searches out a suitable spot, says "Let's move a little further up." After a few more paces, she says, "This is good." We step off the tow path and onto a strip of patchy grass.

Physically, this is not one of my better days. Heat, pollen allergies, and perhaps something in my breakfast augment the constant dis-ease of a body with malfunctioning organs. I toss my white cane to the ground and lower myself to one knee—the victory stance of a quarterback in the last moments of a winning game or a hero about to be knighted. Then I take to both knees in a gesture of supplication and prayer. I unpocket the ring with its turquoise inlays, find her hand awaiting mine. I reach out and say, "Will you be my wife, Robin?"

We have been together for a year now, and she is intimate with my body in disrepair. Eyes and kidneys taken by decades of mishandled diabetes, a donor kidney tucked into my abdomen, constant blood-glucose monitoring, and three insulin injections each day—I can scarcely fend for myself.

Yet, my body is translucent to her, she sees through the dark glasses, past the bruises and scars, around the damaged and missing organs. She sees something beyond the reach of myopic microscopes and all those colored plates in Grey's Anatomy. There is something in me that cannot be measured, and it is all for her.

Ever-so-quietly she says, "I will marry you." Her voice is strained, tearful perhaps. And during the moment I hear tears of bliss, not fear. But we both know Death has been loitering, glancing at his Rolex, ever since I was a toddler. Now he will be the third wheel in our marriage.

I kiss her hand and slide the ring on.

She returns the ring-gesture by slipping mine on my finger. Then she helps me to my feet.

We stroll along the canal, eventually decide to head back to the bed and breakfast because the heat and low blood-sugar levels are wearing on me. We come upon the horse again. His breath is heavy with the exertion of drawing a great weight. I know his type. He is a Rocinante who, in his off-hours, daydreams of being Trigger.

Our autumn wedding day is overcast, confettied with spritzes of rain. But this does not deter us. Robin pulls into the chapel entrance of Saints Peter and Paul Cemetery, circles the building, and heads up the central drive to my family's plot.

A few thousand will soon witness our exchange of vows. They are lined up, row after row, gathered together in kinship groups, toe-to-toe with other attendees—all attired in their sartorial best. They must delight in the sound of Robin's approaching Subaru, my muffled classic rock emanating from the closed windows. The Who or Joe Walsh must be a welcome relief to the ceaseless stillness. Music, lively music, is the only respect I can give to the deceased, and I'm picturing so many ghosts mouthing the lyrics, faces broadening into wan smiles. Our wedding is a gala event for a lawn full of seniors, reunited couples, and even the rare little ones.

Life's been comparatively good to me, so far.

"Remind me what we're looking for," Robin says.

"Second or third intersection. Right-hand corner. Maybe one row back."

"I'm looking for your family name?"

"No. Toppitzer. My Aunt Catherine." I do not need to remind Robin that my aunt was a mortician, spent much of her life among the dead, brought many to this place. But listed under the serifed sweep of her name are a half dozen other extended family members, people I know and still love: my grandfather Jack, an advertising executive who died of Parkinson's; my uncle John, a rumored Vietnam War codebreaker and a confirmed bank robber; and my grandmother Mary, the woman who gave me shelter from my troubled father, who substituted for my abused and madness-driven mother, who gave me a safe home when I lost my kidneys and eyes in my late twenties.

We pull to a stop. I hear Robin undo her seatbelt and adjust herself as she, presumably, seeks out the gravesite and says, "Let me come around to make sure you're not stepping out into mud."

She cuts the engine, the song dies out, and she climbs from the car into chill and a landscape of etched granite and autumn grass. She opens the back door, removes the cake fashioned from carnations. Robin then comes around for me.

With my hand on her shoulder, she leads me around pockets of mud and over uneven grass. We come upon Granny, placed in the midst of the Ciarrocchios, the Ruffos, and the O'Briens, doing her best—as she always did at serious gatherings—to entertain a crowd of stiffs.

Robin says "Hi Mary," and then "Hi Kitty," to my mortician aunt, whom she knows only by reputation. Robin moves away from me, and the slight whisper of fabric and flower petals tell me she's placed the cake at the grave.

When she returns, Robin says "Feel," as she draws my hand above her ear where's she's tucked one of the carnations.

I saw for nearly thirty years. I know endearing when I see it.

We stand, holding hands for a few minutes. Robin is studying the names on the family plot, I'm seeing the ghost of my grandmother's face as it was in the last of my sighted days. I'm expecting a sign from our shared time—a cardinal from her sunflower-seed feeding days, something buzzing off the page of her beloved Yeats' "The Lake Isle of Innisfree" and its "bee-loud glade." Instead, I hold the umbrella against the drizzle while the two of us stand alone.

No presiding officials are needed: my SSI health benefits are gone if I earn a living or marry an earner. We have no need for a presiding emissary of God: Robin is half-Jewish, half-other, and all-secular. I was raised Catholic, but I'm more into Jesus the hippie-philosopher and his "do unto others" aphorism, and part a follower of Monty Python's Life of Brian and its "blessed are the cheesemakers."

As for family, Robin's schizophrenic mother has long been deceased, her abandoning father has been long absent, and my father would not be welcome for reasons too numerous to enumerate. My eccentric mom—who fled when I was six—has been in constant contact, and if invited, would attend with more of the gift she has given me all along: dark humor. But what had seemed, when conceived, a nuptial worthy of a Poe short story or the union of Percy Shelley and Mary Godwin now feels like the wedding plans of a marginalized teenager or an eccentric. So, I am glad Robin's sisters live on the West Coast, that my sister resides in Boulder, and my extended family of cousins have all drifted to South Jersey and then down the coast after my grandmother's death. Ours is a quiet party.

"Are we ready?" I ask.

"I am."

"Who goes first?"

"I will," Robin says. "Move the umbrella closer over me while I read my vows." Then she unpockets the index card she has her wedding promises written on and swears, "In the presence of this beautiful and awesome universe," to make me her husband in the traditional ways, in the "for better and worse" and the "for richer and poorer" ways, and "in sickness and in health."

Her words float there, under the shielding umbrella. They settle upon me, are absorbed by me, become part of me.

"And when death parts our bodies, still will you be my husband, and I your wife, until the end of time."

These are not uncommon promises. They are spoken on so many sunny days, in posh hotels or serene park settings, by kids in their twenties and by remarrying middle-agers. Here, now, the words of love have taken on new meaning, have attired themselves in defiant optimism.

I have come to our wedding moment with an advance vow, to myself, not to joke away my tension, to reign in the one-liners and glib asides that are my tendency during times of excitement. And though I often tend to be baroque, colorful, and filigreed, I am to the point, laconic, manly in my promise to her. "Upon my grandmother's grave, I swear to love no other, to be with no other, forever." Then I remove the ring from my pocket, take Robin's hand, and slip it on. I repeat, "Forever."

Robin takes my hand, holds it for a moment, then places my wedding ring on my finger. She draws me to her with a few words, a "You may kiss the bride" kind of thing, and when our lips meet I'm, as always, an adolescent boy sharing my first kiss. The sensation is exciting and a little surprising. I am amazed at and frightened by somebody wanting me.

We stand together for a few minutes, the drizzle sounding like a cascade of rice, the clouds our wedding party.

"Guess there aren't any birds. No cardinals or anything?" I ask.

"I'm sorry," Robin says.

"Not even a crow? There were tons of crows in Granny's neighborhood."

"I'm really sorry," she says.

Soon, Robin says, "Goodbye Mary. Goodbye Kitty."

I say, "So looong, Granny," the way she drew out her goodbyes to me. "See you Kitty."

Robin leads me back to the car, starts it up. The music is on, old friends like Frampton or Fogarty strike up the dance. When we head down the lane, I'm feeling a little melancholic. Maybe planning our wedding on the anniversary of my grandmother's death, at her graveside, in the rain, wasn't my best idea. But I hold firm to my purpose. This was an event as much for spirits as for bodies.

Robin says, "There are two balloons in the sky."

"Hot air balloons? Today?"

"No. Two silver party balloons. Spinning. Like two gray-haired ladies waltzing."

I find this hard to believe. October? In the intermittent rain? "Who's having a party outdoors today?" I ask. And with a tone that hints at knowing, add "Who would dream up a thing like that?"

One Stage (Spring)
by Emily Rapp Black

And then you cried all the time—
some fine thread tweezing through
ecstatic numbness:
a letter that reads like a painting,
an unexpected kindness, a book
you finally read, finding
death in every line, fingering the
red-gold tangle of rotting hair
in its plastic bag like an unhinged lover. Dead
hair from a dead boy.

Birds fight for nest space
on the roof, in the just-budding trees,
and you hate them. You are
everywhere and nowhere. You
don't know what to do. You knit
invisibly, in metaphor, in the body,
this useless, winding endeavor.

You wear the world on your finger
like a thimble, tap doors,
test the strength of dark windows
rattling like a sign you don't
believe in but look for, still. You make your lover
pull mice from the kitchen traps.

The day is a weapon: the couple
unstrapping their dark helmets
in the parking lot,
the toddler brushing a stray
curl from his forehead.
A cloud in motion. Light.

Your head is a balloon, a bomb, a gun.
Altitude and depth have no meaning.
Suspended over landscapes you feel nothing.
At night your body expands like a raft.

And this singular unfairness: even in the desert,
grass continues to grow.

erased boy
by Isabelle Jia

we are warm bellied mistakes
lying next to ripe milkweed angels.
wild bulbs of light with their
wings folded like tulips but i still feel
moonless.

the taste of red hibiscus seems so
foreign like it's wrong to think
i found a goodboy.
he gives me sweet citrus like
kisses by an empty lake.

they tell me there are no goodboys
lacking a dog. but what they don't know is
i am the dog.
what i meant was i am the good boy.
or maybe i was just a boy
or maybe i wasn't anything at all.

7-Eleven Blues
by Jackie Craven

Don't the dead have an expiration date?
says a lady at the convenience store. Vapor rises
around her face. Her pale hands hold a carton of Half & Half.

The milk I purchased already smells off
and all the way home I ponder the problem of ghosts
who linger in the dairy aisle, turning sour.

A seatbelt alarm goes wah-wah-waaaah
because my Chevrolet mistakes the one gallon weight
for the husband I buried long ago.

I'd buy a new car, but he's still in this one,
crooning through the broken radio—Sorry sorry, oh-oh so sorry—
notes off-key, apology past due.

She Who Hears the Cries of the World
by Winter Ross

It was not a good day to die—It was too beautiful. The Denver smog was behind us. Before us was the pass, its peaks snow-capped even in July. I'd driven 1,200 miles to deliver my two children to their father for a summer visit. The Boyfriend, along for the ride, had entertained the kids in exchange for an opportunity to get away from the humidity of the East Coast. My sadness and anxiety about being separated from my little ones had motivated me to schedule a retreat at a Zen Center within a day's drive of them.

We drove by a group of people on the side of the road. A flat tire, I thought, as I glanced in the rear-view mirror. But the reversed image reflected the truth. Startled, I recognized the posture of a man performing CPR and braked. Boyfriend, who'd been keeping his eyes closed against the sting of gritty contact lenses, looked over at me from the passenger seat in surprise. It was no time to slow down. The van needed momentum to climb through the thin air.

"Someone's hurt back there," I explained.

"Nothing we can do about it." He pulled at his beard.

"You know I was an EMT. I'm going back."

He shrugged, "It's up to you."

99

Taking a deep breath, I swung the wheel of the van hard to the right to gain extra road for a U-turn. Still, the wide turning radius of the vehicle brought it close to the mountain's edge.

The complaining tires flung sandstone into the canyon below but the van obeyed. I pulled into a wide space across from the gathering and got out. Brushing the hair out of my face, I glanced both ways for traffic and ran across the road to the fallen figure.

He was a big man in his late 50's, stretched out on his back on the red soil. I took in the twisted bike on the ground nearby. Too old and out of shape to be biking up a mountain, I thought. Should've known better… probably a heart attack.

A young man, blond hair obscuring his face, knelt at the bicyclist's head, breathing for him through a plastic mouthguard. A middle-aged man in a Department of Wildlife uniform, leaned hard into the bicyclist's chest. I bent between them. "I'm an EMT, if you need help." Both men hesitated. The younger stopped for the count and looked up as if to make way for me. "No. Don't stop!" I said, "Unless you have to. You're doing fine."

I'd come from sea level and could barely breathe for one. I knew I couldn't put air into those dying lungs as effectively as the twenty-year-old across from me. The body on the ground was heavy and solid. I could see it took all the government man's weight and strength to reach his heart. I wasn't strong enough to help much in that position either.

I slid my palm beneath the bicyclist's neck, made sure the airway was open, then felt along the soft jowls for the carotid artery. "I think I can feel what you're doing, but no pulse," I murmured to the man grunting beside me. He glanced sideways and nodded. Sweat trickled through his thinning hair and down into the collar of his uniform. The broad chest beneath his hands barely rose between compressions.

"You need to breathe a little harder," I coached Younger. "That's good. If you get dizzy, stop and I'll take over, okay?"

"Thanks, I'm alright." he whispered over the bloated face between us.

So, I just crouched there between the struggling men, trying to be helpful, my fingers on the bicyclist's damp wrist. I never felt a pulse. I could have checked his pupils but I didn't. I didn't have to. I didn't want to look into a dead man's eyes.

I found myself looking, instead, up into a sky of such deep blue that I could sense the stars behind it. A chill came over me as I imagined the bicyclist looking down on us: three strangers kneeling in the desert dirt around his body, agonizing over our inept attempts to bring him back. Was his lingering consciousness comforted by the compassion of these strangers?

Forcing myself to take a breath of my own, I looked around. Vehicles were parked haphazardly. I noticed another bike flung on the ground. A thin man, watching through tears, twisted his biking hat between his hands; a man in jeans stood with a ten-year-old boy squatting near his patched knee. I looked for Boyfriend. He leaned against a stray U-haul trailer with his arms folded, a spectator. Blue Jeans picked up the bikes and put them in the trunk of an old Buick, where a woman waited behind the wheel. The boy didn't move.

"Ambulance and sheriff are coming," the wildlife officer gasped, nodding toward his green pickup. Its radio antennas shone in the sun. "It won't be long."

Almost as he spoke, a white truck with a gold star laminated on the side swerved into the pull-off. Clouds of dust and gravel tore from the wheels. The sheriff banged open the truck door and ran toward us. "Hey, Bob! Let me take over for you, there."

Wildlife shook his head, sweat spinning into the dry air. He had a grimace of irony on his face. "No, man. I have so much adrenalin going, I'd explode if I quit."

"You sure?"

"I'm sure."

"You okay, son?"

Younger nodded and kept breathing.

The sheriff noticed my fingers on the bicyclist's wrist and raised his eyebrows. I shook my head.

He turned back to the truck to report to the ambulance coming along behind him somewhere in the rough forest at the bottom of the pass.

The ambulance crew, two men and a woman, were from the village. Although they toted high-tech equipment and wore orange jumpsuits, it was clear they weren't used to handling life or death situations every day. An IV had to be inserted twice by hands that were visibly shaking. Their patient vomited reflexively, and the tube pressed down his throat had to be readjusted. Electrodes hastily taped to his skin wired him to a red box full of gauges.

"Everybody back! Clear!"

The big body stretched out stiffly, convulsing. I looked away. I saw the ten-year-old, his eyes wide and face as white as the dead man's, still sitting in the dirt unattended. I moved to block his view and caught the kid's eyes with my own. I heard the next "Clear!" behind me.

"This is not something you need to watch. Go back to your mom and dad."

With a look of relief, the boy got up and headed toward the Buick without a word. I watched him, wondering at parents who'd leave their child to witness this and thinking how amazingly easy it was to order someone else's kid around and get an unquestioning response. My own would have ignored me.

"Clear!"

From the corner of my eye I saw Younger, standing now, sway. Both hands covered his face. I walked over to him, put my arm around his back to steady him. We stood together silently, averting our faces at the next "Clear!"

"What am I going to tell his family?" the thin man moaned. "What am I going to say to his wife? It was my idea to ride today. How can I face them? The ambulance was too late! It's taking too long!" He turned a tear-streaked face to me. "He's dead, isn't he? Don't you think he's dead?"

"I think so." I answered hesitantly, trying to soften the obvious. "Don't blame yourself. It's not your fault."

One of the paramedics shot me a hard look. "There will be a counselor at the hospital to talk to him," he said in a tone that told me to shut up. "Let's get the gurney."

It took six of us, straining, to lift the bicyclist's body onto the gurney, the gurney onto the ambulance. We almost lost him once, tipping at the step up to the wide orange doors. The body rolled toward me, the blue-white lips brushing my arm. Finally, the gurney slid in. I gave one paramedic a hand up into the back and slammed the doors after her while the other two climbed into the front. The ambulance arced onto the road, its siren screaming down the mountain air. The sheriff, his yellow lights whirling, drove after, followed by the tearful man and the family in the Buick.

After the echo faded, Younger wandered the turnout, stooping to pick up bloody pieces of gauze, bits of white tape, strewn tubing. His companion, who had waited quietly in their Volvo, packed up their first aid kit. Younger looked at me, then up at the sky. "All this… and for nothing. What good did we do?"

"You did the best you could do. That's good enough."

"Yeah, I guess you're right. Thanks." He'd removed all evidence of the tragedy. The pull-off was pristine as an environmentalist's campsite. He ducked into the Volvo and waved as they headed on over the pass.

I scuffed across the road to the van, where Boyfriend had re-settled himself. Mica twinkled in the black asphalt at the road edge. I walked around the van and skidded down the bank toward a low wall of willow. Puffs of red earth drifted away from my feet, rabbit brush scratched at my knees. I couldn't see the stream but knew willow grew only beside water in this dry country. I pushed my way through the narrow-leaved branches and squatted as close to an eddy as I could. With my hiking boots sinking into the sand, I washed the dead man's drying vomit from the back of my hand and forearm. The shallow water was fast, clear, and cold enough to numb. Beyond my reddening fingertips, fool's gold sparkled in the sandy bed. I reached to touch it, but wavelets caught the sun and threw painful shards of light into my eyes. I turned stiffly, shook my hands. Rainbow prism droplets flew, evaporating before they hit the ground. I ran my palms across my eyelids and into my tangled hair. Sighing, I lurched back up the bank and hauled myself into the driver's seat.

Boyfriend sprawled on the passenger side, head back, eyelids clamped. "My eyes are killing me," he whined, opening one a fraction to regard me. I ignored him, reached for the keys in the ignition, and glanced in the rearview mirror. The road and turn-out beyond were eerily empty—as if the past had been a mirage. Already it seemed a shimmering dream in the day's heat. It had to have happened, I told myself. The van was facing the valley we'd already traveled. I cranked the wheel laboriously to turn back uphill.

At the top of the pass, I looked out across the plain below to another mountain range: the Sangre de Cristos. Legend has it that two hundred years ago, a priest, mortally wounded by natives, took refuge on a raft in some lake down there. He had watched the snow on the peaks turn deep pink with alpenglow as the sun set behind him. "Sangre de Cristo," Blood of Christ, were his dying words.

Down valley, we drove past a pink stucco café, and I spotted a payphone on the outside wall. "Do you wanna stop for breakfast?" Boyfriend prodded. Eat? Is it still morning? My shoulders ached, my hands gripped the wheel as if they were melted on.

"No. I need to talk to my kids. I need to hear their voices."

"What do you mean, 'No'? I'm starving!" Boyfriend glared at me from his eye slits.

"We're expected for lunch at the Zen Center," I reminded him. "You can wait." I parked in front of the phone. I dropped a quarter in, but all I got was the ex's voice on an answering machine.

Up in the Sangres, junipers and ponderosa pine stretched out their arms and waved alongside the four-wheel track to the center. I knew this road. I'd dreamed about it years ago. A carved wooden sign said, "Welcome to Dharma Sangha." We left the van in a small parking lot, climbed the path, unlatched a gate, crossed a tiny lawn, and opened a rusty screen door to the back entry. Low shelves were lined with shoes and sandals. We slipped out of our boots and padded into the kitchen.

"Welcome! Welcome! Come in and sit down!" A monk in tee-shirt and shorts bowed formally, giggled, then gave us both hugs. His shirt was decorated with a portrait of Yoda, the wise little master from Star Wars, and the words, "May the Force Be With

You." I couldn't imagine him in a long black robe. He rubbed his shaved head. "Is something wrong?"

"Put me to work!" I pleaded. "Give me something to do. I can't sit."

"Sorry, hon. That's what we do here!"

I tried to laugh, but I felt too dried out.

"You won't believe the morning we had!" Boyfriend interrupted cheerfully. "This woman is a hero!" The other two monks in the kitchen put down their knives and hurried around the counter to hear his story. Their salad preparations would be postponed by speculations of exactly which mountain pass had claimed the life of the bicyclist. Surrounded by craggy peaks that regularly took the lives of climbers and hikers, they were keeping score. Boyfriend had hooked his audience. "They musta shocked the guy five times."

I backed out of the kitchen, left the performance behind, and entered the open space of the monastery's main hall. Giant ponderosa logs formed the ceiling vigas. The vigas supported a long room that jutted from an earth berm to the open hillside. I blinked in the white light coming in through the windows. The entire southern wall was glass. Black paper cutouts of swallows were taped high on each pane to warn real birds away. A painful crack, running from ceiling to floor in one panel, was either testament to the futility of communicating with nature or a memorial to a pre-cutout casualty. I could see past the lawn, beyond a tangled garden of herbs and poppies, to the sagebrush floor of the valley. If I squinted off into the distance, I could just make out the Great Sand Dunes nestled at the foot of the mountains.

Silent children. Seas of sand. Corridors of dreams. Bleeding mountains. Gold for fools. A dead man's kiss. Suddenly I felt like a bird hitting the window, feathers scattered, stunned. The light flared in rhythm with my pounding head. I had to shut my eyes and turn away.

When I opened them again, I saw a figure begin to emerge from the shadow of the north wall. It seemed to move toward me as my eyes became accustomed to the dimness. It took my complete attention, finally, and filled my frame of vision. Before me stood a life-sized statue poised on a low pedestal. Kuan Yin, the Buddhist goddess of compassion, gazed serenely at me from the darkness. The lustrous eyes were not heavy-lidded and inward looking like those of the Buddha. Instead, she stared steadily out from the shade to the harsh landscape beyond the monastery. The flowing robes, cast in black patina bronze, glowed with polished detail. Her left hand held a budding lotus. Prayer beads trailed down the folds of her gown and ornate hems lapped like waves around one bare foot. Her right hand held a small pouch from which flowed a stream of water. Slender fingers opened gracefully toward the ground in a gesture that suggested both offering and acceptance. She seemed to be waiting patiently for whatever the desert brings. Waiting, with water, for whoever crosses the pass.

I felt the peace of this Bodhisattva flow over me like a cool wave. The images of the panting wildlife officer, the little boy wide-eyed with horror, the trembling hands of the paramedic, the young man swooning in my arms, and the tears of the thin man, faded as I met the deep gaze of the goddess known as "She Who Hears the Cries of the World." I brought my palms together before my face and bowed. The taste of salt tears brought me back to myself.

When Yoda-monk entered the hall with a vase of flowers for the table, I straightened and quickly brushed at my cheeks, embarrassed.

"May I help?" I asked.

"Sure, sweetie. Come back to the kitchen. You can grab the kettle and cups. We'll make tea."

The Astonishment of It All
by Marian Armstrong Rogers

This warm, sunny day my husband Sam and I are sitting on a bench in front of Starbucks on Main Street in White Plains, sipping coffee and watching fountains of water lift and curve as if dancing to the music flowing from speakers mounted on the building.

Twenty-five years ago, this block was empty, the earth lumpy and strewn with debris from a demolished building. An old, scarred bench sat at its edge so construction workers could take a break. We had sat on that bench, Sam and I, while he begged me to keep seeing him even if marriage were out of the question. "We can have pockets of happiness," He'd said.

"Do you remember?" I ask now, and am immediately sorry. In this pleasant moment, I've no wish to remind him of the Alzheimer's whittling at his memories.

"Of course I remember," he answers.

And maybe he does. It doesn't matter, today it's enough to be sitting on this new bench, mesmerized and delighted by dancing fountains that were only a dream in someone's mind when I was a dream in Sam's.

That summer, we went to White Plains often, old roots pulling me back to the city where I'd lived most of my life, and where I felt a measure of peace. It was about a twenty-minute drive from the condominium we'd moved into the previous autumn, a move that had left Sam restless, irritable, and incessantly complaining: "Apartments always run down." "No one takes care of places like this." "In ten years, this place will be an eyesore!"

The thoughts had lodged in his brain and would loop round and round, be repeated over and over, driving me crazy since it was I who had insisted on moving us back to Westchester, even though it meant leaving a spacious townhouse for a small apartment.

So, I began taking Sam to a philosophy discussion group we had enjoyed in Pawling, where we'd lived before moving here—an exhausting two-hour trip by train, since I no longer drove at night, but worth it because though I took Sam, knowing he missed our previous life, I needed the stimulating conversation even more than he did. And, too, I was fond of the facilitator, a professor I admired and considered a friend.

One night, realizing I had responded to a subject of special interest to me a bit too long, I said, "Oh, I'm sorry. I don't want to dominate the discussion."

"Well then why don't you stop?" the professor said. It felt like a slap.

"Okay, I will," I answered, fighting not to cry, not to make a spectacle of myself, not to alarm Sam. I said not another word.

I'd thought myself emotionally strong, with the taxing move to Westchester that had frayed my nerves behind us, but after that night I went into a tailspin, crying for days, hiding in the bathroom so Sam (who was now easily upset), would not see me. Until then, I hadn't minded taking Sam anyplace at all—possibly I was in denial—but now I noticed couples in our building going out together to shop or lunch or for dinner in the evening, the wives gracefully stepping into cars their husbands had driven to the front steps. And I wanted my husband to pick me up and take me someplace.

It wasn't his fault that he couldn't do that anymore, but neither was it mine, and a simmering resentment at all that had happened, was happening, and would continue to happen, lodged in my heart like a low-grade fever.

As Sam's neurological muscular weakness increased, he fell walking home from the corner grocery, breaking his arm; fell on the front steps, hit his head, got a shiner and proudly said, "I look like I've been in a barroom brawl!"; and fell while stepping up a curb as we were returning from lunch in town with Pawling friends. That date ended in the emergency room, Sam with a badly bruised side, and I, having landed beneath him, with a sprained right wrist, and broken right leg.

I soon learned that Sam's short-term memory was now short indeed, as every morning, seeing me in a wheelchair (my balance too poor for crutches), he asked, "What happened to you?!"

Usually I would say, "Oh, I fell and broke my leg," or "Don't worry, I'll be better soon. Don't worry, it doesn't hurt." But once, feeling deprived when Sam was unable to get the wheelchair over the metal strips of the patio doors so I could sit outside on a gorgeous warm day, I told him in a flat voice, through clenched teeth: "You. Fell. On. Me!"

"Oh, say not so!" Sam said then, like one of his beloved Shakespearian characters might have done, downcast, and sorrowful.

Two minutes later he had forgotten and was in the kitchen getting cereal and making coffee, still able to do these things, able to make sandwiches too, though the ham or cheese or mayonnaise or mustard might disappear until I found it in a cabinet, a drawer, or sometimes in the freezer, where coffee filters were almost always found, and once, in winter, his wool hat.

One day, guilty and sorry over some mean thing I'd said (I don't recall what), and wanting to erase the sadness I'd drawn on Sam's face, I quickly said, "Don't mind me, Sam. When I don't feel well, I'm mean as a striped snake."

"I never saw a mean snake," he said, laughing out loud.

Another day I complained about something done or not done in the kitchen and he yelled: "It's my home, too!" I was glad. It was such a normal response.

Sometime during those difficult days, my resentment melted away as neighbors brought meals, and daughters Laura, Catherine, and Beth, came to bathe me, and stepdaughter Holly took Sam on Saturday or Sunday so I'd have a day of peace (not easy for our daughters to do in this age of liberated women with responsible positions outside of the home).

When Holly took Sam, I welcomed the solitude, feeling lonelier when he was home, where he had become unnaturally polite and was offended when I was not. Now I was supposed to say: Would you mind putting that light out, please? Not, Get that light, would you, Honey? It was like living with a stranger— and love?

One morning Sam came out of the bedroom and into the kitchen where, fully functional again, I was getting our breakfast.

"Good morning, Love," I said.

"Who told you to call me that?" Sam asked.

"Call you what?"

"Who told you to call me 'Love'?"

"Sam, I'm your wife, we've been married more than twenty years."

He paused, looked at me questioningly—probably wondering why this 'stranger' standing at the stove in her pajamas said she was married to him—then, after a minute or so, shrugged and said, "Well, I must love you then."

It was said in such a matter-of-fact way, as if he'd said: Well, the sun is shining. Well, the newspaper is at the door, that even though I was shocked, I burst out laughing.

———

Sometime that year, I joined a meditation group at the local hospital to nourish my starved soul. I would set Sam's breakfast place, and leave cereal on the kitchen counter with a sticky note on which I'd drawn a smiley-face with wings: "At meditation, home soon, Love, M." When I got home, he would have eaten, and would be sitting in his favorite chair in the living room reading the Times.

Until he wasn't.

It seemed sudden, Sam's need to be gotten up, to be told to shower, shave, what to wear, when to eat. Arthritic legs kept him from wandering, so I could safely leave him for a few hours, but now he would lie in bed all day, if I didn't get him going. Needing to vent about my increasingly diminished life, I started keeping a journal:

<u>Journal Excerpts: 2007</u>

- Sam still makes good coffee! He brought me some, I am pleased, and he is pleased that I am pleased. How simple life seems at times. How simple and pleasant it is in this moment.

- I am ill, ill, ill, ill. If I could be alone, no one to take care of… would I get better?

- I long for someone who can <u>remember</u> that I'm ill!

- At least Sam doesn't wander off (yesterday I wished he would!)

When my small book-light for reading in bed began bothering him, I moved into the guest room, leaving both our bedroom doors open at night. When his wandering became a nightly event, I'd wake and listen with trepidation, afraid he would go into the kitchen and turn on the stove. Once, hearing him there, I hurriedly got up and asked, "Are you hungry, Sam?" He was looking for the bathroom. Once, I faked sleep while he stood at my bedroom door for God knows how long at God knows what hour. It was chilling.

"Are you alright, Honey?" I finally asked.

"Yes," he answered, and went back to bed.

Then, one morning, Sam flatly refused to get out of bed when I called him. So, for both our sakes, I distracted him:

"Rise and shine," (cheerful voice, big smile, no matter how I felt).

"No shine today."

"Glow? Gleam? Twinkle? Shimmer?" I'd say then, and laughing, he'd play along, forgetting that he didn't want to get up.

One rare morning in 2008 he looked at me and said, "You are a pure joy." I felt all the love he'd once had, I felt like he'd come home to me. But still:

<u>Journal excerpts: 2008</u>
- No_inner resources left… what to get up for?
- I may not love Sam, but I care about him. I could not leave him and be happy.
- Oh I <u>do</u> love Sam, just so tired I can't feel anything.
- Today is our twenty-second anniversary. I didn't remind him. No cake.
- He's so locked up. How am I ever going to do this if he won't let me love him?

———————

But a mind is a strange and unpredictable thing, or rather a brain, even a brain leaking memories the way eyes leak tears. When I had fully accepted that to expect anything from Sam was an exercise in futility (it was around the time I was sick with a stomach virus and asked Sam for a glass of water. He filled the glass, and drank the water), and when, far less willingly, I had accepted that the Sam I loved was gone, and the love I longed for from him impossible, something happened.

I don't know what, or why, or how, but I suspect some part of his brain, the self-protecting part that had always guarded his inner self, his deepest thoughts and fears, relaxed or was annihilated by the Alzheimer's he had refused to acknowledge or discuss, even when he was able to.

Years ago, I had told Sam, "I love the way your mind works." He couldn't remember that, sometimes he didn't remember my name, yet one evening he had a lucid moment during which he touched my arm to stop me as we were walking into the living room, and looking worried, asked:

"How will you love me now?"

"I will love you gladly," I answered instinctively. (A lie? A hope?)

For Sam, it was like the walls of Jericho falling, his fear, in that moment of awareness of what was happening to his mind, suddenly exposed, a sigh of relief when he heard that he would still be loved.

A minute later, the worried frown gone, his eyes sparkling with merriment, he said, "And I will love you madly."

It was a rhyme and a joke that became a bedtime ritual, and it was Sam who began it, saying with a grin, as I left to go to my room that night after I'd tucked him in like a child, "Wait! I love you madly."

"And I love you gladly," I responded, chuckling.

I refer to it as a nightly ritual, like our morning wake-up game. But it was far more than that; it was an affirmation of love said every single night for the two-and-a-half years we had left to us.

Affirmations are powerful when repeated daily for weeks, months, years, which might be why on Thanksgiving the following November, we fell into a day of romance as if we were still those middle-aged lovers who sat on that scarred bench in White Plains long before the fountains danced.

Glum, I had declined dinner invitations from our daughters, telling them I wanted to stay home and relax, so Sam and I would have our turkey at the diner. On Thanksgiving I didn't even want to go to the diner, so I threw on jeans and a sweater and rummaged in the kitchen to see what I could scavenge for a meal. There was a small chicken in the freezer, which I dropped into a pot of warm water to thaw; some salad greens; Stovetop dressing; potatoes; a can of cranberry sauce; even left-over pumpkin pie, bought a few days earlier when I'd stopped at a bakery on the way home from a medical visit.

Perfect. And easy.

While the chicken and potatoes baked, I put on CDs of scores from plays we'd seen and loved: The Fantastics, Phantom of the Opera, Cats, music being what I turn to when I'm feeling particularly low. Then, surprising myself, I decided to make it a special day, setting the table with china and candles and cloth napkins.

Music filled the apartment. Our neighbor Dominick heard it and invited us over to spend the afternoon with him and his family, but our dinner was already cooking, so, knowing Sam had Alzheimer's, he left and returned with CDs of songs from when they both were teenagers: Pistol packin' Mama, lay that pistol down. Mares eat oats and does eat oats and little lambs eat ivy, a kid'll eat ivy, too, wouldn't you? Sam remembered most of the words of those old songs and sang them with gusto.

After we ate, I put on CDs of singers I'd loved: Cole Porter, Peggy Lee, Frank Sinatra; Sam reached for me, folded me in his arms, and we danced—awkwardly, two stiff old folks—but lovers again. That evening, we held hands while watching a televised program where Chris Botti played his trumpet as sweet as the angel Gabriel, and Andrea Boccelli sang, "Like the stars in the sky, we are meant to shine." It was a day lifted clear out of ordinary time.

In sharp contrast to our peace and gentle joy, that day was lifted out of ordinary time for others, too, lifted into nightmare and heartbreak. There had been a massacre in Mumbai, which used to be Bombay, and in my imagination was the mystical land of snake charmers, gurus, and other marvelous things. Terrorists had attacked seven hotels; more than a hundred had been killed; hostages had been taken.

And yet my journal that day begins: "What an absolutely perfect day." Because that was my reality: a day when Sam and I danced, and held hands, and listened to exquisite music—a day I had thought could never happen for us again.

In bed that night, I thought about the suffering souls in Mumbai, prayed for them, prayed that some of the joyful energy of Sam's and my exceptional day had entered the energy of this sad and needful world.

There would again be times when I would scream to my journal, call myself stupid for choosing this crazy life of mine (I'd known Alzheimer's ran in Sam's family, and he was already fifty-nine when we married). There would be times when I'd want to tear my hair out.

But, as impossible as it sounds, there would also be this: during the coming dreaded years, I would grow to love Sam more deeply than I'd ever thought myself capable of. And, even as Alzheimer's took almost all his memories, he would love me back, somehow continuing to recognize love, and—when I took him to a nursing home near the end of 2010—its absence.

Obed

a short play
by Rebecca Pilling

Cast of Characters:
JULDIE. A woman, anywhere between 22 and 102
OBED. A tomcat

[The lights come up on JULDIE sitting in her living room, wrapped in a plush throw blanket, her feet propped up on an ottoman. A carton of ice cream sits empty beside her; a bag of chocolates rests forgotten near her feet; on the table next to her is a glass of wine, half empty. Her cat, OBED, lounges on a nearby rocking chair. The TV is on. It's a sitcom. As the episode ends, JULDIE laughs at the final joke. She turns and looks at OBED.]

JULDIE: It's funny.

[OBED says nothing. OBED is a cat. Cats do not speak in JULDIE's world.]

JULDIE: I wish you could understand it, Obed. You'd think it was funny, too.

[OBED stares at JULDIE. JULDIE'S eyes widen. She looks spooked, like she just saw a ghost, or someone said something unkind about Michelle Obama; JULDIE loves Michelle Obama.]

JULDIE: Obed? Do you understand?

[OBED blinks his eyes and turns his head away from JULDIE.]

JULDIE: Ohmigod, Obed, you do understand, don't you? You understand the show and the jokes, you even understand what I'm saying now, don't you? Don't you?

[OBED licks his right shoulder twice, then lies back as he was before.]

JULDIE: You understand everything! [Realization dawns.] And you don't like it do you? You don't think the show is funny! You find the humor beneath you, that's why you don't laugh at the jokes! You're too intelligent for this sort of comedy. It's too base, too crass, too… too… too human. That's it, isn't it?

[OBED turns his head toward JULDIE again. JULDIE gasps.]

JULDIE, in a hushed voice: Cats truly are the superior creatures on this planet.

[JULDIE gets up, knocking the chocolates to the floor and flinging the throw blanket onto the couch. OBED watches JULDIE walk over to him. JULDIE holds out both her hands. OBED closes his eyes as JULDIE caresses his face and scratches behind his ears. Yes, once again, JULDIE is worshiping OBED in the manner he deserves. Every time JULDIE ruffles and smooths his fur it is the deepest reverence. JULDIE is figuratively prostrating herself before OBED, and OBED basks in her adoration.]

[Suddenly JULDIE giggles and scoops OBED up into her arms and rocks him like a baby.]

JULDIE: Oh, Obed! If only all that were true!

[JULDIE carries OBED back to the couch with her, where she continues to snuggle with him. She rubs her face in his fur, scratches his ears, and pets him all over. Grumpily OBED succumbs to his fate. JULDIE might be a primitive being, but OBED secretly loves JULDIE as much as JULDIE openly loves Obed.]

[But her taste in comedy is still trash.]

[A new episode starts. Lights fade to black.]

One Night and a Quarter of Tomorrow
by Susan Cummins Miller

The night you left us
the ironwoods wore a cloud
of tiny lavender blossoms
that looked gray and insubstantial
in the moonlight.

After the late-night news,
we sat on the porch, watching
creamy saguaro buds unfold as slowly
as a solemn high Mass. You told me
how it pained you that those flowers
had only one night and a quarter
of tomorrow before they closed
for good. A microcosm
of a woman's life.

That's all I remember except
that it was Mother's Day
and I'd brought no gift--just myself,
sitting next to you on the porch swing,
listening to the old stories
one last time--how you skinny-dipped
with your sisters in warm Minnesota lakes, sang
with a big band at college, fished for pike
with Boppa . . . .

We rocked and laughed together until,
around midnight, the bats fluttered in
to bury their wrinkled faces
in soft saguaro blossoms
overflowing with pollen.

Hurry
by Thomas Kearnes

No one seems too concerned that we're lost. GPS is useless up here and none of our cellphones can pick up a signal. Clancy waits for us at base camp to return Sunday afternoon. He always gets stuck with the lone-wolf duty and pretends he doesn't know why.

Winston's map is nothing but happy thoughts and horseshit, so we set up camp atop a large, rocky hill. The problem, Winston admits, hours too late to win my respect, is that our planned campsite had turned into swampland some time after the map was printed. A boy asks how old the map is, but Winston ignores him and leads the others in an Air Force drill song. Irene, Irene, she's one of the best. And every night I give her the test. Too bad Irene isn't here with real coffee and smokes.

We've been backpacking the border between Arkansas and Oklahoma. Small, stumpy trees heckle us, and the troop takes a good long while to find soft earth among the rocks to pitch its tents. The moon hangs low in the black sky, every now and then a thin cloud veiling it like a widow's face. I enjoy nights like this. Back home, I sometimes slip out for a smoke after Hilary and Kenneth fall asleep, and wonder how many others gaze at the moon with my wonder.

From the edge of the fathers' campfire, I watch them perch on their sling chairs that fold up like wallets. I'm used to them ignoring me. Any fool knows why. Damn straight, I'll never tell my son, my only child, to curb his ambition. Hilary and I make a point of telling Kenneth, often and sincerely, that the world can be his—all he has to do is reach.

"Arthur, you need a seat?" one of them asks. "You seem mighty winded after today."

"I'll be sleepin' soon enough."

"It's not a bother."

I sip the watery coffee. "Kenneth's gonna wonder where I am."

Another jackass leers from the behind the campfire, his face slippery behind the smoke. "Better watch your boy, Arthur. Leave him alone too long and he might earn another merit badge." The men laugh and slap their thighs. Carry on like a kid your whole life and having your own kids won't change a thing.

I ponder how to respond. Every shithead here has a son in the troop. Milton is a hefty boy with a uniform that smells like bad milk. Billy boasts about his luck with girls, never mentioning the allure of his father's lake house. Grover is so dumb that Hilary suspects his mother drank during pregnancy. They know Kenneth left their sons in the dust. Of course, they're nothing but peaches and cream to his face.

After another sip of coffee, I clear my throat. Pure quiet save for the crackle of the fire and the crickets. "Hilary still has a few to sew on his sash."

"Get too many and they lose their meaning." Billy's father, named Bill, doesn't bother to make a face that matches his concerned tone. "You shouldn't get your Eagle until you're a man."

"I guess that's why they call it Boy Scouts." The breeze gooses me. I drain the coffee from my collapsible cup.

The fathers grumble like kids called in from recess. One of them spits a glob of tobacco into the flames. There's a brief sizzle. Cigarettes are forbidden at all Scout events.

Winston claps once with a goofy grin that can't be real. He believes a scoutmaster's main job is to keep the fathers nice and docile. I bet Irene could do better. "Speaking of Kenneth, it surprised me when Clancy mentioned that he was speaking at your boy's Eagle ceremony." Winston plays at sounding disappointed, making me think he isn't playing at all. "I never knew they were that close."

What bullshit. I know Winston keeps an eye on no-frills Clancy and my live-wire son. That's probably why they volunteered the man to remain at base camp, walkie-talkie ready should the troop stumble into shit. Of course, even after it was plain that we were lost, not even Winston radioed for assistance. Maybe he wants to undermine Clancy's connection with my boy by suggesting something ugly lurks at its core.

"Clancy supports my son," I say. "What more you wanna know?"

Bill chuckles. "I guess that makes your boy Nephew Tom, don't it?"

Panic flashes in Winston's eyes. "C'mon, guys, let's keep it civil."

"If you're just joking," I say, "how come I'm not laughing?"

"Don't be so delicate, Arthur," one father says.

"What kind of example you settin' for Kenny?" Grover's father adds.

There's more, but I don't pay attention. I'm not a dummy. The troop shit itself when Kenneth made his decision. In Boy Scouts, it's a big damn deal. The speaker presents the Eagle badge to the scout after singing his praises. Oftentimes, he's photographed with the scout. Some of these clowns won't share a tent with a black man, let alone a picture. I'd be lying if I said I'm not tickled my son showed off his brass ones, but I'm worried the boys—and their fathers—might try to influence him, and not very kindly. They're already steamed that Kenneth reached the top rung before starting high school. Shining an even brighter spotlight on his big night is considered foolish. Hilary wonders what Clancy plans to say about our son, but I tell her if Kenneth trusts him then we can, too. No way in hell would I let any other father have that privilege.

At first, my curiosity gnawed at me. But I put off the question when driving him home from choir practice. I forgot it altogether while quizzing him for next week's spelling bee. It wasn't until we spent all last weekend assembling his science fair display that I worked up the nerve. He stared at me like I spoke in tongues. Finally, he shrugged and said Clancy was the only father who wasn't a douche. I told him to find a nicer word if Hilary asked him herself.

I make a show of stretching then say that I'm headed for bed. I suggest Winston bring real coffee to the next campout. The kiss-ass says goodnight, but the other men distract themselves by poking in the blaze. I don't see Kenneth until the moment we collide.

My son yelps like a smacked puppy. His arms and legs shoot out like sparks, and he giggles at the silliness of it all. I'm sure his outburst drew stares, but he isn't worried. I've never known my boy to worry over these rednecks.

"Your pills?" he asks. "Did you remember?"

"You know I wait for bed."

"It's past ten."

"Why aren't you asleep?"

"If I crashed, I couldn't remind you. Mom says you forget all the time."

I'll never know how it feels to walk beside a son who looks like me. Running errands in town, I sometimes cross paths with a man and boy who obviously share blood. I imagine these fathers must feel like real men, too much greatness for just one generation. When Kenneth and I are out, people can't hide their surprise that we're kin.

He looks like Hilary. Rather, he looks like all the men in Hilary's family. Bony, black hair, flat feet, a flurry of elbows and knees when he walks. I don't look forward to holidays with her family. Everyone in the room shares a single face—by nightfall, I can't remember my own.

I send Kenneth back to our tent, promising I'll be there soon. I want a few more moments beneath the moon. There's no doubt they're watching me speak to my son, guessing our words, passing judgment. I hope they spend half that time thinking about their own sons.

Hurry

An hour after I crawl inside our green tent, I'm finally confident my son has drifted to sleep. I grab the open New Yorker rising and falling upon his small chest and stash it at our feet. Hilary bought him a subscription last Christmas on the condition he tell her everything he learns. She's afraid Kenneth might one day resent our one-size-fits-all educations and trot off to Dallas or Houston, anywhere the country's great minds gather.

I don't worry about that as the cold air passes through his parted lips. His eyeballs dance beneath their lids. I stew on the same thing I've been trying to forget this whole hour: today was brutal, but tomorrow might be damn near impossible.

<hr>

We arrived at that state park late last evening, giving us just enough time to check in at base and set up camp. We came in cars and trucks, some of the fathers (and their boys) sharing a ride. No one rode with Kenneth and me, even after I told the troop we had room. The men, the ones who cared enough to give up their Sunday football and twelve-packs, bunked with their sons. I don't know what the boys, including my own, thought of this, but any other arrangement would turn into a popularity contest, and I knew Kenneth would get the leftovers. I thought about him burying his head inside a sleeping bag to avoid Milton's armpit assault.

The next morning, after we packed the sleeping bags, the tents, the personal articles, we started out on a zigzag trail that Winston assured us follows the map. Behind our birdbrain leader, the fathers led the way, a knot of middle-aged men with sturdy thighs and guts hanging over their waistbands. I wasn't surprised to find myself at the back, already forgotten, already panicked where my next breath might come from.

Following us were the boys. The patrol leader, a know-it-all senior named Terrence, didn't waste time demanding the boys shout drill songs, instantly making them men. It was the first time I heard of that floozy Irene. The moon was high, the lights were dim. And there she stood all slick and slim. I was scared to look back for Kenneth, scared I might lose my footing. I'd never face the mirror again if my own son had to help me to my feet. Finally,

I glanced over my shoulder and saw Kenneth bringing up the rear, not singing, not part of the troop at all, his eyes sliding all across the scrubbed, raw landscape. Pride boomed in my chest, and my next breath came easily, like a kiss at prom.

Winston finally let us rest, not long after we passed one of the dirt service roads that winds around the hillside. Rangers and rescue personnel can take these roads, he said, if necessary. By the sneer in his tone, I understood flagging out on this trail wasn't a wise move. Kenneth sat with me, keeping lookout while I sucked from my inhaler. I wasn't about to give these bastards another reason to pin a bullseye on our backs.

"We've got hours left to go," my son said. "Mr. Winston doesn't know where we're going."

"We may be the only two who can admit that."

"If you need to slow down, I'll double back and check on you."

Sometimes it staggered me how decent my boy was. I didn't want the other fathers to know—his goodness was something Hilary and I created, so we should be the ones who enjoy it. His dark eyes searched my face for doubt, but you don't raise a kid all these years without learning to hide that. The February sun was dim, a yolk smacked against a pale blue sky. Thankfully, the chill wouldn't come till nightfall. Kenneth asked me if I needed one last puff.

The chain of command among these smug bastards filtered up the news that I was starting to fade, my chest tight and breathing a struggle. I was drowning in the wilderness. Winston slowed our pace, declared like some do-gooder asshole that a true scout assists the weak, the ill, or anyone who was leeching off the others. The boys carped that we'd still be hiking after sunset. I wanted to tell the little shits that Winston's bogus map was to thank for that.

Terrence, the patrol leader, was right at my heels. I glanced over my shoulder but the kid refused to meet my eye. I knew it was only decorum that kept him from trampling me like road-kill. A metal band squeezed my lungs, kept out the air. It wasn't yet sunset, but we were definitely approaching dusk. With huge relief, the procession stopped as Winston once again pretended that his map might help us.

Fortunately, the fading light forced our troop to slow down, and I didn't have to face the indignity of my son passing me. I knew I couldn't avoid catching his eye as he looked over his shoulder, worried about me. When we settled on a campground, the fathers watched me roll out the tent. I tried not to pause for breath as Kenneth shook out the other end, but I had to gulp down that night air. I needed it.

"What's the matter?" my son said, brazen and sly. "You guys forget how to pitch your own tents?" He smirked and winked at me, like I was in on the joke.

I tell Hilary she'd be damn proud of the way Kenneth conducts himself on these little strolls through the unknown. I know, she says. We did a good job with that one.

I made my coffee, trying to trick myself into anticipating it like the real stuff. I stood outside the fathers' informal powwow. Kenneth had retired to our tent the moment we cleared dinner. The boys had no use for him, and he had no use for them.

On Sunday morning, our breakfast gear returned to our packs, Winston gathers us around, fathers and boys. He doesn't have the map. At this point, maybe he's worried someone might crack wise. He explains that it's about five miles back to base. Clancy's waiting. Easy, right? He winks and I hope his eyelid gets stuck. Then, in all seriousness, he adds we have only three hours to get there. To get a break on the group rate, Winston promised we'd be off the grounds by one that afternoon.

Terrence pumps his fist in the air and barks that his men are ready. Flabbergasted, I realize that no one's gonna question what will happen if someone can't keep that pace. Winston's conservative speed, and the onset of night, spared me yesterday, but I have no safety net today. Without thinking, I scan the group for Kenneth. As usual, he's standing at a distance from the others, pack erect on his back, his face blank like a sheet. I know he's giving me space, would never give the men cause to think it was him taking care of me.

As the fathers and boys double-check their gear, I pull Winston aside. Already, he's looking at me like I wet myself and it's his job to tell me that it happens to everyone and it doesn't make me any less of a man.

"Five miles in three hours?" I say. "We'll be movin' at quite a clip."

Winston lays his hand on my shoulder, and from the corner of my eye, I see Bill and one of the new fathers snicker. "If you need to take a break, maybe hang back," he says. "That's fine. Not every man is built from the same buckshot."

"I don't have a map."

He guffaws. This is a big damn joke to him. "Well, maps haven't done us much good this time, huh, Arthur?" He slaps my back so hard, it stings. "Your boy's a pretty capable young man. I'm sure he'll look after you."

With that, Winston strides away and joins the other fathers. It doesn't matter now, but I can't shake the feeling he's been looking forward to cutting me loose this whole trip. He's just been waiting for a circumstance that would keep the dirt off his hands. He has a son, that bastard. Locked up in juvie hall for his second DUI. He thinks if he never mentions the boy, we'll forget.

As the troop lines up, fathers followed by scouts, Kenneth slips in beside me and assures me I can do this. He reminds me that even these assholes wouldn't leave an ailing man to expire on a hillside. "I'm the one they want to exterminate," he says, "not you." I know that's supposed to pick me up, but it crushes me.

We've been hiking for fifteen minutes, at a faster clip than before, as promised. Good news is we're heading downhill. Another switch is the fathers keep stealing glances at me, different ones, never more than one at once. I just glare at the bastards. I know the moment my lungs seize up, I'm in trouble. Terrence shouts in my ear, commanding the scouts to start in on those marching tunes. I warmed her up the best that I could. And when I got in her I knew she was good. I've never heard this nonsense before, but I can see where it's headed. It's plain as a welt on your ass they're not singing about a woman.

Not long after, I start to fall behind. I haven't slowed my pace, so they must've picked up theirs. I watch those bastards' backs file down the trail. Before I can take my next gulp of air, Terrence sweeps around me, barks for the scouts to keep up the pace. They all pass me. Billy, Grover, Milton and his distinct odor, all the others. I'd expected the troop to gradually leave me behind, deserting me by degrees, but I assumed they'd at least make it look like happenstance. Now even the boys pick up speed as I halt in my tracks, clutching a tree trunk for support. My whole torso rocks as I try to forget those traitors and worry about my next breath. During all this, my eyes shut. Like the doctor said, I stop everything that isn't helping me breathe. Opening them, I find Kenneth beside me. He places his hand on my back.

"Don't make a fuss," I say.

"Those douches are gone. They don't care."

"I need to rest." I sit heavily upon a rock. "Not sure how long."

"I can wait."

Five years ago, after my heart gave out and I pitched over in my workshop, my head banging the edge of the workbench, I woke to find Hilary holding my hand. They juiced me back to life. Kenneth was only in second grade. When the doctors told my wife things looked bad, I made her promise we'd keep our son in the dark. He shouldn't spend his childhood living under a cloud. No way could he focus on his achievements and worry about me. Hilary begged me not to come on this hiking trip, and I could see her point. I knew, though, that if I left Kenneth to face these jackasses alone, worry would weigh on me worse than any trouble getting wind. It's clear, though, he can face them on his own. I forget that at the start of every day, but I remember it before my head hits the pillow.

I shrug off his hand. "You better hop to it. Lord knows they won't wait."

"What about you?"

"I'll make it there soon enough."

Kenneth's eyes flash with panic. It pains me to think how many years I have to endure that look from my child, his fear that he'll lose me for good. He glances down the trail, but the troop has disappeared. All we can hear is more nonsense about this Irene woman. I rolled her over on her side. And on her back I also tried. A steady breeze wanders through these ugly little trees. Kenneth puts his lips to my ear, as if the whole troop was close and curious.

"You'll make base camp before any of those bastards. I promise."

He doesn't bother to explain, zipping down the trail, looking as far back over his shoulder as he can with a pack obstructing his view. As my breath comes a little easier each time, I calmly watch my son grow smaller and smaller, farther and farther away. I close my eyes and breathe before he disappears entirely.

I check my watch. It's half past ten. I estimate how close the nearest service road might be. On our hike uphill Friday night and all of Saturday, we crossed three or four. My breath steady and my heart strong, I hike. It's plain as day I'll never make base camp, so I don't rush.

There are more birds here than I'd noticed before. All the different calls colliding remind me of a conversation. Those bastards, they're too busy marching and singing to notice all this beauty. If only my son were here to tell me the name of each bird, the name of each little ugly tree. He knows all those things. Hilary sewed those merit badges on his sash years ago.

It takes me a half-hour to hit the first service road. When I notice the trail opening out onto the dirt-and-gravel lane, I decide maybe God is good after all. There's even a wide, low bank of stones to sit on. After a few minutes, though, I realize the service road won't do me any good if there are no cars. If I do spot one, what am I supposed to do? Hail it like a taxi? Only park employees drive this road, and maybe passengers aren't allowed. My spirit sinks and I consider starting the hike again. Maybe if I make it to the next service road, the troop will be at base camp by then and come looking for me... but only because they must.

I'm thinking all these things when a quick, sharp horn blast spooks me. I whip around and see a pale green Dodge Ram I almost recognize. The windshield is dusty, and the angle the sunlight hits it makes seeing the driver difficult. The truck rolls up beside me.

His arrival is what my son would call bon chance.

"You too good to march back with the other crackers?" Clancy grins and slaps the passenger seat beside him. I try to sling my pack into the pickup bed, but the weight tips me backward. I try again, this time with both hands. Clancy is still laughing as I climb in.

"I wondered if I should stick out my thumb."

"Only select members are allowed on these roads."

"The sick and tired?"

Clancy shakes his head. He can't imagine a grown man downing himself like that. "After we got here Friday night, your son said you might need help, especially today. I've been keeping an eye out." He shifts gears and we hiccup forward.

My jaw flops open, my body tossed by the unpaved road. As much as I fear the day when I must rely on my son just to keep ticking, it feels good to know he'll be there.

"When the posse arrives," he says, "take him aside and say thank you." We bullshit and laugh. We wend down the hill toward base camp. It's a longer trip there than I guessed. I would've never made it before sundown, let alone by one o'clock.

Clancy is confident like the soldiers on recruitment posters. Only difference is, you laugh when he's around. It's a surprise when he quietly asks if we can discuss something "real quick." I ask what's on his mind.

"It's about your boy's Eagle ceremony." Clancy gazes far past the truck's hood. "I'm humbled he asked me, and I know I said yes, but…things are hard enough for your boy already."

"Clancy, you'll break his heart."

"Some of these assholes pulled me aside, asked me questions they wouldn't dare ask any other father."

"Winston's stooges won't get their paws on my son's Eagle award."

"But has Kenneth ever said why me?"

"Same reason I think it should be you." We lock eyes after he whips into the parking lot by the park ranger's office. "You're the only one who's not a douche."

I make sure Clancy is back on board before I load my pack into the minivan and stroll into a paved seating area with stone tables and benches. Not comfy, but it gives me a view of the various trails dead-ending at the pavement. At far corners of the area, other scouting troops gather, rowdy and proud. One day my son should experience the satisfaction of being a true member of a team, but that can wait for a better "team" than the jackasses marching my way.

Winston's knees pop high like he's on the drill team. He's joined the boys recounting that town slut, Irene. Irene, Irene, she's the best in the land. The best F-15 in the fighting command. They seem proud of themselves for finishing, and I can't ruin that for them. I'm not surprised the whole troop parades past before I see Kenneth. He hangs back, a member of this troop in name only.

He got me home safe. I'd like to tell Hilary, but I wonder if I could hold back the tears.

"I am exhausted, and I am irritated!" Kenneth collapses on a bench at my table and lets his pack tip backward to the ground. "Been waiting long?"

"Clancy came in the nick of time."

"Bet they're shocked shitless to see you," he says. We turn to enjoy the troop's bafflement. Everyone from Winston to stinky Milton can't believe it. Kenneth rolls his eyes and turns back to me. "This was your last hiking trip, Dad."

I ponder whether to object. Once Kenneth puts his mind to something, there's no changing it. I ask if he's thirsty. There's a snack hut at the edge of the seating area. Not right now, he says. It's only half past twelve. We still have a bit to enjoy the many birds and little ugly trees.

"It's too bad Irene can't join us," I say. "I hear she's one of the best."

My son laughs hard and loud. The troop looks our way, but he's too busy cracking up to notice. He'll break some hearts one day. He's already broken mine. He turns thirteen this summer. Kenneth will be a man soon, but I hope he knows there's no hurry.

Good Morning, Beautiful
by Kate Hodges

The sunlight wakes Chis up. Last night, they were either too drunk to remember to close the curtains, or in too much of a hurry. He can't remember which. He watches her sleep: blond hair spilling across the pillow; mascara smudging her cheeks. Her lipstick faded away hours ago. Hidden in the shadow of her chin and shoulder are tiny scratches from his stubble.

He pulls back the blanket a bit and nudges her. "Hey there, good morning." The blankets smell like her perfume. Lilacs. Lilacs for Lilah. She stretches, and then reaches for the extra pillow to cover herself.

Chris pulls it away and kisses the top of her head. "You're beautiful."

Lilah yawns. "Coffee. We need coffee." Chris grabs his shirt off the floor and places it on her shoulders. She slides her arms in. He smooths the collar down, letting his hands rest on her shoulders for a moment. She gets off the bed and starts to walk across the room, stopping at the desk under the TV to grab the kettle. He gazes at her. "I like you in my shirt."

She walks into the bathroom to fill it with water. He collapses back onto the unmade bed. The sheets chide him. Silk and Scarlett. Fuck. What did I do? What did I do? He pulls the covers over his head. Now what? She's here. In his shirt. His phone buzzes. His wife. Ignore. "Please God, don't let her find out." God may forgive everyone, but his wife won't. The call invades this space. His wife does that, finding places that are just his, and she comes and claims every spot.

"Hey, Sleepyhead, don't go back to bed without me." Lilah plugs the kettle in and switches it on. She pours the instant powder into the mugs. "The breakfast is free. I thought we could eat before we go."

Chris emerges from his blanket cocoon. "Can't. I know it's Saturday, but I have to head into the office to pick up some files." The kettle whistles.

Lilah's expression is hidden behind the steam. She stirs the coffee and hands him a cup. "I have a busy day too."

He checks the time on his phone, "We'd better get a move on."

She gives back his shirt, "You might need this." He puts it on. He fastens the buttons, takes a sip from the mug, and makes a face.

Her voice is low. "I thought it was okay."

"I've had better."

Lilah reaches up to help with his tie—dark green—the same shade as his eyes.

He steps back. "I'll do it."

She bites her bottom lip, then tugs on her dress, and watches as he puts on his armour:

Boxers.

Trousers.

Belt.

Socks.

Shoes.

He takes another sip of coffee and gives her his crooked smile.

"Every time you smile at me like that, it makes me want to crawl back into bed with you."

"I wish I could carry you back right now."

"If only…" She sighs.

"Anticipation makes things better…" He takes her hand and brushes a kiss over her knuckles. "Or maybe not. You ready?"

Lilah grabs her purse. "Lead on MacDuff."

"Actually, that's wrong."

"What?"

Chris explains, "It's Lay on, MacDuff. It's an attack cry."

Lilah takes a giant step to keep up, "I like how you know stuff."

Before She Fixes Lunch: Aubade
by Laura Lee Washburn

Each morning while she finishes sleep,
he heads downstairs. He lifts each room
by its two near corners
and snaps it brisk into the air like a sheet.
In the kitchen the coffee cups
stack in firm white rows, the plates
pair by colorway. Blankets
square up on the backs of living room sofas,
dog toys pile under his favorite chair.

While he snaps along with oatmeal and walnuts,
she breathes the linen scent of rest,
the dog cuddled into the small of her back,
the cat warming her feet, the halftones
of her sleep playing like a film, reminding
her of him, of him.

       Time to get up,
she says to the dog, all mouth
and bound in morning. Time
to get up, she says to the cat
who flattens himself across her chest.
Any moment, barking, nips

at her toes when they touch the floor, the scent
of cat food, small pins in her hip. The wind
picks up; she's headed for the door,
a half glass of cranberry juice already poured
and waiting. He's somewhere
in his morning, and they're both headed for noon.

Kata Hatiku

In Indonesia
by James Penha

Here the seat of all emotions
is heartless, it is hati: the liver,
just as in kanker hati: liver cancer
there is hati-hati: liver! liver! be careful!
and hatiku milikmu: my liver belongs to you
and kata hatiku: these words from my liver
and rindu hatiku tidak terkira: in my liver
the longing for you never ends. And so
how do we dare to think we fall in love,
you in your liver and me in my heart,
except that we make of our bodies one.

Hillbilly Love Story
by Timothy O'Leary

In retrospect, I never should have put that snake in Annemarie Kitsap's mailbox. It wasn't like it was a rattler or cottonmouth. Nothing that would jump out and fang you. Just a big bull. Ferocious looking, but harmless. Prized in these parts for their propensity to devour rodents and truly dangerous reptiles.

In my defense, I meant no harm. Regard it as a romantic gesture; the clumsy flirtation of a lovestruck kid. Truth is, I always adored the girl. Even before she inspired that warm tingling down south, I'd stare at her all googley-eyed, captivated by the curly red hair that shot out her head like a forest fire; skin too white and pure to sprout from this hot county; porcelain features so sharp she appeared otherworldly, like a beautiful gift from aliens.

From birth, Annemarie was a force of nature, attacking life as if it owed her more than the rest of us. By the time she was four or five, adults were actually afraid of her. Instead of cooing about what a pretty child she was—and there's no doubt she was the most beautiful little thing anyone had ever seen—they'd circle as if approaching a foamy-gummed Rottweiler. Annemarie cared less, so self-assured she didn't require hugs or affection. At Sunday Services, when a visiting pastor said, "My, what a stunning young lady," Annemarie looked at him as if he'd just passed gas in an elevator, muttering "Tell me something I don't know, Jesus-man."

Our spread bordered the Kitsap's farm, and since Annemarie and I were only a year apart, our folks threw us together whenever they were feeling neighborly. Annemarie regarded me with the disdain of an angry older sister, acting as if my mere existence was God's plan to annoy her, but I happily accepted her eye rolling and sucker punches, thrilled to be in her sphere, her insults and outright cruelty just fueling my love. A happy cuckold by age four.

I was Jane Goodall, and Annemarie my rare primate, as I observed every aspect of her progression. I marveled as her rail-thin, little-girl body retracted and expanded in all the right places, her farmer jeans abandoned for a tight denim uniform that served as inspiration for me as I trailed her down school hallways. Sometimes I'd sneak through the soybean fields that separated our farms, and climb into the sweetgum tree that afforded a view of her bedroom, transfixed by the Annemarie bedtime ballet, straining young eyes to catch the entire performance. The delicate way she removed her clothes, to be replaced with one of four tee-shirts I knew by heart. My favorite; her Dad's old white wifebeater, barely covering those hopeful breasts. Her hair-brushing ritual—red silk freed to drape soft shoulders. Finally, she'd prop herself up in bed for twenty minutes to read before the room went dark, and I'd rush to the library the next day to find whatever was of interest to her, on the remote chance she wanted to engage in a literary discussion.

I could write a bestselling book called "The Wonderful Taste and Aroma of Annemarie," detailing decades of covertly inhaling her strange and delectable scents. Johnson's Baby Shampoo wafting off those Shirley Temple locks when we were toddlers. The tang of cinnamon from the wad of gum she'd sometimes rip from her beautiful mouth and shove into mine, seemingly with malice, but an act that gave me indescribable pleasure. The sour, sensual aroma of her armpits, when she'd roughly throw me into a headlock to deliver an Indian rub. When I was nine, she tackled me behind the barn after her folks' anniversary party, pulled up her gingham dress, and peed all over my head; an act meant to humiliate, but to this day one of the greatest experiences of my life.

Annemarie's perfume evolution: her mother's eau du-something in grade school; the sweet trace of Charlie that defined her junior high years; the Spice Girls Body Spray in high school; and finally Dior J'Adore, the signature spoor of a more adult Annemarie. Throughout this progression, I was her constant secret Santa, saving up my scant allowance to leave gifts by her locker.

But my devotion and attentiveness seemed lost on her. I knew, someday, she'd understand our inevitableness, but teen years are difficult. As we aged, Annemarie's attitude toward me morphed from disdain into outright hostility. I remember her yelling, "Get away from me, you goddamn freak," during sophomore year, when I took my usual seat on the bus behind her, a spot chosen to afford the perfect vision of her elegant ears. After that, when she saw me, her face would screw with hate, and she'd extend a hand as if to shield herself, which devastated me more than you can imagine. At one point she inserted family into our relationship. One day when I returned from school, my folks were waiting for me. "Annemarie's parents complained. Leave that girl alone," Dad ordered.

But of course, that was impossible. And ridiculous. I looked forward to the day when the Kitsap's were family, and we could all have a laugh around the dinner table over Dad's silly order. I knew our fates were intertwined but could understand how others might have difficulty comprehending the relationship.

What I really needed to do was regain her attention, which wasn't easy. There were so many distractions in Annemarie's world. A girl so beautiful and brilliant is assaulted on multiple fronts by people that can't help but desire her. And that's when I came up with the snake idea.

As little kids we played together in Felt Creek, capturing tiny water snakes and transporting them to a bigger pool to watch them wriggle to freedom, sometimes even racing them like slimy racehorses. Though Annemarie didn't share my complete fascination with all things reptile, I admired the fact that, unlike every other female I'd ever met, she was fearless about creepy-crawlers.

And so, putting the big bull in her mailbox was just a playful love pat; a reminder of good times we'd experienced together. Yes, a bit of a jolt, (and perhaps in back of my mind I was enacting a little revenge) but it was the kind of thing I was sure she'd appreciate. I was prepared for—even wildly anticipating—retribution. I stuffed the snake into the oversized receptacle, and retreated behind a tree across the road, to see her reaction.

But I'd forgotten that Annemarie's old grandmother was visiting from Sevierville, and watched in horror as the old bat hobbled out to check the mail, probably hoping to discover her Social Security check, or perhaps an advertisement for a Hoveround power chair. Annemarie was always the one to retrieve the letters, and it never occurred to me someone else would open the box. I wasn't in position to see the old lady's face, but as she flipped open the door, I heard her scream, "Lordy," (that's an old folk curse around here), then she stumbled hard, falling flat on her back. The snake was as surprised as she was, probably half-insane with fear in the hot metal jail, and it sprung out, landing flat across Grandma's legs. As the old gal raised her head, the bull crept up her stomach, and slithered across her face to escape.

I'd heard the term, "stroked-out," but had never witnessed it. The closest I'd seen was in seventh grade, when Marty Goebel had an epileptic seizure. He was at the chalkboard, stressed-out, when Mrs. Geller tried to get him to conjugate a verb, and suddenly he was on the ground, shaking like someone hooked jumper cables to his nuts, and frothing something fierce. Grandma's mouth stayed dry, but she vibrated in place just like Marty.

Annemarie was thirty feet behind her and dashed forward when she heard the scream. She watched the snake slide over the old woman's body, and saw me turn and dash into the forest, terrified that my practical joke had put an old woman in her grave.

Some good news. Grandma lived, so I'm not a murderer, although her face is frozen in a crooked scream. She also lost the ability to speak, though she did develop a grunt-based language that her family understands. From what I remember, she wasn't a big talker anyway.

But the episode left me quite unpopular with the entire Kitsap family. Within an hour, the sheriff was knocking at our door, and I had trouble coming up with an answer when Daddy asked, "Why in the hell would you put a snake in someone's mailbox? What in God's name is wrong with you?"

"Annemarie," I wanted to scream. "Annemarie is what's wrong with me." But I knew he wouldn't understand. Nobody could.

My folks and I had to appear before a judge, and I was fearful that I might be sent to the boy's prison in Dandridge. I'd heard horrible things about what went on in that place. My mother always described me as having "fine features," which I knew in prison was synonymous with "hello little bitch, come give your daddy a kiss" so I wasn't looking forward to incarceration. Luckily, my attorney managed to convince everyone that a strict boarding school would be a better option, and it was decided that I'd travel four-hundred miles to attend Fork Union Military Academy, with the stipulation I never return home until I was at least eighteen, and that I maintain a hundred yards between myself and any Kitsap for the rest of my life.

Can you imagine never being able to get within a hundred yards of Annemarie? I call that cruel and unusual punishment.

After the proceedings Mr. Kitsap jabbed his dirty farmer's finger at me and said, "If I ever see you on my property, I'll shoot you down like a dog with rabies." I figured he was just trying to impress Annemarie with his best Atticus Finch impression, but made note that I needed to avoid their farm when he was around.

Annemarie's attitude was more distressing. I'd hoped that she might see this for what it was. A misguided attempt to gain her love. Instead, I'd inspired a new level of hatred. As we walked out of the judge's chambers, she slid a hand to the back of my neck, pulled me close, and whispered, "I'm going to kill you. Not right now. Maybe not this month or this year, but I will kill you." And she dug those beautiful nails into my neck till blood ran down the back of my shirt. It was terrifying, and for some reason I felt myself grow hard.

Fork Union Military Academy beats prison, but not by much. It's a place constructed on rules—which runs counter to my personality—and I hated the silly uniforms. It made you feel as if they were planning to refight the Civil War and we were the first line of defense. I wasn't raped, though there were a lot of disgusting consensual sins committed in the woods surrounding the place. On holidays my family would come see me, since I couldn't go home. It made my mom cry when we had to spend Christmas in the Fork Union Days Inn, and when I'd politely inquire about Annemarie, she'd get this hopeless look on her face, her tears flowing even harder. But I couldn't stop myself from asking.

They offered to come get me when I graduated, but I told them I'd take the bus. I didn't mention my little detour. I'd heard from my sister that Annemarie was a freshman at Austin Peay State in Clarksville. It had been over three years since I'd seen the girl, and I was hopeful that by now our issues would be forgotten, replaced by mutual yearning. I was excited to let her know I'd be attending Austin Peay in the fall, even prepared to suggest we could share an apartment.

I hadn't anticipated the difficulty I'd have finding her. I thought I could just wander around campus, our reunion appearing happenstance. Wow, Annemarie, how are you? I didn't know you went to school here. I'm just checking out the place since I'll be coming here in the fall. Sure. I'd love to have lunch. Stay in your dorm tonight? Yeah, that would be great, as I'd just planned to grab a cheap motel.

But there were almost ten thousand students, so I needed to do some detective work to find her. I knew she was an English major, so I chose a discreet spot in front of the liberal arts building, knowing sooner or later she'd come by. Sure enough, at around 3 pm, I saw her exiting a side door.

"Well, look who the cat dragged in," I yelled in my most energetic and mature voice, though to this day I've no idea why I picked such a hackneyed greeting, like something you'd hear from an eighty-year-old-geezer surprising a war buddy at a Rotary luncheon. Nervous, I guess.

Annemarie was walking with two friends, those adorable lips in mid-giggle, when she saw me. Her reaction wasn't as I'd hoped, her eyes flashing from fright to rage. "What are you doing here?"

she screamed. "You stay the fuck away from me, you creep. I will call the police. You're not allowed anywhere near me." She and the other girls turned and headed toward a back parking lot. I didn't want to cause a scene, so I casually followed at a safe distance. They jumped into an old Tercel, Annemarie driving, and I made note of the license as they sped away.

Of course, this was a major setback to my plans. It was obvious that Annemarie still harbored resentment, and I needed to take action to get our relationship back on track. I'll admit that my solution wasn't ideal, but when is an eighteen-year-old in love ever rational?

That evening, I hiked to a swampy field outside of town, and gathered up all kinds of snakes in a pillowcase I'd borrowed from The Motel 6. Nothing dangerous, but a collection that would impress the most seasoned herpetologist: a thick corn snake, several bright water snakes, even an eastern hog-nosed snake. The next afternoon I was back on campus. It only took me a few minutes to locate Annemarie's car, which I was pleased to discover she hadn't locked, probably because there was absolutely no reason for anyone to break into the thing. I did find a gym bag stuffed behind the driver's seat, and I paused to zip it open and inhale my love's tart aroma. My plan was to release the snakes in the car, which might jolt Annemarie out of her angry funk and return her to better times. I was leaning across to the passenger seat, just about to dump the bag, when I heard her voice.

"I told you I was going to kill you," Annemarie said, her voice surprisingly calm, considering what she was about to do. I've always assumed I'd be very tense right before I shot someone. When I saw the gun, I lunged away, but I was hard to miss from three feet, trapped within the confines of that little car. The first bullet, which was probably aimed at my head, caught me in the right shoulder. The second was much more lethal, coming in right below my belt buckle, tearing-up my insides.

And that was the last time I ever saw my beautiful Annemarie. She pushed her head into the car, as I lay splayed across two seats, snakes slithering in the blood that was pooling on the passenger floor. "I told you," she said one more time, assuming she'd killed me.

But that's ancient history, though certainly the defining moment of my life. The little .32 caliber bullet is still lodged a fraction of a millimeter from my spine, governing my existence. The doctors say it can't be removed, and warn me that someday it'll likely shift and kill me. But dying might not be so bad, since living as a paraplegic doesn't have a lot going for it. They moved me back to my parent's farm, confined to my damn bed, with an occasional foray in a heavy metal chair. Dad died five years ago, so mom has to attend to me, cleaning-up my piss and shit, just like when I was an infant. The cheerful soul I remember has morphed into a sad old woman who cries every night before she dozes off. I know because I require very little sleep. I lie here, late at night, listening to my mother's agony.

And later, when it's painfully quiet, I concentrate hard, and sometimes I'm sure I hear Annemarie, a quarter mile away, home for a visit, getting ready for bed. Annemarie pulling on that tee-shirt, thumbing through the books on her shelf. And later, as she reaches to turn off the light, I sense that she's thinking of me, regretting all the tragedy that's come between us. Right before she dozes off, I can hear her mouth a sweet, "Good night, my love," as she pulls the covers to her chin.

Another Country
by Evan Balkan

As he wheeled his suitcase through the terminal at Heathrow, Sebastian was already a tad giddy. For here he was in London to accept the Twenty-Ninth Annual Euthenics Prize for "work befitting the great spirit of selfless scientific endeavor for the betterment of humanity." This, after his waterless toilet—solar-powered, self-cleaning, and capable of converting human waste into fertilizer—won the quarter-million-dollar prize.

Settling into his hotel room, he paused and cleared his throat: "Every twenty seconds, someone around the world dies of a diarrheal disease." Again, his voice lower and graver: "Every twenty seconds, someone around the world…"

Sebastian felt an almost overwhelming urge to add, "Am I right, people?" He'd always had a begrudging admiration for cheerleaders and stand-up comics who were able, by force of sheer inane will, to cajole an immovable audience into "giving it up," and "letting it all hang loose." This was a problem with his line of work: the conferences and the awards were always rather staid affairs; the same array of faces, drawn and pale with pinched eyes and tired brows from so many hours in the lab, the same terrible jokes he had once loved so well:

Have you heard the one about the sick chemist? If you can't helium, and you can't curium, you'll probably have to barium.

Or:

An ion meets his atom friend on the street and says he's lost an electron. "Are you sure?" asks the atom. The ion replies, "I'm positive."

This last one, he recalled, actually caused one of his colleagues to shoot Yoohoo out of his nostrils. Nevertheless, he would eschew the jokes and get on with it: "Every twenty seconds, someone around the world…"

He stopped. No reason to do this. He'd be ready. He'd committed his entire speech to memory already, running it over in its entirety as his plane hurtled across the North Atlantic.

He unpacked his clothes, set them in the dresser, and ironed his shirt and pants for the next day. He had dinner in the hotel restaurant, noting the extensive wine list, and got to bed early. He wasn't very tired—only seven o'clock in his body—but it was already edging up to midnight GMT and he'd need to be downstairs and ready to go by 8:30 am.

"Every twenty seconds, someone around the world dies of a diarrheal disease."

The audience nodded silent agreement.

"I've been told to always start with a joke, but there's no joking about this threat to human health."

More solemn nodding.

Sebastian stood next to his winning prototype, pointing out its functions to a rapt audience. "Here," he said, tilting the solar panel toward the audience and blasting with a ray of fluorescent light a gray-bearded man with a pince nez. "The panel absorbs the solar radiation, which powers an electrochemical reactor…" Sebastian fiddled with the mechanism while behind him, projected on a massive screen, images of the reactor tilted this way and that. "The reactor breaks down the waste into fertilizer. There is a hydrogen byproduct, of course, which will be recycled into cells that can then be drawn upon to provide power to the reactor on days in which there is not enough solar radiance in the atmosphere." Great murmuring rippled among the crowd. While often indistinguishable to the untrained ear, Sebastian recognized the murmuring as awed appreciation, not skepticism (he'd heard those murmurs before as well). Best to soak up the approval now; he recalled how his nanotube pathogen test for pancreatic cancer was at first enthusiastically received and then how quickly the small but loud chorus of doubters had come forward, questioning his claims about test speed and reliability and cost, and how his work hadn't yet been run through the grinder of peer-reviewed journals.

"And here," he said, tapping the reservoir at the top of the bowl and quieting the murmuring. "This tank receives the treated gray water, which can be used for irrigation."

A hand shot up from Graybeard in the front row, now fully recovered from the temporary blinding.

"Yes?" Sebastian said, though the official Q&A portion had not yet been announced.

Graybeard stood, half turned toward Sebastian looming above him onstage and half toward the audience. As he spoke, he danced slightly so that he could address both parties at once, davining like a quiver recently relieved of its arrow. "Let us say this toilet is put into use in some poverty-stricken bush village far from cities and towns…"

"That's the idea," Sebastian said, smiling, solicitous. The audience chuckled.

Graybeard turned entirely to the audience. "Let us assume so, then. What happens when the toilet requires repair? Is the idea to train one villager? And if so, where do the parts come from?" He sat, then abruptly rose again.

"The electrodes themselves have a ten-year estimated lifetime," Sebastian replied. "And all of the parts within the toilet are very easily reparable. It's unlikely there would arise a frequent need for new parts."

A young woman with a long brown ponytail and thick black-framed glasses stood up two rows behind Graybeard. "Having worked in many remote areas in Africa," Ponytail said, inflected with a midwestern American accent, "I can attest to the extraordinary ingenuity one finds in native people who must reuse as a matter of necessity. It is here in the UK, in the US, in Western Europe. Here we reuse and recycle out of a sense of environmental obligation but the idea of yet another plastic bottle or a grocery bag being easily available and obtainable is never in question. But if you live in the Togolese bush, for example, you repurpose everything and extend one product's life into many lives. I would feel confident in backing our esteemed speaker and say that you will find villagers all over the Third World who would require no mechanical training. So long as the toilet operates when they receive it, they will manage to maintain it, I am certain."

Ponytail sat back down as a tremor of subdued applause rippled through the auditorium. Graybeard, undeterred, raised his upturned hand with exasperated incredulity and shouted, "And what is the cost of this mechanism?"

"The approximated cost of the waterless toilet is twenty-two hundred US."

A gasp went out across the auditorium, but this one Sebastian found unreadable. The emcee, the distinguished A.S. Wang of Durham University, strode on stage as if he feared a riot might break out. He held his hands in front of him, presumably to stem the tide of growing discontent, and then raised them closer to his face as if he half-expected a barrage of Bunsen burners to come careering toward him. "There will be plenty of opportunity to ask further questions at the appropriate time," he breathed into the microphone. "We will repair to the Q and A session after the awarding of our young distinguished scholar series, which, as many of you know as past recipients, honors the work of our youngest generation of scientists studying in programs across the UK."

A parade of children herded onto the stage. They formed a row next to Sebastian and Dr. Wang—some two dozen of them, a panoply of mostly Asian ethnicities: Burmese, Indian, Pakistani, Bangladeshi, Chinese, Korean… each one nervous and uncomfortable and very much bespectacled.

"Here they are." Dr. Wang said, beaming, walking around to grasp the hands of each of them, oblivious to their palpable discomfort as their spines rattled under Wang's overzealous two-handed grip. Up and down, bouncing and juggling, a rogue's gallery of discomfort, a veritable UN of social unease.

Sebastian took the opportunity to slip backstage and accept the bottle of Evian being thrust at him. "I am so sorry we did not have this available for you on the stage," a young student said, an Ursa Major of acne across his cheeks and forehead.

"It's okay," Sebastian assured the wreck of a kid. "Really. It's okay."

Fresh beads of perspiration had popped out all over the kid's forehead. He emanated a reek of anxiety—his deodorant, had he chosen to apply some that morning, having already well expired, or proving itself incapable of keeping up with his over-driven apocrine glands. Sebastian shuddered. It was a repellant spectacle, and it was one that Sebastian feared was still his own reality—residing dormant just below the surface, ever-ready to pop out like a plague of locusts sprung out of years-long slumber. Sure, in the world of scientific advancement, Sebastian was sometimes regarded as a veritable movie star—fairly good-looking and possessed of an outer confidence that managed to hover just the right side of arrogance. Better yet, he was a nice guy, genuinely so, having never fallen into the trap of so many uber-intelligent nerds and geeks before him: diving headfirst into assholishness as reasonable reaction to a childhood spent being the butt of so many jokes. Now, here in adulthood, the very attributes—intelligence, mental acuity, inventiveness—that in any other person are regarded with admiration, and in the unattractive, socially awkward, nerd types, garnered nothing other than contempt, now turned themselves, more often than not, toward a generally nasty disposition. Sebastian wasn't that way. Here, among his kind, he was fawned over and admired. And yet, to the outside world, he knew, he was hardly a few rungs up from the sweating kid proffering the bottle of Evian.

It was an odd and sometimes difficult line to straddle. While he had no trouble voicing an opinion or keeping up with normal conversation, he was aware of the exhausting mental game he was forever engaged in: whenever speaking with anyone not in his field of expertise, where lingo and various -eses were perfectly acceptable, he had to perform a balancing act between coming across as condescending due to his superior intellect and dumbing himself down to the point of being patronizing. Either way was a losing prospect. To find that spot between, he discovered, was a difficult task. And so the obvious path was to stay here in the world of lab and conference. Venture too far into the sub-world—the sports bar, the boardwalk, the midlist state college classroom—and you risked exposure. And yet, he often wanted to visit those lands, to believe he could roam freely among this world and that. For he knew, he could never forget, in that other world, that is where Joanna Benson lived. And Joanna Benson, even after almost two decades, had never entirely left his mind.

Sebastian's recent Internet searches had revealed that Joanna was now living in Baltimore, a divorced mother of a little girl. The fantasy persisted: he would find her, reach out to her, offer her and her girl sanctuary in a troubled world. It worked for Forrest Gump and the love of his life—until she died of AIDS, that is.

"What does a subatomic duck say?"

It was Ponytail, and she was standing a few feet away. She had sneaked over while Sebastian was signing a program for Sweat Boy.

"I'm sorry?"

"You said you should always start with a joke, so 'What does a subatomic duck say?'"

"I don't know."

"Quark."

He smiled. "That's a good one." It wasn't, but she was so earnest—and, he noted, kind of cute.

"Christine," she said, and held out her hand.

"Sebastian."

"Yes, I know."

They decided on the hotel restaurant. As they were seated, she insisted on splitting the tab with him. "Please," he said. "I asked

you to dinner. I will pay, and I will not hear one more quark about
it."

She blushed, pleased that he had enjoyed her joke.

He would order the wine first. Wine, the perfect melding of
nature and human involvement, was one of his passions. He had
calculated by the age of fifteen that a knowledge of wine was a necessity for adult life. The memories of boozy parties at the Benson
house before Joanna's parents split up had left a deep impression
on Sebastian, then just a child: one could be thoroughly indiscriminate about it all, taking whatever was handed him without
reservation and downing it in one massive, disgusting, gut-churn-
ing gulp. (He could recall one of the adult oafs being handed
a drink that glowed with a repulsive neon color and seemed to
have swirls of something vaguely fecal floating in it and, without
asking what he was about to imbibe, simply bellowed, "Bottoms
up," taking the entire thing down in three gulps, his ponderous
Adam's apple escalating from jawline to the dip of his collarbone
and back again while everyone around him cheered. When he was
done, he slammed the glass down with such force that it cracked
through). Wine, Sebastian decided, wine. Slow, savoring sips.
Knowledge that took in not only Bacchus and mythology, but
also geography and horticulture, terroir and tannins. It wasn't just
Napa and Sonoma and the Loire Valley, but Pinot Noirs from
Oregon, Italian chiantis and orvietos, Spanish tempranillos, sau-
vignon blancs from New Zealand, Argentinean malbecs, Austra-
lian shiraz, German and South African Rieslings, the list went on
and on and he knew that he had only scratched the surface; there
were wines being produced in Romania and Israel and Moldova;
even China and Uzbekistan had large outputs. In the US, every
state in the country, incredibly, had wine production—though
the idea of a Wyoming Frontenac or a Nebraskan edelweiss gave
him the shivers.

Sebastian scanned the extensive list, running over it two times
to make sure of his choice. While he took his time deciding, the
waiter and Christine sat and stood, respectively, in anticipatory
silence, twice turning to one another and emitting embarrassed

little laughs before Sebastian declared: "We'll do a Pauillac, the Château Pichon Longueville, Comtesse de Lalande. 2004."

"Verrrrry good, sir," the waiter said, taking the menus and hurrying off.

Christine gasped. "Um, I couldn't help but notice that wine is, like, $300."

"No, no," Sebastian said. "$285, approximately."

Christine squirmed. Her face reddened. A slight fog coated the insides of her spectacles. "Um…"

Sebastian gently placed his hand on hers. "Don't worry," he said. "Really. I've just received a prize. It has a generous monetary value attached. I appreciate your defense of me back there, so you get to be the recipient of the awards committee's largesse. Least I can do." He wanted to add, "I don't expect anything of you," but the only reason someone ever says that, he reckoned, is precisely because they do expect something and hope to secure that expectation by way of paralipsis. He could guess at the source of Christine's discomfort and he didn't want to make it worse. She had to be thinking: This man just bought a $300 bottle of wine. Plus dinner, plus dessert, plus tip. This will easily exceed $500. Surely he is going to expect a swap of this sumptuous feast for sex. For crying out loud, we're both staying in this very hotel.

If these thoughts were in fact swirling around her head, he hoped to stave them off, or at least calm them. He did this by launching into a description of the wine itself, to let her know that it was no blind choice driven by vanity or a desire to soon have her submitting to his every lascivious whim, but rather his choice had been driven by his deep knowledge of the product: "The Longueville is an excellent Pauillac. The estate was originally classified as fourth growth, but the performance of the wine means, qualitatively speaking, that it is essentially a second growth, and has been that way for a good twenty years now. Ah," he said, noticing the waiter's return. In tow was the manager, there to offer his congratulations to the Mister for his superb choice and to observe his charge ceremoniously doing the honors of decanting. All of this had the effect of heating Christine more. She had to remove her glasses and surreptitiously wipe them on her napkin.

"So, you're from Chicago?" Sebastian asked.

"Naperville."

"Ah, nice." He had no idea if Naperville was nice. But he smiled agreeably anyway and with deep confidence in what he was saying. Sebastian was self-aware enough to realize that the small act of standing on a stage, accepting a prize, being the toast of the town, made him infinitely more attractive and confident than he actually was in either case.

"Tell me about your work," he said.

She had been working with the CDC in infectious diseases in West Africa but had been removed because of an Ebola outbreak.

"Ah, yes," Sebastian said. "Interesting. Sad, of course, but interesting."

"You always want to stay. But at a certain point…"

"Yes, I understand."

"Our lead physician was stricken, actually. Rushed to Berlin, then Emory. Barely survived. So we left. But I hope to get back." Her hands flew about her as she spoke.

"Ebola is fascinating. Bloodborne, yes?"

"Clear signs of coagulopathy and impaired circulatory system symptomology," she said, tearing a hunk from her bread roll.

"Bleeding from mucous membranes and puncture sites?" he asked, taking a sip of water. He eyed the wine, settling and plum-colored and lovely.

"Roughly half of reported cases. Small punctures. Fruit bats, usually."

"And the bleed sources?"

She was riled up now, bursting with excitement: "Hematemesis, hemoptysis, melena. Diffuse bleeding is rare, usually exclusive to the GI tract." She picked up her fork, using it to punctuate her words like a maestra leading an orchestra.

"I see you have sinistral leanings," Sebastian said, referring to her use of her left hand to stab the air. "Me, too," he added, waving his fingers.

"True of much genius, yes?" She smiled.

I could like this girl.

"Pardon me." They both looked up, lost as they'd been in their dinner table talk. It was Graybeard. "I was sitting over there..." He pointed to a far-off table, desolate and small, set for one. "I wanted to personally offer my congratulations."

"Thank you," Sebastian said.

Christine didn't say anything, looking suddenly chastened.

"You're welcome." Graybeard walked away, leaving Sebastian and Christine to sit in silence. It was the tone. Offered in such a way that the content of the message, clearly, was to be taken in opposition to its literal wording. It was snide and it momentarily ruined the mood.

Sebastian poured out small bits of the wine and prodded Christine to try.

She sipped. "Mmmm, good," she said.

Sebastian glanced at Graybeard, sullen and glowering across the dining room. His glare confirmed that Sebastian was the victor: award, expensive dinner, the girl—the spoils.

He poured their glasses to three-quarters full and drank. "Good indeed," he said.

The wine paired nicely with their choices of meal: grilled veal sweetbreads and pan roasted magret of duck for appetizers, a main course of Grilled Herefordshire Lamb tenderloin with French Green Lentil Cream and Crispy Grit Cakes, and to finish it off: what the waiter claimed was the restaurant's "famous" chocolate bombe: Dark Chocolate Olive Oil Mousse, Crème Fraîche Chocolate Cake, and Orange Caramel. He actually made a kissing pantomime with all five fingers pressed to his lips as he described it.

"And I'll have a glass of Blandy's Malmsey Madeira," Sebastian said. He turned to Christine: "You want one?"

She blushed and shook her head. "I think I've had plenty. More than plenty. One more sip, well, I can't be held responsible for my actions."

Indeed, after Sebastian had paid the bill—in the end, roughly $635—and they entered the elevator, neither said a word as Sebastian pressed his floor, 14, and Christine pressed nothing.

They had started on "L," of course, and so there were thirteen opportunities for her to press a button. But even after one or two, the act of it would have come across as a calculated decision, and not in his favor. Had she simply pressed her floor—he didn't even know which one it was, but if it had also been 14, surely she would have remarked at such coincidence—when they first got on, well, message sent and message received. But as they zipped through—1, 2, 3, 4—and still no push of her finger, it spoke more loudly than the numbers themselves.

But suddenly the elevator jerked, groaned, and stopped, somewhere in the indefinable space between floors 9 and 10. A harsh, clattering deadened stop.

"Are we stuck?" Christine asked, her voice fluted with panic.

"I don't know," Sebastian said, pressing indiscriminate numbers to no effect.

"Oh, God," Christine muttered. "Oh, God!"

Sebastian kept pressing, watching Christine out of the corner of his eye, the way she tipped from foot to foot as if she had a bladder threatening to burst; the way several strands of her hair had loosed themselves from her tight bun and had fallen over her glasses; the way she had begun smoothing the sides of her shirt in a jittery and insistent way.

"You okay?" Sebastian asked, his finger still doing a tap dance across the buttons: 16, 2, L, 11, 4—to no effect. Finally, his eye registered the red Emergency Call button, so he depressed that. The result was a shrill bell that only heightened the encroaching aura of hysteria.

"Oh, God," she called.

"Christine?"

"Okay, okay, okay, okay," she repeated, and began walking tight circles in the elevator. "You see—okay, okay, okay, okay— you see, I suffer from claustrophobia and, well—okay, Christine, okay, just breathe, okay. You're okay..."

This was the last thing Sebastian wanted to hear. He had always suffered from a touch of claustrophobia himself and the only thing beating back the crescendo of nerves was his self-imposed need to be calm for his companion.

"It's an irrational phobia, I know," she said, her voice more controlled but still tittery.

Sebastian had to bite back the urge to correct the tautology: Of course, all phobias are, by definition, irrational. That's what makes them phobias. He knew this sudden nasty impulse derived from his own sense of encroaching panic. He loosened his necktie, thinking all the while how ludicrous a move it was, how terribly clichéd, and how it accomplished little. Sebastian took notice of the elevator walls, how they seemed at once to move in on them and then retract, a living, breathing thing, like a beating heart. He pushed the alarm bell again, which did nothing other than enrage him. Somewhere, that stupid bell was sounding up and down the elevator shaft and it signified zilch, really. He could envision a cluster of people standing in the lobby pushing buttons with irritation, hearing the alarm, seeing that one of the cars had stopped moving, and doing nothing other than continue pressing the button. Hell, it's probably what he'd be doing if the situation were mercifully reversed. Eventually, one person might register the bell, put two and two together and go to reception to report the stuck elevator, but then what? A bellhop with a crowbar would be dispatched to save him and Christine, both beating back full-on panic with only the barest of threads?

"Isn't this thing supposed to have a phone, or a call button?" Christine asked.

Indeed, there it was, just next to the panic button. Sebastian depressed the silver button.

"Yes?" came the staticky reply. The fact that a real voice answered immediately allayed, somewhat, the feeling of impending asphyxiation.

"We're stuck in the elevator."

"Okay, which car, sir?"

"How on Earth would I know?"

"Okay, sir. Just sit tight."

"Do we have any other options?"

"Help will be on the way."

"Okay, are you hanging up, or—?"

There was no response.

"Now what do we do?" Christine asked.

"Apparently, we sit tight." Sebastian stared at the ceiling. "Look, we have oxygen. You see the holes up there? We can't die in here. We'll be fine."

Christine exhaled and then flung herself at Sebastian, not really kissing him, but rather pressing her sweaty lips on his while strange staccato whistles leaked from her nostrils. She backed off him and began unbuttoning her blouse. When she was done, she let it drop to the floor beside her, revealing an assertively unsexy beige bra, precisely the brand and style Sebastian's mother used to favor. He could see them in his mind's eye, strung across various hooks and faucets to dry behind the green plastic shower curtain in his childhood home. When he wanted to shower or bathe, he had to unhook those bras from their perches and set them in a pile on the toilet seat. What a Freudian opportunity presented itself here in the form of Christine. How wonderful to fondle the not so soft material of the brassiere and return to the Oedipal cocoon.

He moved toward her, then stopped. "You have a small patch of psoriasis on your shoulder."

"Yes," she said nodding and smiling, as if her psoriasis patch was a dermatological trophy delivered by divine fiat.

"Five minutes in a tanning booth. Clears it right up."

"You're sweet," she said, smiling, the tension released like the slow unletting of the tied end of a balloon. She gave him a kiss on the cheek.

He reached down and, brushing her calf, picked up her shirt and handed it to her. "You don't have to," he said. "We don't have to."

"Isn't this the way it's supposed to work? I mean, a stuck elevator? We start here and then head to your room. Isn't that what people do? In movies, at least?"

"Believe me, this is not lack of interest on my part. You're a very attractive woman. It's just, well, if you want the truth, I'm in love with someone else."

It felt natural coming out of his mouth, but it somehow registered as a huge surprise to him. He smiled. "I've always been in love with her. Irrevocably, I'm afraid."

Christine put her shirt back on. "Yes?" she said. "Tell me about her."

He'd known her since they were little kids. He used to go over her house, first for rollicking neighborhood parties his mother had been invited to, and then play dates with just Joanna, and she was the only one who was consistently nice to him when no one else was. And the thing about it, what made her such an amazing person, this Joanna Benson, was that she didn't need to be nice to him. She was the most popular girl in school. The only people who didn't like her were those who were jealous of her. She was a pure soul, a beautiful person.

"You keep using past tense. Is she still alive?"

"Oh, yes, she's still alive. It's just that we haven't spoken or seen each other in a long time. She's married now. Well, divorced."

"You should call her."

"Maybe I will."

"But still," she said. "I can't help but wonder at it…"

"What's that?"

"You say I'm attractive to you."

"Most definitely."

"And here I am. And she, well… what, Sebastian? Do we live in our own lonelinesses forever? Lord knows, I do it, too. Have done it ever since I can remember. But is this what we are doomed to do?"

Sebastian paused, and then: "Why risk a broken heart when you can have one that just thumps along, all utility and nothing else?"

The car started up again. They listened with relief to the movement of gears and pulleys doing their glorious work. The car lurched to the next floor and opened. A queue of irritated people glared at Sebastian and Christine as if they had been responsible for keeping the elevator from moving.

"I'm actually on 6," Christine said.

"I can ride with you…"

"I'll take the stairs, thank you."

"Of course."

They entered the stairwell and paused on the landing. Then, they shook hands. She went downward, he up. "Goodbye," they called.

The three flights were an effort, the booze and the adrenalin smashing and swirling in Sebastian's bloodstream.

He hadn't realized it before, just how drunk he was. The buzz had left him completely during the elevator ordeal. But as he entered his room and sat on the edge of the king-size bed, the sheets and blanket still tucked ruthlessly around the corners, the walls swirled about him and he had to close his eyes.

He lay back on the bed and let the world spin. He would be sick.

But no matter. He knew now: It was another country, one that could provide no real succor. He wanted back home, to the cocoon of loneliness that cut wide, and deep, and delicious.

Bloodsister

D. Dina Friedman

In the second grade closet, we pricked
our fingers, pressed the pads,
becoming sisters. At my bolted

desk, I'd wait for your twist,
catty corner toward
my seat, trying to

assess your lips. Even
when you smiled, more gone
than the chip on your tooth,

the gummy gap between
a hint of sharp poking through.
I couldn't smile. My lips

were glue, too often struck
when your face turned to scowl,
an inverted U, I couldn't

frown back at you either, only
in the mirror, behind my closed
door. I loved you badly,

willing to bleed and wait
for that slight spinal shift
that marked your turning, wanting

to be your hair back then.
Not the bound barretted
bangs, the perfect, untangled ends.

Monsters are Always Invited
by Kate Larsen

You know, Frankenstein's monster just wanted to be loved, Elizabeth says.

I thought Frankenstein WAS the monster.

Common misconception. He is, in a different sense.

What senses are there for monsters?

Well, a monster isn't your BODY. It's your MIND. Elizabeth taps her temple and bugs her eyes out over her dinner plate, fork aloft.

So, I suppose Dracula just wanted a call girl, hunh?

Probably. Dinner and a show! She cackles. Poor Lucy.

Who's Lucy?

His juiciest victim. She looks up under long lashes and waggles her eyebrows. Except Mina. Everyone was all in love with Mina.

How come?

Her hair. Lucy was just brunette. She twists a finger in her pale locks. Everyone wants us blondes. Victoria rolls her eyes and clears the table.

Only the clanking of dishes as Elizabeth sprawls paper and schoolbooks across the table damp from the dishrag, pencil bobbling between her crooked teeth, over and over. Up and down. The sky blacks the tiny windows, the air bites Victoria's skin when she steps out to smoke.

Night air makes nicotine easier to consume, smoke twists between pinpoint stars, curling and unfolding and stroking itself in a striptease, tangled in its own toxic charm. In her mind her own form, nude, soft pale flesh against the curling dark hair of a man and the tangles they make between pinpoint stars they can never see. Inside, the books are packed away, sleepy dark circles grace Elizabeth's deep eyes and she announces her retreat to the bath.

Mrs. Cline is going to kill me, she sighs, shoves a book into the bag until its seams groan. She wants to build airplanes but all she can remember are the classics, the numbers and shapes evade her. Imaginary number? She shrieked one night. What the fuck? And she went to work that night instead of bed, sitting on the corner stool with glassy eyes while the regulars yelled at the game on TV and ordered one beer at a time. She even got to borrow a pair of heels and smoke cigarettes while she waited, her drags slow and precise and unpracticed. They both slept the next day, sometimes you need one off, Victoria said, and it's okay, when your brain is running a marathon every day.

Elizabeth comes out to smoke after her shower, and as always Victoria hesitates. They both know she should tell her not to, but they both know she'll steal one later anyway, so why not enjoy each other's company?

Elizabeth crawls into bed around one in the morning, like usual, unless he's there. She always whispers first, calls her sister's name, even if the only answer is soft snoring. He isn't there that much. She folds her arms across her chest and nestles her face between her sister's shoulder blades, folds her knees up to her elbows.

There are so many worries for young girls that they don't know, can't see. The school is a ten-minute walk, but Victoria drives her every morning. Lets her smoke in the car so she will.

Did you finish your math?

No.

What will she do?

Flunk me, she groans.

You need a tutor.

We can't pay a tutor.

Duh. Someone will help you if you just ask.

Sarah who washes dishes at the Italian place next door brings her after school. You never know. She needs a ride. In the corner of the kitchen by the fryers she scribbles and flips through textbooks and sleeps, finally, until Sarah's shift is done and she can drive her home.

The neighbor lady is old and has cats and on Saturday nights she stays up late watching something on TV and she keeps an eye on the door across the hall and there are only two keys to the deadbolt and one is inside and the other is downtown in a dingy barroom. The impasse is reached here: the pink bra found smashed deep in the bottom of the sheets, at the edge of the bed where the top sheet folds over the bottom. The panties that match, lace trimmed with black and tiny bows, so tiny you could bite them off with your teeth. And so Victoria dug deeper: not the backpack, that bottomless pit of knowledge, but in every corner and every fold of clothes in the dresser, and she found the pills and the condoms and pictures on the phone and was struck at once by the loss and the beauty, the exquisite and perfect delicateness of Elizabeth full grown, white-gold hair and creamy skin in a way she never wished to see but now knew as lovely. So, she said nothing, and they drank beer on the couch and watched How I Met Your Mother all night. The neighbor lady knew everything and petted her cat while she told. But a girl can't stay in a barroom on weekends, that's that.

So, Victoria closes at two AM and folds tips into her pockets if her shirt is cut low and she doesn't frown the way she'd like to. The TV glows blue in the living room and her sister isn't in her own bed, she's in the big one, waiting, a pile of comforter and pillows with a tuft of hair poking out.

When the tutor is found, Elizabeth has to go home after school, they can't have a whole pile of teenagers taking up space in the kitchen, there's only one chair by the fryer and they can't be at the bar if they can't drink, that's that, says Craig, filling his own glass from the tap and counting at the register. Sorry.

But it's okay 'cause he's a nerd, she says, and Monica walks that way home anyway. The neighbor lady is waiting in the hall with her cat when Victoria gets home at midnight, did you see that boy she brought home, it's not the same one.

Good, she thinks of pictures not meant for her eyes.

He left at five-thirty, she clips out, stroking her cat. Kinda goofy looking. Thickest glasses I've ever seen, she wipes her nose with a hanky. Least that other one was cute.

A body can get used to anything, and security slips in, the world is okay, the grades up, look, even Mrs. Cline left a note on my last test. That's that. It's okay.

Good, and as always, so proud. You're really going to go somewhere.

God, I hope so.

Me too.

And it is okay, it's okay until it's not and how do you ever really tell for sure? Victoria knows the second it happens, roiling like vomit in her stomach and she does puke, barely makes it to the trashcan by the register and drops two full, foaming beers that shatter against the polished hardwood. Craig's head whips around across the room and the cook is picking up glass and she pukes again, on her knees in front of the garbage and the other waitress has brought her a glass of water and is pulling her up by her elbow. I have to go, and she bolts out through the kitchen while Craig swears at her, drops the keys twice at the car door for trembling, and is headed home.

At six PM, she is in the parking lot, snatching her purse and slamming the locks on the car door, the aging elevator rattling so slowly down that she takes the stairs two by two, heaving for breath at the top of three flights, jeans swishing together and the neighbor lady meets her in the hallway without a cat and her eyes are like tennis balls. I have the worst feeling—but Victoria pushes the old woman aside and shoves open the unlocked door, and the neighbor lady follows her in, a silent slippered wraith.

Books and papers trail from the breakfast bar to the kitchen and living room floors, pens rolled in all directions. No TV, no sound. No breath. Elizabeth is not on the couch, not in her room, there is no hair peeping from beneath the comforter of the big bed. The neighbor lady pads quietly behind and Victoria can't speak, her throat is dry, so she croaks out a name and her fingertips push the sliding glass of the mirrored closet door aside. There is Elizabeth, white gold in the deep dark of sweaters jeans dresses shoes. The tiniest sob escapes beneath her hair, and her sister's small hands attempt to scoop beneath her arms, a child, but her arms clamp tight to ribs and she is halfway rolled out into the light before her legs manage to crawl. The neighbor lady is close behind, and no one sees, but tears roll down her cheeks and her hands twist each other a painful white.

Elizabeth sobs again and presses her face hard into her sister's chest, a babe snuggling at the breast, salt tears and snot soaking the fabric of the bar shirt, fingers wrenching at her back, twisting skin and cutting with nails. Her sister strokes her hair, holds her cheek, and shush shush.

For long minutes they are a pile on the floor, the neighbor lady on the chair of the computer desk behind them.

Elizabeth wipes at her face with the heel of her hand and that's when her sister sees the bruise, long thin purple fingermarks smeared on white flesh. She catches the arm and their eyes meet, a storm of icy blue. Victoria doesn't have to say it, but she does, you have to tell me what happened, so that you can tell someone else, softly. Fresh tears flood Elizabeth's face splotchy red and her mouth crinkles back from her teeth, peels open into a silent wave of grief.

I told him no, is all she can cough out. I said no! she buries her face again and the neighbor lady hiccups behind them.

I heard a huge ruckus, she cries and wrings her hands, and I knocked on the door but nobody came, and I heard her scream and I couldn't get in and I didn't know who to call and she wouldn't answer the door after he left.

We have to go to the cops, Victoria announces, what seems like a long time later. We have to. We do. Her sister sniffs up whatever is in her nose and wipes the rest on her sleeve. The neighbor lady runs or shuffles across the hall for her purse, ridiculously huge, bigger than she is, and the elevator ride is solemn. Victoria calls on the way, to ask what to do, and at the hospital the doctors are as probing as he was, but it's science when they do it.

It is a long night, and they order pizza on the way home that nobody eats, and the neighbor lady stays for a long time and mixes raspberry vodka into hot tea and goes home, finally. They hold the two doors open and look across the hall at each other for a moment, a cat mewling and twisting about the old woman's ankles.

They go to court because that is what women do, but if Victoria were a brother, she'd buy a gun. She wouldn't need one, she has hands that itch to claw and choke and tear. She does buy a gun, though, and they both learn to use it, and Elizabeth's doll face is gorgeous in fury as it is in pain, firing the thirty-eight over and over, sinking hot lead into the bullseye or close enough. A gun would have been good before, or perhaps not at all—as useless as it is now.

The second bedroom houses only a bedframe, the box springs and the mattress with the blood stain hauled away to be burned, or whatever. They sleep curled next to each other in the big bed, and often Elizabeth's fingers, cold and delicate as porcelain, reach out to touch Victoria's spine, her cheek, her arm, her black hair in the dead of night, their icy arrival waking her every time. But Victoria isn't there in the day, when the other girls whisper or yell slut and the boys smirk and look at her easy. Blood of my blood, flesh of my flesh. The purple bruises on her sister's throat burn a fury into her because she can't take them away, make them her own, she can only watch as they slowly fade.

Craig lets the girl wrap silverware, sits beside her, on Saturdays now. He makes her laugh… and he's very good at math. He pays her to wash dishes on the weekends but not school nights because she needs sleep, he says. So, Sarah drives her home and she waits across the hall and pets the cat and watches Dateline with the neighbor lady who both deadbolts and chains the door. She finds this silly.

No one's going to break in, Elizabeth says, puts down Tolstoy. Even Dracula had to be invited in. It's not who gets in, it's who you let in.

They both cry, Victoria cries for not understanding, for things that can't ever be fixed, for not being there, which is the worst part except for not being able to wring his scrawny neck without going to prison. She cries for not being smart enough to orchestrate the perfect murder.

She'll be okay, says Craig, as they watch her tease the cook in the kitchen. The laughter is good and pure, real laughter, for the first time in a year. Too bad she didn't get your dark hair, he looks at Victoria from under his eyebrows. But she's too smart to be set back by this for long. Too bad there are so many slimes in the world, he sips foam off a fresh beer. That's just it, it's just too bad.

It's too bad I wasn't watching her, Victoria's guilt finally voiced.

Don't do that. He whips his head around to glare at her. You can't. She has to be in the world without you sometime.

I just don't trust the world.

No one does. Why would they? That's just survival instincts.

I can't believe I didn't kill him.

Craig's face grows dark and hard. You're a woman, he says. You're too small. That's why this whole mess happened. Delicate little princess hands. Everyone loves us blondes.

Dr. Van Helsing went all the way to Romania to save Mina, Victoria broods over pizza rolls and Oscar weekend on the Sundance channel. Didn't he?

Yeah, he did, not looking up. How'd you know?

I read the end.

But not the whole book?

She looks at Elizabeth sideways and they laugh.

He's at a different school now, she says softly.

Oh?

Yeah, his parents made him change schools after the court stuff.

Good.

I guess. I wanted to stab him, Elizabeth whispers.

Me too.

I took a knife to school once.

Oh?

I was going to follow him into the bathroom. Her eyes are empty and stare at nothing. And when he wasn't looking, I was just going to stab him.

Mm hm…

He was sick that day, one of my friends asked someone who knows one of his friends. He was gone all week. Then he changed schools.

Where on earth did you get a knife?

From the kitchen. It's in my backpack.

She nods. And the knife stays in the bag. It's something, like the gun stays in the glove box.

Blood of my blood, it poured from my veins too, from a place more bestial, where it boiled under my skin and heated my heart to a maddened frenzy. Because I can't take it away from you.

But the boy walks free.

Until prom committee starts their work, and Victoria picks Elizabeth up much later in the day.

It takes that long because Victoria's days off are short and there's no school on Sunday except for good families. But the day does come, and the knife in the backpack can just stay there with the pepper spray on the keychain, that's supposed to drop grizzly bears.

Victoria's no good at following or being discreet and really it looks nothing like the movies. But she's too little, Craig said so, princess hands, so he's the one who gets out. The car slides along the curb behind three or so parked ahead, and Craig rolls the black ski mask down his face, slides it delicately in place, and slams open the door and is running down the sidewalk before she hits the brakes.

He is tall and skinny and Craig is built like a pit bull. He bares his teeth as the nerd turns and his fists are sunk into his mouth and his groin and they are on the ground and Craig's hands are around his spindly neck, shaking him like a dog shakes a rat.

How do you like that, he screams. How do you like that. He releases and leaps backward to his feet all in one motion, I know where you live, he howls. I'm coming for you again, and kicks him in the stomach as he writhes on the ground, spitting blood. Tell me to stop, bitch, Craig snarls. Tell me you don't like that. Tell me no! and he spits across his nose and the tires squeal on the asphalt like in the movies as they leave and Victoria doesn't realize until they pull into the shared parking lot of the Catholic church and the bar that she's been crying the whole time.

Craig's body heaves with breath as he rubs his knuckles. Wasn't a fair fight, he says to his knees.

No, she says. It wasn't. Her hands shake as she searches the center console and unscrews the half-pint. She wipes her lip with the heel of her hand and passes the bottle. Thank you, she says, her thirst quenched.

In the Haunted Toy Shop Late One Spring
by Susannah Carlson

My boy's inside before the doors fully open,
Power Rangers sneakers sparking on linoleum.
I lag behind, savoring his gangly frame,
His head still too big for those
Slight shoulders, those bird-wing bones.

Something inside me swells to aching
Sweet and fleeting as wet winter grass.

He's earned the gift he is choosing.
So new to the world, this little old soul.

The aisle of yellow Tonkas draws me.
Evocative as music. I stop to feel:
Sandbox of my girlhood,
Broken backhoe.
Wet sand and cat turds
Cool the skin of memory.
Sour grass and Hi-C
Sugar the ghost of my tongue.

And he is gone. My perfect boy.
Swallowed by the labyrinth
Of this haunted store.

Around a bank of plastic horses,
Beyond the Playmobiles and Legos,
I find him in that pinkest place.

Human simulacra line the shelves,
Some speak or wet or cry.
My youthful fear of mannequins
Blinks twice and turns its face my way.

And there, at the end of the longest aisle,
I see my beautiful child,
In too-short pants and too-long tee,
His body, still adjusting to the weight of air,
Taking shape like a butterfly's wing.

He turns and shows me his chosen prize:
Ballerina Barbie in pink satin and tulle,
Trembling in her box between
His small and dear and growing hands.

"This one, Mommy, please?"

The Writers' Wife
After reading Galway Kinnell's
"The Call Across the Valley of Not Knowing"
by Carly Gates

For years I have imagined that red house, sinking
into the dark earth, and I've placed her there,

Kinnell's first wife, her belly swollen with life.
She reads for the first time his poem about lying together,

two mismatched halfnesses, as her husband dreamed
of another woman, his true half, still moist with youth.

How must she have felt, their second child thrashing
inside of her—did she already agree with him

that her happiness lay in sleep? In dreaming
of lying in some other room, of a less fickle moon?

She must have once gladly held the blossom
of his empty heart, kissed the wound of his mouth

full of poetry, full of nightmares, but how long
could she last when he sliced open the scab

each time the flesh tried to heal, viewed happiness
as blindness already fat and soured?

How long could anyone? My husband's patience wans.
I watch for the glowing ember of his cigarette

as he paces outside, surprised each time it reappears.
We cannot blame Aristophanes, Kinnell, only ourselves.

No moon can brighten our nightmares:
writers who sink with our houses, spouses who escape outside.

Kinnell's wife tears out the root of her heart, buries
it for earthworms. This darkness closes like a fist.

A Drawn and Papered Heart
by Beth Konkoski

It pays fifty bucks an hour and the class is three-and-a-half hours long. Not the sort of thing you tell your mother about, but we'll make rent. And it isn't as bad as I expected. I was nervous but the first night, we stopped for dinner, and after two beers and some enchiladas, I relaxed. I told Richard about the zit on my back. "Will they notice? Draw it?"

"It isn't about perfection," he said, finishing his third Corona. Do colleges care about professors drinking before class?

Tonight, I slip out of my jeans and into the white robe I have carried over the mountain to this community college in the desert. Richard teaches Life Drawing 201 here at night, after a day of high school art classes, because they hired him and college teaching looks good on his resume. But he complains. "Nobody down here willing to model. How do you teach a fucking life drawing class without a model?"

And that is where I fit in. The curtained space I stand in has art room props on a shelf behind me: dried flowers, a Papier-mâché dog sculpture, a tarnished silver ice bucket, arms and legs from a mannequin. It is a small, thrown together changing room, the size of a shower, comforting the first night when I was so nervous about undressing, but now I feel a little foolish, hiding back here to transform from person to model. Why don't I just take off my clothes and leave them in a pile by the stool? I guess that would feel more intimate, letting my jeans slide off my thighs in front of the students, mostly young Mexican boys with perfect skin, and hair that falls like rain when they take off their baseball caps. They are beautiful, each of them, but especially Antonio. I try to find poses that will keep me looking his direction, able to see the squinting, dense focus that crosses his face when he draws me.

Before stepping onto the wooden platform, I look around on the shelves for props to hold. Last week, Richard went nuts when I wrapped my arms through an empty wooden picture frame, its gilded surface shedding gold paint on my shoulder. "The angles, the angles," he proclaimed, making me shift at least five times with my body contorted inside the rectangle. I had expected modeling to be dull, maybe some time to think a little about the three classes I still need to take for my master's in Special Ed., so I won't lose my job. Then there's the visit from my parents to worry about. Their attitude toward Luke has not improved since the wedding, and they will require an especially well-planned story if I am to cover up his ill-fated military career and current job as a surfer of channels in our apartment. It isn't like I'm okay with where he's at. I'm just trying to have a little patience.

The hours on this small stage aren't slow or empty at all. I realized the first night, hot under the lights and keeping my calves flexed while I crouched on the edge of the stool, that I am part of the finished product in an active sense. Somehow my energy shows up on their pages, and the drawings are always better when I focus on how I am positioned and who is drawing me. I have to push the pose out at them and think about it, watching the sweep of the second hand on the clock so I move on a schedule: eight poses at thirty seconds, six at two minutes, four at four minutes, and two at six minutes. We run through this pattern then take a break. The second session begins with four minutes and moves to the final, almost impossible sixteen that feels like six hundred. When my mind drifts, Richard knows. When I walk around the easels on break and see what they draw, I can tell the poses that deflated me or kept me too much in my head.

There is a vase tucked behind a pile of duck decoys, and I pull it toward me. The bottom scrapes like fingernails on the metal shelf and kicks up art dust, a mix of all their erasing and scribbling and sharpening. It smells of brush cleaner, chalk, and failure, this dust that settles on my arms and travels deep into my lungs when I pose. The vase is large enough to hug, and painted with metallic gold paint. I don't believe it has held flowers in this decade, as it smells dry as a late summer creek.

A single rose sits across the stool. The outer petals curl like a lipsticked mouth, just a small pout off the head of the bloom. I touch its velvet, then lift it from the stool and look around. Antonio's eyes meet mine above his easel.

"For Valentine's," he says. And his gaze returns to the page even though he has nothing yet to sketch. A pulse kicks alive in my groin and at my collarbone, like I've been doing a quick set of jumping jacks. At the stool, I cannot quite decide what to do with the rose or the vase, and the lights are small lasers on the back of my head, their heat traveling through my hair to spike me.

"We're ready?" Richard asks. The students step to their easels and face me. The rose and vase are an impossible match. The mouth would hold three dozen, so I place the single one on the floor and let my robe slip off as well. I balance on the stool with my legs out like a frog's, the vase hugged tightly against my breasts, my face turned so a cheek touches the rim. I stare at nothing on the classroom wall.

Antonio's rose has reminded me that I did not buy Luke a card for Valentine's Day, our second as a married couple. But he has been so difficult since his discharge, not even waking up when I leave for work, on the couch with Styrofoam takeout boxes beside him when I get home. He seems like a different person these last months, and helping him feels both awkward and exhausting, especially since he barely answers my questions about the simplest things, like getting the mail or buying a paper for want ads. "I hear you" is his preferred response, if he answers at all. So, the idea of romance has not been much on my mind, but still, six years together, two married, and I blow it off. It is all I can think of for the thirty-second poses, and this makes me hold them too long. Richard must cue me, cue me, cue me. The irritation is thick in his voice.

On the dining table, when I was a child, I would lay out all the Valentine cards in the box my mother had purchased, trying to match the message of the card with the right person from class. One year I couldn't decide on the card for Robbie Gleason who had come up behind me on the playground and grabbed my elbows, pulled me to him, and whispered, "Will you go out with me?" The only place to go in the fifth grade was the skating rink, so we spent the winter skating circles together after his hockey practice, my hand clenched in his through mittens so thick we could have been holding wooden sticks. As the rink shut down one Friday night, we skated a circle in the dark and he snow-plowed in the far corner, pulling me into the shadows where he pressed me against the wood, his cold lips like a flint the instant they touched mine. I can see myself at the table, searching for the right card, getting annoyed as I shuffled and reshuffled, finally randomly putting them in envelopes and signing names on the front only. Nothing on those cards could tell him how his kiss had made me think of summer and warm coals even as the wind blew against us. And I was scared to give him something noticeable, something from the drugstore in town that would state things clearly. On Valentine's Day he left a heart-shaped box of chocolates on my desk—To Shelly, From Robbie. The box is still in the closet of my old room. He had not been afraid.

"Michelle." The voice pulls at me and I jerk myself off the stool. "Please." Richard's impatience and superiority are a vapor in the room. He points to the clock with his sharp, goateed chin, an artsy look he cannot pull off, and scolds me with the narrowing of his eyes. I am glad I turned down his suggestion that we sleep together after class the first night. At the time I felt a little bad about how harsh I sounded saying no, but he knows I'm married. More importantly, he is at least fifteen years older than me, and I don't think I hid that thought very well. His face sort of emptied and he mumbled, "Of course not," as he led us to his car. In the teacher's lounge at school the next day, he apologized without looking at me, but wanted to know if I would still model. "You're good, and I don't want to lose a model or be weird with a colleague," he said before walking away. I wondered how sleeping together would have left us "not weird," but it wasn't really worth going into. Luke wouldn't have liked me still riding over the mountain with him if he knew about the proposition, but I am not in the habit of telling him everything I experience. I have assessed the risk and weighed the options; I'm pretty sure I can overpower Richard if he ever presses it, so I don't worry. I turn my focus to the clock and the angles of my body until break.

"I liked your shoulders in this one." Jose points, and I see the solid twist of torso, a neck long and looking away. They never draw more than an outline, a suggestion of me in space. Richard says they are learning how the body connects and doesn't, how different it looks from what they expect. I hear him telling a student that he wasn't looking carefully, hadn't really seen. Tightening the belt on my robe, I step away from the circle and into the hall. I will walk to the bathroom for something to do.

"You didn't look at mine tonight." His voice sounds like wings in the dark.

"Sorry." I step to where he leans against a bank of windows. Outside, the sun has turned everything to some scrambled art tapestry of orange and vomit pink. The clouds look like crumpled laundry.

We are only a few feet apart, and I can see a pulse in his throat. His arms cross at his heart and he doesn't look away. He has been in my thoughts all night. If I'm honest, before tonight. I want to dig around in the space behind his eyes, to feel the shine of his hair across my skin.

"Thank you for the rose."

"You're welcome. He looks me in the eyes now. "Valentine's Day is for beauty." The classroom door opens, and we are both startled by Richard searching, spotting, scowling.

"Time," he says like a referee. Antonio hustles himself toward the call, so I am unable to say anything. I just follow, watch him move in his jeans and let his words repeat inside my head. For the second half of class I am anchored on the stage, imagining what Antonio will think of each pose, how he will shift me onto paper. Even the sixteen-minute poses feel short as I breathe my way around what I will say to him after class. At the end of the night, there is never an inspection of work, just the hurry to be done and away. But if I dress quickly, I should be able to catch him in the parking lot while Richard closes up the room.

The night is almost chilly when I step outside. I can see a group of students walking together toward the scattered cars in the lot. Their voices sound as young as kids on a playground as they toss goodbyes around. I hurry to catch up. Antonio peels off toward a pick-up truck near one of the light posts. I am ready to call his name when the passenger door opens. High heels click on pavement.

"Antonio?" And then a spectacular girl in a leather mini dress emerges from behind the truck's cab. Her body flashes through the dark like a meteor in its confidence and layered gold. "It took so long," she says.

"Gloria." He steps toward her, kisses her with his hands cupping her chin. She wraps herself around him, into him. A little leap and her legs circle his waist. He boosts her higher on his hips and kisses her harder. They crash against the side of the truck and I can hear them both moan. I am grateful for the dark and the moment of not calling his name.

Back on the sidewalk, I drop Antonio's rose into the blue recycle container and pace quietly in the shadows, waiting for Richard, who will drive us back over the mountain.

If I Had Three Lives

by Sarah Russell
After "Melbourne" by the Whitlams

If I had three lives, I'd marry you in two.
The other? Perhaps that life over there
at Starbucks, sitting alone, writing—a memoir,
maybe a novel or this poem. No kids, probably,
a small apartment with a view of the river,
and books—lots of books, and time to read.
Friends to laugh with, and a man sometimes,
for a weekend, to remember what skin feels like
when it's alive. I'd be thinner in that life, vegan,
practice yoga. I'd go to art films, farmers markets,
drink martinis in swingy skirts and big jewelry.
I'd vacation on the Maine coast and wear a flannel shirt
weekend guy left behind, loving the smell of sweat
and aftershave more than I did him. I'd walk the beach
at sunrise, find perfect shell spirals and study pockmarks
water makes in sand. And I'd wonder sometimes
if I'd ever find you.

Camping For the First Time
by Bill Stenson

fam .i .ly ˈfam(ə)lē: a group involving parents and children living together in a household.

Theo and Silvie McDonald and their two boys, Richard and Manson, for example, are a family. Richard is ten and Manson eight, and the McDonalds have been a family for as long as Richard has been around. The marriage was a hurried affair. This family knows another family, the Sharmas, Leela and Tariq, and their six-year-old girl, Beet. Tariq was born here but Leela has only been in the country for seven years. These two families haven't been good friends for very long. Just a couple of years. It doesn't take long to be friends with some people before you know certain things.

These two families, when they get together, do what most families do. They cook for one another (biryani rice and tandoori chicken when Leela is cooking, roast beef and Yorkshire pudding when it's Theo and Silvie's turn). Tariq doesn't cook. They watch fireworks, swim in the river, and hike to the very top of small mountains. In the winter months, they sometimes watch movies together, often Bollywood movies, because Theo and Silvie like them as much as their friends do. One day in the middle of summer, they decide to go camping.

Leela has never been camping before. She doesn't understand why anyone would spend time away from hot water and flush toilets. Tariq knows all about camping, he says, but admits he's never been. For both, it will be their first time. The McDonalds own a large tent, just one, but Theo borrows a second tent from his brother. They have a camping stove, two coolers, and an axe to chop firewood. There are enough sleeping bags for the kids, but since they don't know if they will ever camp a second time, they decide the adults will make do with blankets, top and bottom. The forecast suggests camping is a good idea.

Theo reserves the camping spot ahead of time. He likes to plan. The spot is large enough for both tents, and it is an easy walk to the lake, which is swimmable this time of year. If Theo has one complaint, it is the aluminum campers that surround them, one with its own TV antenna. He notices Leela eying the monstrosity. Envy he surmises.

The first night, the McDonalds organize themselves in the largest tent. This makes sense to everyone since they have two boys. Tariq finds the whole camping experience exciting, and he takes his time explaining to Leela how they will make a temporary home for a few days. Mostly the kids swim all day long. The adults jump in to play with them, then sit and watch the sun drift across the sky. Manson didn't get suntan lotion everywhere he should have and his one shoulder is burnt. Richard applied the lotion to his brother's back and should have known better, Silvie tells everyone.

The kids have known each other for such a long time, in the context of a kid's time on Earth, and they are having so much fun, they decide on the second night, the kids can talk themselves to sleep in the small tent and the adults can stay up until they're talked out and then share the large tent. The adults agree that the kinds of friendships children establish at that age are not to be taken for granted.

There is a campfire ban because of the hot weather, and a park ranger snooping around to enforce it, so they settle for their propane stove and two flashlights. Tariq was looking forward to using the axe, and he uses it to chop wood that someone else will burn. They can hear racoons rustling in the woods all around them. One boldly explores the possibility of food, and Theo throws a rock and hits it on the head.

Leela isn't much of a drinker (she gets lightheaded, she says) and only sips on the white wine she and Silvie have agreed to share. Tariq and Theo are drinking beer for the second night in a row. I love this camping business, Tariq says, rubbing his hands up and down his biceps. The lights from neighborhood flashlights and stoves, spotted between the surrounding trees, are extinguished and the kids are talked out. Leela picks up the flashlight and heads toward the outhouse. She returns and says she's ready to sleep, is almost eager to sleep, knowing when they wake up in the morning there will only be breakfast to deal with and then the camping trip will be over. She hands the flashlight to Silvie, so she can repeat the journey. I like the silence out here, Tariq says, and Theo looks at him critically, a look not taken in because of the dark. Theo can hear the TV in the camper beside them. It's not loud, but it's not silence. Not even close.

Theo and Tariq have one more beer to work on. They both agree there's no sense taking beer back home. They can hear Leela and Silvie giggling about something for a few minutes and then there is only quiet. An hour later, the comparative merits of field hockey and ice hockey have been exhausted, and as if they need something to agree on, they decide it's time to call it a night. Neither has a flashlight so Tariq goes to one side of the tent to pee and Theo moves over to the camper and pees on the rear wheel.

Tariq gets back to the tent first. What vague light existed outside in the wilderness is gone. He rubs one hand along the blankets and finds the one Leela has hand sewn with images of peacocks, and realizes Leela is sleeping right in front of him. There is room over by the side of the tent, and when he squeezes in under the blanket Leela moans in her sleep and moves over to let him in.

Theo takes in the last of the camping experience. He likes the smell of a campground. Even the neighbors in their aluminum houses he ignores while he searches for, but can't find, the moon.

When he gets into the tent, he can tell where Silvie is sleeping just by her breathing. She never snores in her sleep, but her breathing is hoarse, as if she is threatening to.

In the middle of the night Tariq realizes there is more beer in his bladder than he had thought. Despite his intentions to be graceful, he stumbles out of the tent and has moonlight to guide him to a copse of trees to relieve himself one more time. When he's done, he stands absolutely still. Never has he been in such a dark place and been able to see the stars and the moon so clearly. The stars look like they are just above the tops of the trees. When he parts the flap to the tent, he sees that there are two people on one side of the tent and one on the other, but he feels all mixed up inside because it is as if the world has reversed itself, or maybe he has entered the tent from the wrong side. He climbs in under the blankets and hears bodies turning over in their sleep. He lies there with his eyes wide open and he feels a hand reach out and bring his hand to settle on the side of a leg. He knows right away that the soft leg his hand is resting on does not belong to Leela. How could he know this in the dark? he asks himself, but he knows this is not the question he needs to answer.

Tariq is the first up in the morning. He doesn't know who is sleeping and who is pretending to sleep and he doesn't care. He gets out in the fresh air and goes for a walk. When he gets back to the campground, no one is about so he makes a pot of strong coffee. Everyone agrees that breakfast at the campground is too much trouble and that it's best to head home and have breakfast there. Theo drives them back to town without saying much. He drops the Sharmas off and takes the van back home. Can we eat real toast and peanut butter? Richard asks. Silvie says they can make whatever they want.

The phone rings at eight-thirty that night and it is Tariq. We need to talk, he says. Leela and I. We need to talk about the camping trip.

Richard and Manson are bagged and fast asleep when Tariq and Leela arrive just after nine with Beet, groggy, but still awake and wrapped in a blanket. Leela lays her down on the sofa in the living room and puts the blanket over her. Go to sleep, she says, and turns off the light.

In the beginning, Tariq does most of the talking, but they all take a healthy turn at explaining what happened. What is real and what is not real is a deep mystery, Tariq says, and it is our responsibility to know the difference. Everyone owns up to what is real to them and it is almost midnight when they all agree what needs to happen next. The three kids are almost like family now, so they decide they will get to remain a family. There is an extra bed in the house that Beet could sleep on, but she looks so peaceful lying on the couch, they leave her be. Silvie packs enough for a night or two, and goes home with Tariq. They will have a picnic in the park around one the next day and explain things to the kids, who are more than adaptable and will adjust in due time. One week at one house and one week at the other. It will be an adventure for them Tariq says, and in his mind, he is mostly thinking of the kids.

———••———

The three kids attend the same school, which is a big help. Beet is beginning grade one and she is nervous. Both Richard and Manson have had the same grade one teacher, Miss Fairweather. You have nothing to worry about, Richard assures her. She likes girls better than boys, anyway. Just keep your fingernails clean and you'll be fine.

The week school starts, the kids are with Theo and Leela. The school is close enough that they can walk, but Leela insists on driving the three of them, and she follows Beet right into her classroom and stays there until Miss Fairweather tells her she needs to leave.

Other than one day late in September when Beet disappears and shows up at her mother's door at bedtime, the three kids adjust well. That is, from the parents' perspective, at least. That doesn't mean the kids don't talk among themselves about the change in corporate structure. At Theo and Leela's place, things are a tad cramped. Manson and Richard are used to having their own room (which they have at Tariq and Silvie's) but now they have to sleep in the same room so Beet can have a bedroom to herself. The reason given is that she is a girl.

Beet is daring, cute, and wriggly, and Richard enjoys having her around most of the time.

I guess we're brother and sister now, Beet says one day when they are at Theo and Leela's place.

Goes to show how much you know, Manson says.

Well, Richard says, we're like brother and sister in a way because we live in the same house but we're not brother and sister in another way because we're not made from the same material.

Manson is sitting by himself in an overstuffed chair and covers his ears with two pillows.

What does material mean? Beet asks.

Well, your mom, we call Leela, gave birth to you, and our mom, you call her Silvie, gave birth to me and Manson. That's why.

So, if I went to the hospital when Sylvie was there, and she brought me home, then we would be brother and sister. Right?

Well, not exactly. Our dad has a role in all of this. And your dad, Tariq, was the one who made you, and that's why Leela and not Sylvie brought you home. Does that make sense?

I'm not sure, Beet says.

You guys are nuts to be talking about all of this, Manson says. Let's talk about getting a dog.

Are we going to have another brother or sister? Beet asks.

Well, that's not up to me, Richard suggests. I doubt it somehow. When enough time passes, and parents see what they've got, they figure enough is enough.

But what I mean is, if Mom has a baby with Theo, then the baby would be our brother or sister, right?

Leela pokes her head into the living room and explains that supper will be ready in twenty minutes. Richard gets a kick out of such announcements. He wonders if it is supposed to build up anticipation in some way. Most of the time the whole neighborhood knows, just from the smells coming out of the kitchen, when a Leela-made dinner is being served.

Well, if Dad and Leela have a baby, it will be a half-brother or half-sister to you and to me and Manson.

Why would they only have half a baby?

It would be a regular-sized kid, it's just what they call it.

What about if Daddy and Sylvie had a baby? Would it be just half a baby too?

Yes, it would.

Then maybe they can all do it and together we'll have a whole brother or a whole sister. I think a sister would be the best because I already have two brothers.

There won't be anymore babies around here, Manson says, so just forget about it. When we get a dog, it will be a whole dog for everyone.

Leela leans into the living room. Supper in ten minutes, she says.

———

Leela is the kind of woman who likes to take her time. Some mornings she will make chai masala tea and never get around to drinking any. She cherishes the aroma. Theo has built his life around being organized and efficient and he buys his coffee in the drive-through. It is soon apparent that if Theo wants to gain satisfaction with Leela he will have to play along with her reverence for tantric sex. Beds are for sleeping, Leela says, and wholesome sex can take place anywhere, and it does the week they don't have the kids. Thick rugs, fat chairs, the bathtub, wispy, dried out grass beside a gurgling stream. Sex is a mating of energy fields according to a tradition that has been around for five thousand years, and some nights, Theo figures that's how long it takes before they actually get down to it. Many nights they never do. The lotus position is new to him and takes practice. Theo thinks of Leela as mysterious and beyond explanation. Leela is stunningly beautiful, so Theo does his best to be a good student.

Silvie finds Tariq attentive, a man with a variety of detailed plans that manifest themselves with care and attention. Sometimes Silvie's personal appetite for sex has resulted in a Coles Notes version of what Tariq is used to. This confuses Tariq at first, but he tells himself Silvie is honest. He finds there is time to watch the sports every night now, and as a result it is like he is living a completely different life from the one he has known.

Since the reorganization of their lives, not once have Theo and Tariq discussed with each other this part of their existence. Silvie and Leela, when any kind of sexual reference surfaces, communicate their satisfaction with a look, a cocking of an eye, or for the truly exceptional, a tongue grazing lips.

The varying speeds at which the renovated coupling takes place happens when the kids aren't around. The kids don't think about their parents sex lives much. Richard, being the oldest, makes an effort to understand things but gives up easily. The three kids have been plotting for months to get a dog, one that will live in whatever house the kids are living in. Theo has his name on a waiting list for a Neapolitan mastiff for a while until Leela's boss tells her how big such an animal can get. They settle for a Heinz 57 from the pound, a dog the size of a beaver who likes to be around people, but Leela is allergic to the dog, so he lives inside one week and outside the next. His name is Charlie.

The house Theo lives in, the one once inhabited by Silvie and Theo, is smaller but worth more because it is in a better neighborhood. It occurs to Theo that he owns half the house. Silvie owns the other half. Legally. If the houses had the exact same value, then it would be logical to put Leela's name on the title and have Silvie legally own half of Tariq's house—the one originally inhabited by Tariq and Leela. He's not sure if it's wise to bring this up with Leela because it is obviously in her best interests that this happen, but he realizes she has no idea of the value of either property and hasn't given it any thought. He also is reluctant to mention it to Tariq or Silvie because if his supposition about the value of the two houses is validated then Silvie might not agree with the plan. Theo does not intend to move anywhere, because of his job, but if Tariq and Silvie decide they want a bigger or fancier house or a house on the other side of town, it could be a problem.

You like your job, right? Theo asks Leela one night after a long session on both the couch and ottoman that has left him exhausted.

I have a good job, she says. I'd like a better one, but for now I'm happy and I get paid well.

And Tariq likes his work. Doesn't he?

Now that's a long story, Leela says. He hates his job and is always applying for work at some other financial institution but there is always something wrong with every prospective job. The benefits. The pension. He may never change his workplace. It's difficult to change, but I wouldn't bet against it. Why are you asking?

Just curious, Theo says. Just thinking about the future.

Theo just can't let it go. He dwells on it, and the more he thinks about it the more he believes he has something to worry about. With Silvie on the title for the house, she must own half of it, and he's sure this would stand up in court. But with Leela living with him in the house, going on a full year now, then maybe she legally owns half the house. Could it be that Silvie owns half his house and Leela owns half his house, which would leave him with no house at all? He makes a mental note to run these scenarios by a lawyer.

Tariq thinks about the future just as much as Theo does. He can imagine having a little boy running around, one who would take his name into the world. He mentioned it to Silvie once and she told him it was an interesting proposal, but she was a horse past her prime, and besides, she'd had her tubes tied. Tariq heard her out, and after some investigation discovered that she could have the ligation reversed for nine thousand dollars. He hasn't mentioned the possibility to her yet because Silvie spends money faster than the government, and because he does the finances, he knows they're having a hard time keeping up.

I think we should buy a convertible sports car, Silvie tells him. A red one.

There's no point buying a car that can't hold five people, Tariq says. Maybe when the kids grow up. Isn't that when people do that sort of thing? When they're middle-aged?

Well, we'll buy a sports car that holds five people. I'm sure they make them.

Five people and a dog, Tariq says.

Charlie the dog has been a mistake. Theo thought a dog was a good idea, if only to shut Manson up. Tariq didn't want a dog at first. Why would you want to own a dog? he said. A dog is like owning a three-year-old forever. Manson makes it clear from the get go that the dog will be looked after by him and his brother and Beet, who can be convinced of anything. It turns out Manson fusses over the dog for the first few weeks then loses interest. Richard says he'll brush the dog, but that's it. Beet refuses to walk the dog unless someone comes along to pick up the dog poop. The week the kids are with Tariq and Silvie, it is Tariq who does most of the dog minding. He teaches the dog to shake a paw and gloats about it for days.

When the three kids and the dog move back to Theo and Leela's place is where the problem begins. Leela claims she's allergic to the dog. Theo doesn't see visual evidence of swelling or rash, but Leela makes an appointment with the doctor to prove her point. Richard, Manson, and Beet think it is cruel and unusual punishment that Charlie must sleep outside every second week. The three of them build a doghouse and drag it up to the house and right under Richard and Manson's window, so they can talk to the dog and reassure him he's still loved.

This the three kids think is a satisfactory solution for a short time, but when the weather turns foul, they can't stand Charlie out there all by himself. One night, Richard opens the window, fetches the dog, and airlifts him into their bedroom. Beet finds this exciting and says she doesn't want to sleep in her room, she will sleep on the floor with the dog. It somehow works the first night but the second night, Leela, who usually falls asleep early, hears unusual noises and opens the door to investigate. The lights in the room are off and she almost steps on Beet. Once she turns on the light, she can see what is going on. She calls Theo from the living room for backup, but Theo finds it funny. How ingenious, he says. Leela demands a family meeting for the following day.

The kids are invited to the meeting and the dog comes too, though he has to sit out on the porch because of Leela's allergies. They are at Tariq and Silvie's house, and Silvie has made blueberry muffins. Theo has a slim binder with some preliminary assessments on house values, though he hasn't explained why he's come to the meeting with what makes him look like an insurance salesman.

Once everyone sits—the adults on the comfortable chairs, the kids on the floor—Tariq is ready to begin. Everyone expects he will be the one who will make the introductory statement, maybe because it is his house, maybe not, and all eyes are on him. This is not like past family meetings, and everyone is ready to argue with whatever he is going to say, Tariq can feel it. Leela watches Tariq wringing his hands. She holds to the position she does not deserve to be itchy because of Charlie the dog. Silvie is less invested in the dog issue because she's not itchy and she finds the dog amusing. It is her opinion they should say goodbye to Charlie and trade him in for a cat, or if that doesn't solve the problem, a lizard. Theo doesn't care so much about the dog issue, but he wants a solution because he believes until they decide on the fate of the dog there is no room in people's minds to consider whether he owns half a house or no house at all. Time passes and nothing is said. Tariq isn't convinced he knows where to start. They hear Charlie get to his feet on the front porch. The dog barks three times, as if to suggest he has a point of view in all of this, and everyone, especially Beet, laughs. The dog speaking up reminds Tariq that before Beet was born, he and Leela had looked after his uncle's dog for a month and there hadn't been a problem of any kind. Tariq wants to declare that in his humble opinion, most of the world's issues are nothing more than fabricated myths that obey or defy the customs of the time, and how easy it is for us to get caught up in the mess of it all, and that we need to break away from these myths the best way we can. He thinks he should start with something no one in the room expects him say. Like camping, for example. Maybe they should all go camping again because it is the kind of activity that takes you away from what you are caught up in, which you may not really be caught up in at all based on the myth theory he believes but would need to explain to the group in front of him, a group that examines him closely now because it has been a long time coming, this introductory speech, and there is a tension in the room because every one of them understands that silence does not last forever.

Tenth Anniversary

by Alison Stone

To celebrate, we watch ourselves—
bright, slim-waisted. Matching in white.
Your jaunty bow tie, my crown of flowers.

The circle's cast.
Our daughters hum
inside my ovaries and my young mother
beams as we kindle one pillar
with two wicks. Now, as then,
my breath catches
at the priestess's billowy sleeve,
the sliver of air between satin and flame.

We make two sets of promises. The first
we've written: Your pledge to guard
my art. My earnest Spanish.
The traditional vows I've memorized
and speak one line at a time:
By seed and root, by bud and stem…
You echo, our voices weaving,
high and low tones in contrast, the way
your dark skin shines against my paleness
when we make love.

Nested together, legs entwined,
we're wise now, understand
the deal we struck. My sloppy housekeeping,
your temper. My stubbornness,
your loud TV. The push apart, the turn
to stagger back—marriage's excruciating
dance, our small house crowded with a whole
menagerie of betters and worses. Their silky pelts, soft
ears. Their wings and wild cries!

Snarls in the middle of breakfast, crap
on the floor, fur flying as arguments
chase their tails. Love
crouched just out of reach.

The pair onscreen
have no idea.
Rings are exchanged, the broom
placed on the ground.
Hands bound together by silk cord,
we jump.

Tight
by Pamela Balluck

She is his cousins' cousin; he is her cousins' cousin. They have considered themselves tight, but never before like this. As Rachel and
West sit talking on her grand aunt's sofa, she is somehow seduced
with Scotch tape he applies to the front of her clothing, which
he then slowly peels away. She laughs, surprised he would touch
her like that, so deliberately. They are standing now—she to say
goodnight—and she is even more surprised when he bends and
kisses the base of her neck. They have had their share of vodka.
She grasps his biceps and holds him at arms' length. "You don't
know what you're doing. Look, West. It's me, Rachel."

"I know who you are," he tells her. "And you are mine."

Until this moment, she had thought he was gay.

Rachel is "smoking hot," whispers West in the pitch-black of
his room at the family gathering house on the Tiburon Peninsula.

She whispers, "You're crazy. You're drunk."

"I am drunk. But I have waited for this."

"I am old, West. This is Rachel. Are you serious?"

"Rachel, whose body is girl-superhero hot."

She whispers, "Superheroine."

"Superheroine hot," he enunciates.

She imagines the shapes that his mouth's making against her ear.

"And she is mine. If she'll let me."

"'She.'" She whisper-laughs. "Seriously?"

Tonight, Rachel is not so drunk. She thinks out loud in the whisper she has gotten so good at this long weekend, "This would not be happening if you were not drunk. If you were sober, you would not want this to be happening. I can't believe this is happening. Oh my god. Oh god."

He whispers, "I have always wanted to fuck you."

She whispers, "Always? At Kit's wedding, you wanted to fuck me? You were, what, twenty-three?"

"Twenty-four."

"Me, forty-whatever? Are you serious?"

"Stop asking."

It annoys him that she counts back only a few years, as if Kit's wedding is where they first met, as if she's only known him since he became a man who makes champagne speeches. She has not before last night ever thought of him as a man who would talk to her this way, who would actually stick it in her, and now she's filled with him, hangs onto him, but will barely move, and will barely let him move, afraid to make noise, because they're in a house full of family. It's tantric. He's arrived. She's got him.

So many of them are together around the Tiburon house on the Bay built by Aunt Syl's grandparents, who came to Tiburon with the now-defunct railroad. Rachel's father's maternal great-grandparents settled in Santa Monica at the same time. North and south, they were the first of the family's West Coast contingent, which eventually spread from LA south to San Diego and north from San Francisco Bay to Portland and Seattle.

West tries not to look at Rachel when her eyes rest upon him; he tries not to look at her when he sees in his periphery that her face is turned his way, unless they're both pulled into the same conversation with others, or unless Rachel is the one to approach him, which occasionally she does, has always, because he's West, because they're tight.

Now that she reads him loud and clear, she is taken up so completely with her actual relatives, or by standing on her own in the water, taken by the views of the bridges, the sails, the ferries, the city she misses. West watches her and wonders if she's thinking about him. She feels him watching her and wondering what she's thinking when she's seated on the stone breakwater thinking about how he touched her and how he might touch her again. She throws for the dog. She yoga-stretches. She turns and waves, smiles up at the house. But she will not go up to him when the others are away. She knows they would not be alone for long. Always, someone's arriving. Hear a car? Hear a ferry? Here they are.

———

Rachel will not make a move that would lead anyone to view her as "aggressor." She speaks low to West on the Bay-facing porch, says she's never before been with anyone more than a few years younger. She has "cougar-cliché" anxiety. She moves the bench swing in a rhythm that's turning him on. "It's a predatory term," she tells him.

"You're not the predator," West says. "I am."

She says, "I reach out, put my hand on your face right now, on your knee, on your arm, someone will look out that window, come out that door, or up those steps, guaranteed."

And here West is, hard again.

He loves the way she has begun to look at him, but she's careful not to reach, is not willing to be seen as the reacher. She did not ask for this. But she loves it. She didn't ask for him. But, she wants him now.

———

West's alcohol consumption has been an open topic of concern this long weekend, and today he laid off just to demonstrate that he can, but almost everyone has gone upstairs to bed, and he wants his drink. He asks Rachel if she'll join him, and she says she'll have another beer. She has had nothing stronger today, tonight.

"What's the point?" he asks her.

She likes beer. "I don't need vodka," she says. "Why do you?"

Cousin Mariah sees West with the bottle frosty from the freezer, says goodnight there in the kitchen, heads up the stairs, and now it's just the two of them. It's been like this every night, since Rachel arrived, later than the rest, and made her bed in the living room.

Rachel says that she'll have a fresh beer but West talks her into joining him in vodka. He tells her, since she's so afraid of getting caught, better to look like he got the older woman high than the other way around. The other way around? The wish is he wouldn't drink, but no one imagines he'd drink anything other than his vodka.

Rachel repeats under her breath, "'Older woman.'"

He complains that all the fizz drinks are gone and there's nothing to mix the vodka with but the kids' grape juice. He drops ice cubes into tumblers, and Rachel insists on watching him pour the vodka into hers, and on seeing how much he pours into his, next to hers, before he adds the juice. Rachel, who usually drinks vodka nearly neat, tastes it. "It's disgusting," she says, pushing it away. "What a waste of vodka."

"I can't drink vodka plain," West says.

"You might as well," she says. She's wearing a yoga camisole, low-waisted, long jammie shorts, and slippers. "Sexy, huh?"

"You don't have to wear sexy," West says.

When Rachel walks past him into the living room, toward the couch, he pinches at her shorts and yanks downward, but they stay put, and she keeps walking. He says, "Drawstring?" as if it's a personal affront. He follows her into the living room, bringing the drink she abandoned. He says, "I have wanted to pull your pants down all day. You are so tight," he tells her, remembering last night. "Why are you so tight?"

"Underused," she says.

"Why?"

"Good question."

They both wonder whether he would have gone after her this way sober. Apparently, not many have the nerve. It bothers her that they'd need nerve. Her therapist might ask: Does it?

Rachel doesn't want to be impaired—she wants to think, talk, be conscious—but here she is, anyway, biting at his lip, straddling him on the matriarch's couch, half-dressed, her breasts in his hands. She won't go back up to his room, and she won't fuck him down here with no walls, no door. But he's got her and he tells her, "You are mine."

Rachel is afraid West may have woken up the house when he tripped on the stairs, after she whispered him awake, shooed him away and up to bed around four this morning.

Since 7:30 this morning, people have been departing in shifts to SFO or to Oakland, for flights back to Rhode Island, LA, and Seattle. West is flying off next. He has apparently woken up intoxicated. He soundlessly gargles black coffee before swallowing.

He avoids looking directly at Rachel, who, in the dining room, is staring into her computer at the table in the same jammies he removed from her last night—her hair piled high—and she is sure no one can read her, because of her glasses, and because she's using the laptop to screen herself from eye contact not just with West.

Cousin Mariah looks angry but smiles so hard through it, her ears appear as if they might pop off, because she doesn't want to cry through goodbyes, and because no matter what West and Rachel may have done, she loves them. Nonetheless, Mariah calls into the dining room, "Rachel, did you have fun with West this weekend?"

Rachel looks up from her screen, smiles with teeth, and says, "I did!"

When it's time for West's group to leave for the ferry, Rachel steps up, front and center, to pass out heartfelt hugs. Mariah and Rachel try to pretend they haven't lost their battle with tears ("When will I see you again?"). Rachel reaches for West last; her kiss on his mouth and her full-bodied hug in front of others are new, but same as she gave her cousin Mariah, not sexual, and what she'll offer Aunt Syl, Cousin Cindy, and Cousin Marcus before she leaves for Denver.

West says, "G'bye, Cousin Rachel."

Has she ever before heard him call her that?

When Rachel finishes packing her suitcase, she finds tucked there, inside a high-heeled shoe, a plastic Scotch tape dispenser with a tiny, scrolled note in the roll's hole: Stuck.

What is she doing?

Canaries Built Our House of Shame
by Daniel Loring Keating

There is no eulogy. Shame in life is shame in death. Shame, she taught me when she was living, is nothing if not the quiet embarrassment of those around you. A blush rises on my cheek, the heat a contrast in the cold, moisture-less air. I may now own some of her shamelessness, but the concept of some isn't one she would have understood, and so, in a way, she was always alien to me, and me to her. She understood as much. She told me once that we were as alike as nature and as different as a daisy and a rainbow. She said that didn't frighten her. I told her it aroused me, and smiling, she made love to me, on a blanket made of burning dead leaves in a field where time had forgotten its anger and the sun hung on just a little longer, for our sake.

I am so afraid now, my Kaelah, and I know that fear comes from my shame. I am in turn ashamed of my shame. I can see you shaking your head and smiling at my foolish words, words that when robbed of the necessity imposed by broken visions of what "should" be no longer have meaning. I can't see those things because you are dead, and I only know direction now because my eyes can only point in one direction. That is the direction I will travel in, as long as I can, and while that direction now brings me closer to your casket—your physical remains—it does not bring me any closer to you, not really.

I am now amongst people dressed in black, their heads lowered. Mourners. Human refuse. Hatred is calming. One against all others is an equation, and equations are comforting, and aren't real. They're only real in our heads, where meaning is such a necessity that so monumental an unreality as 'two plus two equals four' must be accepted constantly as truth. It doesn't really matter what two plus two equals. It doesn't matter if these people mourn. I hate them, not because two plus two equals four for them, but because it still does for me and if I were shed of that, then hatred wouldn't be necessary.

They didn't love you. They don't now.

I must be the tiger of my youth, striding unafraid through villages and cities and jungles and the fiery end of all things. Strength comes from the knowledge that one is bad, and I am very bad, and perhaps I can use that to endure what I must endure. Your parents haven't seen me yet. Your little sister is sitting next to them. She is the only one who cries. She is the only one who carries a single marigold.

One day she was with us in a park and she said all in a rush that one day, Kaelah, I'll be just like you and maybe I'll come to live with you and we can be a real family not like mother and father not like our uncles not like all that's wrong we can make it right all right together can't we Kaelah can't we?

And you just smiled. Damn you, you just smiled. You are gone. I must stop speaking as though you are not.

Her family is around me and I am alone, the only one in white in a church full of darkness, people who wear their darkness as much in their faces. There are few I know. Kaelah had already left them behind when we met, when we fell in love, when I cried my shame in the form of her name deep inside her where pleasure and love and the future rolled into a single living entity. Their hands are as cold as mine. Their skin is frozen, like arctic photographs left on a snow-covered table. A few of them stir as I pass, pointing, whispering to those next to them. On the whole, they are undisturbed in their deepest of disturbances, the sleep that lives behind their eyes just this side of dead.

I know what is coming when I get to the front row. Her parents must now notice me. I have not made a sound as I have moved but I am distinctive. Beyond my clothes I am a thing, a thing which does not belong, and they sense this even before they see me, and her father stands up. So many of her features are in his face—sunken cheekbones, pencil-thin eyebrows, big, full lips, and eyes as black as a starless sky. His nose is larger. I must focus there.

Go, he says. Leave this place and take your abomination with you. This abomination he speaks of is not a tangible thing or else he would direct his fury at it as well. Or perhaps he sees the abomination, the love I shared with his daughter, as a tangible thing, and the words he hurls at me are hurled instead at it, a writhing, twisting form taking shape in the air in front of me, walking beside me forever, invisible to me now so that I might feel its loss but there nonetheless for these people to hate, to fear, to loathe.

I tell him the truth. I am what she wanted. I was wanted here. These words are very specific. His teeth begin to grit and he begins to transform into a demon, a horrid winged thing with burnt, tar-like skin and leathery wings and a gaze fed by the fear of newborn children, and this creature speaks the name of its God and asks for forgiveness for this wayward youth its daughter took in, for this wayward youth has lost sight and is now blind. And when it is done it is a man, just a man, just what it has always been, and it tells me again to leave.

Kaelah's sister looks at me and cries harder. I want to smile for her, offer her a little chocolate or the flower of a dandelion picked from just outside the church, but I know that the time for affectations has passed for her now and won't come again for some time. What she needs she will never receive again. In time she will adapt to not receiving what she needs and she will grow damaged, and she will devise ways of not dealing with that damage. She will then develop new needs, very likely needs that are more easily fulfilled, and she may even be happy again, although never as happy as she has been. I cannot do anything for her, and I cannot say anything that wouldn't be a lie, so I let her cry, and tell her father, their father, again that I was wanted here and Kaelah had a final request for this ceremony that was not honored, and that an honorable man would have undertaken to accomplish a task set by his dead daughter.

At this he sits down, and I can tell that I have reached him, that I have beaten some part of him that wanted to fight, that I am now the conqueror in this place and the broken souls of all within belong to me. None were as strong as he and none will challenge me now that he has folded. He is no longer a man, though in reality, I suppose, he does still remain a man, perhaps even more a man than he was before. He still cannot cry, but at least he looks now as though he wants to, and at least now he is staring at the casket, which lies open at the very front of the room.

And at last I turn to the casket, and I cannot pretend, my love, that all of this is not a letter in my mind to you. It is cruel how you lie in the coffin, not relaxed but tense, your muscles tight, a look of discomfort in every line of the body I have explored with such acumen as to discover every inch, every imperfection, every unique detail. You look as though you might spring into movement at any time even though you will never move again. You cannot even move these people whose only thought of love is the obligation they think they owe your family, and who are certainly not capable of being moved by anyone else. This failure is not one that would concern you, my love, and I know that were this a conversation we were having, you would do just what your corpse is doing now—not saying a word, allowing me to become increasingly frustrated and angry, until I logic myself straight out of existence.

You will never move again. I will never escape you, not that I would if I could. Like your sister, I have become damaged, and you are my damage, and it is only with you that I may make my meanings and carry on cold while two plus two equals four. And I will do what you have asked of me and then I will run, for defeated or not, there are some things your family cannot abide, and you were always one of them.

I reach into the casket, and to my surprise, Kaelah's skin is not cold like all of ours, but warm. Not warm with life—I am delusional—but warm in the manner of a lamp that has just been turned out. She has been dead for far too long for this to be lingering from her life and I cannot detect the source of it. Seeing the scandalous looks on the faces behind me, I work quickly to undo the top clasp on the modest dress that she was fitted in, and once it is undone and I see people beginning to rise, I take hold of the neckline with both hands and I tear mightily.

There are no undergarments under the dress, and for a second I wonder if someone who knew her had a hand in this preparation, but then I realize that a corpse doesn't require undergarments the way a living body does, and anyway there is a kind of padding present at several locations, presumably to keep the dress shapely and to keep it from stretching across an embarrassing section of her body—like for instance, her nipples, which as I rip the dress and hear gasps of shock and anger behind me, I see are perfectly erect, and finally I do smile because that is my Kaelah, the Kaelah who wanted to be naked at her own funeral, who would be quite pleased with the notion of having erect nipples at her funeral as her lover tears her clothes off.

I feel hands—her father—grasp at me, pull me away from the casket, he shouts words of anger in my ear, but I reach out to heaven, which is a place where canaries fly free and young women eat pomegranate seeds without any fear of retribution, a place where I do not live, and maybe my Kaelah is at peace.

Maple Chaser
by Flo Golod

Now she wants to move to Canada. Join the crowd, Heather. The night of the election, the Canadian website crashed. That's how many people seriously thought they could get out of here.

My sister. What can I say? She's a whack job.

Heather spent hours researching online, so she knew she needed a new gig if she wanted to move to Canada. She'd plant herself on the couch along with whatever cat or dog got there first, laptop on lap, a wine cooler and a bag of chips on the coffee table, reading until all hours of the night, which pretty much eliminated activities like housekeeping and regular exercise. She took one of those interest inventories and decided she should be a librarian. They are now called "information specialists." She ran a database for some jerk who owns a French export company before he grabbed her ass and she quit (she fucked up his database the last day though, which I thought was cool).

I live in my sister's basement, not an optimal situation for a 34-year-old man but I have my issues, too. I spent my thirtieth birthday in jail, in honor of my second DUI. That's the bottom they talk about. So, treatment, AA, and reset at 31. I can talk the bark off a tree, so I got into sales. I could sell you a suit you don't need and make you feel good about yourself even while you max out your credit card. I make more commissions than anyone else in Men's Business Wear but it's gonna take a lot of silk ties before I dig my way out of the drunkard's debt hole.

By way of coping, I am teaching myself to cook, having lived on whiskey and pizza for ten years. I make dinner most nights and this had been a good opportunity for me and Heather to mutually unburden ourselves about the boneheads who buy suits but can't spell "resumé" and the trophy wives who talk about their First World problems while my sister paints their toenails Prosperous Pink or Get Over Yourself Gold.

After one of her tirades that somehow included Russia, the Supreme Court, tariffs, The Wall, and the national parks, and with no mention of how tasty my pork roast and sautéed broccoli was, I pointed a forkful of meat at Heather.

"The Canadians are not interested in French majors who never finished their degree and give pedicures for a living. Have you even applied to library school yet?"

"The universities are too expensive. I'm going to start an online program but I have to take out a loan, so I'll have to up my hours. "

Other than getting to work three days a week and her monthly book club (where, as far as I can tell, they mostly drink wine and bitch about men and politics), Heather is not a highly self-motivated person. Usually, I remind her that since I cooked, she should clear up.

"They still cost plenty and you have to make yourself take the classes. All By Yourself."

"I'm going to school, but I won't finish before he declares martial law. I've got to get out of here sooner."

"Okay Henny Penny, how are you going to do that?"

"I'm on this Canadian dating website." Heather pointed to her laptop like it was a large silver visa. "It hooks American singles up with Canadians."

"But don't you have to get married? You can't like just say, 'Hey I'm sleeping with this guy who lives in Manitoba, so let me in forever.'"

"It's complicated but I can go to Canada on a study permit for six months. Or if I get married, I can visit for six months. I'd have to come back here but I can get in, eventually."

"Do they need more people to do toe jobs?" I did not even broach the issue of a secured marriage deal in six months.

"One of the women who owns my salon has a brother who lives in Canada, and he runs a big salon franchise and she said she'd talk to him."

"So two degrees of separation plus a tight border and then you gotta find a man."

"I'm on it."

I noticed Heather's stick-straight brown hair had red highlights. She was eating about half of what she usually consumed.

I really appreciate Heather letting me live in her basement. Or more accurately the basement of the house she takes care of for her French advisor who may or may not ever come back from Paris. Heather's advisor has a girlfriend there and a husband somewhere in the 'burbs who has no clue. The French Lesbian Drama is better than reality TV. It means we have free rent. We pay the utilities, and I take care of the place.

So, my big sister watches out for me and I, in turn overlook a lot of weirdness. Piles of magazines and papers stacked to roughly my waist, three cats, one of whom has litter box issues, and two dogs who don't know Sit from Steal My Steak. Of course, if the affair ends and her advisor comes back, Heather and I will have to come up with rent and a landlord willing to take on two under-achievers and five animals.

We were getting along pretty well until The Election. I, too, am very unhappy about Fuck Head and worry he is going to take away my health insurance (which I pay for myself, I might add), or that he'll deport my girlfriend's family. However, even by the inauguration, I had figured out that too much news is, like, toxic. Heather's temperature goes up with every tweet and all her left-wing friends post stuff that just makes them even crazier. I fail to see how getting all pissed off on Facebook is going to get rid of Fuck Head.

Heather is a loudmouth on social media, but she goes passive/aggressive in real life. When her clients at that fancy ass hotel spa in downtown Minneapolis started talking about Ivanka's hair and making jokes about sore losers, meaning liberals, my sister started buffing their callouses so hard they squealed. I pointed out that this would eventually get her fired.

I looked over her shoulder one night and she was pecking away at a profile for Maple Match. There were pictures of awesomely good looking, friendly men and women of various ages looking for same. I put my chin on Heather's shoulder, which she used to think was totally adorable when I was nine, but she jerked away and I almost bit my tongue.

"I was just going to check to make sure you weren't posting any fake news on that site."

"Go away. This is personal. I feel vulnerable enough without you spying on me."

"Oversight, not spying, but fine. I'm going to the gym. You should go too so you can get all buff before you meet some Canuk dude with giant thighs."

"Have a great workout. Don't drop a barbell on your toe."

Working out is a major stress reliever, and I am usually capable of a civil interaction for at least ninety minutes afterward. So, I walked in the door and Heather was right where she had been two hours ago, couch lounging and tap tap tapping on her laptop. But the usual glass of vino had been replaced with zero-calorie sparkling water.

"You find the man of your dreams yet?"

"This is very encouraging. There are a lot of guys who live in Winnipeg, just over the border. They sound nice."

"Well of course they sound nice. No one says, "Hey, I'm an abusive pervert and I want someone to dress up in a rubber suit, let me smack you around, and then clean the bathroom, which I defiled.""

Heather sighed and kept tapping.

"Sorry. Give me an example of a nice one."

Heather took a slug of bubbly water, lowered her voice to a lousy imitation of testosterone-speak and read:

"I'm a forty-five-year-old white male. Divorced, no kids. I make my living as an accountant but I'm really passionate about music, motorcycles, and movies. Looking for someone thirty-five to forty-five, professional, active, and ready for the next adventure."

"He sounds reasonable. You won't inherit teenagers who hate you, and he probably earns a good living. He didn't say what kind of music. Please, Heather, don't hook up with someone who listens to folk music. "

"Who cares what kind of music he likes? At least he likes art."

"Ah, how are you going to date someone who lives three-hundred and fifty miles away?"

"Well, first you correspond for awhile, and then if you click, you can call or Skype, and then, well, I could drive up to Duluth and he could drive down."

"Better get the show on the road before it snows."

"Little brother, I am motivated. I'm aiming to be 'in a relationship' by Halloween."

So, July and August, Heather was practically glued to her laptop unless she was walking the dogs or working on her Warrior pose. I have to give her credit. She trimmed down and she looked good. One of my friends asked about her but she got all sniffy and said she wasn't interested in "that kind of guy." My friends are mostly AA guys, which I think makes them a good bet because they're working their program. I wondered how she'd filter out drunks, active or dry.

"I make it clear in the emails that I drink very little and that I'm not interested in someone who drinks more than socially."

"You drink very little as of three weeks ago, and you still slur your words after book group meetings. So, if you're rewriting history, what makes you think Mr. Canada is any more abstemious?"

"I can just tell."

I know when she's entering La La Land so I went to bed.

———————

The accountant didn't pan out. Turned out he really meant it about professional. He asked Heather what her after-tax income was. Understandably, she took offense.

Next up, a social worker from Fort Frances who played chess. He didn't say anything about looks, he read, mostly about "social issues," and he wanted someone to join him in the fight against tar sands mining, and also for making great dinners at home.

"He sounds good Heather. You could go to demonstrations and then come home and make bison burgers."

Heather ignored me because she was typing her heart out to the social worker named Dan.

Things went along with Dan pretty well until they Skyped. What wasn't obvious in the picture, which was probably ten years old, is that Dan weighed about 300 pounds.

"Well that explains the emphasis on great dinners. What are you going to do now?"

"I'm going to play the field. There's no reason I can't correspond with three or four men at once and see who's really my type."

"You're gonna need a spreadsheet."

"Actually, that's a good idea."

Playing the field on a dating site is almost as time consuming as screwing around in the flesh. Having been a playboy for ten years, I am now settled into a nice relationship with Claudia. She was born here but her parents are from Mexico and they are not citizens, so she spends a lot of time working and trying to get them papers. We only see each other twice a week but it's good. My eye wanders at the gym, whose wouldn't? But the rest of me is monogamous. Heather's online love life became ridiculous. She had ten guys on that spreadsheet. She narrowed the competition down to three contenders, another social worker, a mechanic, and, spare me, a poet. Of course, she was way into the poet.

"No one makes a living writing rhymes. What does he do to pay the rent?"

"Modern verse doesn't usually rhyme. Like most artists, he's a server. He tends bar and makes a pretty good living."

"Define pretty good."

"You sound like that accountant. I trust him. We had our first Skype date last night. "

"And?"

"He actually asked me ten questions about myself, a first, and he was very encouraging about library school."

"Does he know you want out of here?"

Heather looked vaguely at a pile of unfolded laundry and shrugged, "He said anyone in their right mind would be freaked out by Trump."

"What's he look like?"

"Well the part that shows on the screen tells me he's skinny, dark hair, a high forehead that might mean balding. He's forty. He has very intense eyes and a big nose. He's not handsome but distinctive."

"So, he's an ugly poet and a bartender. What does he want to be when he grows up?"

"He wants to be a poet."

"I'd like to be a rock star, but it's not listed as a goal on my resumé."

"You don't have any faith in artists. You don't read anything except recipes, news, and sports."

"Okay, so I'm intellectually limited but I'm a practical person. I know for a fact that poets don't make money. Remember Jenna? Her old man was a poet, but he was a professor, and that tenure business meant he made very good dough. So good, he could write books that at tops thirty-four people read, and still send his kids to private school."

"I'm intrigued by Peter. I don't aspire to a middle-class life. I just need to get out of this dying empire and find a guy I can relate to. We can get by."

Heather's long-term planning skills do not impress me.

As communications with Peter the Poet took up more and more of her time, I noticed a bunch of poetry books added to the reading pile. Butt in the air, head facing me upside down between her legs, Heather had achieved Downward Dog.

"Jake, I'm meeting Peter in Grand Marais next weekend. Will you feed the menagerie? And walk the dogs?"

"You realize I'm doing you a favor that might render me homeless if this works out?

"Couldn't you work something out with Claudia?"

"My credit rating still sucks, so it'll be hard to find a place to rent. I don't relish the idea of becoming the sixth person in that household, although they like me well enough. They'd probably want us to get married though, and neither one of us is ready."

"You need to work on your commitment issues." Panting, Heather walked herself out of her Downward Dog and raised her hands up into Mountain Pose.

"You need to get your car tuned up and pack. Where are you going to stay?"

Peter found us motel rooms. He really is thoughtful. He knows it would be awkward to share a room the first time we meet."

"Well yeah, or else he's afraid he can't get it up or that you'll be a psycho or both."

Now she was cross-legged on the floor looking over her left shoulder at me. "I'm not going to dignify that with an answer."

"Will walleye and wild rice make you like me again?"

Heather rolled her eyes and smiled.

I heard her car pull up after midnight, the last Sunday in August. I was due in Men's Business Wear early for the Labor Day sale, so I didn't get up to help her carry her stuff in, which would anyhow just have been a thin cover for wanting to know how the deal went down.

The next day, I dragged myself home after selling twelve suits, twenty dress shirts, and ten ties. Heather was situated in her usual spot, fingers on keyboard, with a kind of doofy smile.

"So, judging from the happy face, it went well."

"He's super-duper. I think even you will like him."

"So, did you stay chastely in your separate rooms?"

"First night yes, second night we shared."

"And…"

"Use your imagination. It's all good. He's coming down here next month. We're working out details."

———

Peter is a tall, slouchy dude with black hair slicked back so he looks kind of like Maynard G. Krebs. I thought what Heather described as intense looked furtive but figured maybe it was just me he didn't want to look at. They yakked and yakked, and she kept putting her hand on his knee when she was talking to him.

I made a nice dinner. Steak, tomatoes with feta cheese and pine nuts, baked potatoes with horseradish cream. Pete picked at his food and when Heather complimented my cuisine, he remembered his manners.

"It's very nicely presented but I don't usually eat red meat."

"I would have baked tofu if you'd told me, Pete."

"No worries. I don't want to be a bother."

Heather offered to clean up and suggested that Peter and I walk the dogs. I could have skipped the male bonding episode. Pete was not a helpful dog walker. I had to ask him to take the leashes so I could do the poop pick up. He dropped one, so I had to chase Zeus while Peter kept tripping over Hercules, who weighs about twelve pounds and likes to wind around people's legs.

"Why did she name him Hercules?"

"Ah, like I think she was being ironic."

Peter looked blank. A humor-challenged poet, and not much on the ball in the irony department. What could Heather possibly see in this guy?

When I came upstairs the next morning for coffee, Pete was gone, and Heather was snarling at some Huff Post news on her phone.

"Where's Poetry Man?"

"He had to get started early. It's a long drive to Winnipeg and he works tonight. "

"You two have a nice time?"

Heather looked at her phone, then at Zeus. Finally, she looked at me,

"Well, it was intense. We talked a lot about what we each want, where we're going with our lives…"

"And…?"

"I told him I'd like to move to Canada. I explained about the online program, which of course I can work on from Canada, and I mentioned there might be a job for me at one of Jeffrey's salons. Something seemed to be worrying him."

"So, it doesn't look like he's going to get down on his knee and offer up a ring anytime soon?"

"I wasn't looking for that. He told me what I already know, that it's pretty hard for Americans to get established in Canada, that it takes about three years and he knows people who've tried it and haven't been able to make it happen."

"So, what's your next move?"

"We're going to Skype tomorrow. It'll work out. Just takes time."

Heather is always encouraged by discouraging men. I offered her a perfectly nice ex-drunk and she turned her nose up. A perfectly pompous poet who doesn't like her expat agenda leaves her panting to win him over. I don't get it.

Claudia and I had taken a rare overnight and gone to a bargain Air BnB in Red Wing and then I had to work a long shift selling suits to Stupids, so I kind of forgot about the poet problem. I came upstairs the next night thinking I'd get Heather a snack and maybe she'd drink a near beer with me. She wasn't in her usual spot on the couch and the dogs were gone. The laptop was sitting open. I tapped the keyboard and the screen lit up.

I started reading this article that wasn't really writing but just a string of bragging scores by USA Americans about having sex with Canadians. Some were gross, all of them dumb. It just didn't seem like Heather-type reading.

The back screen door slammed. I heard dogs slurping water and the fridge door open and shut. I left the laptop, figuring the screen would go dark before Heather got back to it. I almost bumped into her in the doorway. She had a big glass of wine in her hand and her shades were still on.

"You partying?" I asked and reached up to take her glasses off. Her eyes were red. First, she looked down at the dogs, then up at me, and shrugged.

"What's up?"

"I got dumped by email."

"Not even Skype?"

"No, he wouldn't even talk to me. He sent an email saying he didn't think he could get serious about someone who was 'stalking' him for a Canadian residency. He attached this article called "Maple Chasers." It's all people from the US talking about their sexual encounters with Canadians. I can't believe he thinks that's what I'm like."

"I am of the opinion, as you know, that most guys are cowardly dickheads and he didn't look that great to me, but Claudia warned me not to say anything in case you two got serious. However, there is one thing I do not get."

Heather took a long drain of her wine while I expounded. She sniffed and asked, "What don't you get?"

"I mean the site is called Maple Match for Chrissake. What did he think?"

"He did say that he was more comfortable with a long-distance relationship. He said it gives him the time and freedom to write but still have someone to visit and be intimate with."

"And you think I have commitment issues. He at least could have turned it into a limerick."

That got a little smile out of Heather.

I took the opportunity to trade out Heather's wine relapse for a frosted Arnie Palmer I'd just made. "Anything I can do?"

"If you'd make something to eat, that'd be great. I'm going to answer Mr. Canada civilly, and then there's something I want to do."

After dinner, I saw Heather typing away and figured she was cruising Maple Match for a better deal. I did the chin on the shoulder deal, hoping she wouldn't drop my jaw for me again.

She was writing an answer to Assignment One: "What are three ways libraries have evolved to serve changing needs?"

This is How We Will Live, Now That We Are Free
by Ivan Faute

Alexi blew his nose into some toilet paper and threw the wad into the water, still orange from his piss. The last girlfriend hated when he did this. "Why do you have to throw it in the toilet?" she'd complain. "The garbage can is right there."

"It's getting flushed anyway," he'd answer. That was not a good enough answer, and she would then complain about the smell of his urine. It smelled like rotten fruit, she said. She complained often, counting on her fingers the things that she hated about him as if she were making a shopping list. It was after her complaints about his use of toilet paper though that he decided he would never have another girlfriend. Instead, after breaking it off with her, he used them like the blue-tinted paper dissolving in the bowl in front of him. He shook the head of his penis and flushed. The water pressure here was much stronger than in his apartment.

He looked in the mirror. A dark smudge of sleep remained under his eyes. He was wearing a cowboy shirt of ironic madras, alternating blues and browns, set off with pearl buttons rimmed in silver. He pulled the sleeves down and buttoned the cuffs. A swirl of black tattoo ink still showed on the edge of his left wrist when he extended his arm. Though it had seemed, at the time when he had the ink put in, that he would have no problem covering up the tattoo with any sort of shirtsleeve, the shirt styles he felt most comfortable in, those just a little tight across the shoulders, always left a little of the ink peeking out. This was fine when he was out at night, but his boss had looked askance at him. "Those tattoos are for punks and criminals," the boss said in English, straining the words through his thick accent. Alexi nodded and repeated a moral in Russian for the old man, "You can't save the young, they are already rotten." The boss laughed and spat a long line of brown tobacco juice into the Dunkin' Donuts foam cup he carried around with him all day. Even though they were physical laborers, his boss worked only in the "good buildings" and didn't want his clients to be put off by his workers.

While Alexi stood in the strange bathroom and looked at himself in the same outfit he'd been wearing the night before, he thought perhaps the saying could be true. He didn't believe that he could be corrupted; he was rotten to the core already. But he wasn't so sure about these American girls. He knew what he was doing; taking them home at night and then a quick goodbye was no more to him than dinner from the drive-through, but he wasn't sure they always understood. Also, he wasn't sure if he felt good about corrupting them or not.

He opened the bathroom door onto the long hallway. The hallway had several doors along one side. All of these girls had the same condominium with three bedrooms and as many bathrooms, deluxe fixtures, and cavernous ceilings. He had painted enough of them to know they always had too much space in them. Even when someone could fill them up with enough furniture, which a lot of the owners couldn't, there would still be wide, empty spaces between the couch and the coffee table. No matter how they arranged the furniture, it was always awkward.

Alexi couldn't remember which door was the bedroom. The first room he tried was empty except for several Crate & Barrel boxes marked with "X-Mas" in black ink. When he was first being a playboy, Alexi used to slip out with only a kiss on their forehead sometime in the early morning, but that behavior made him feel cheap. Though he still didn't want to stay long enough for conversation, a lot of the women had comfortable mattresses, and he didn't feel bad about taking advantage of that.

The next room he checked was the bedroom he had just left, but the woman was no longer there. As often happened, he had forgotten this one's name. He knew it was something like "Claire," but he wasn't sure he had ever been presented with it properly. He would get around this the way he always did, by using vegetable names as a term of endearment. He used the Russian word of course, and they all thought it was adorable.

"Kartoffel?" he called out, his voice a little creaky from all the cigarettes the night before. He'd stopped buying cigarettes months earlier, but always bummed a few from the others around him. Sometimes now he smoked even more than he had when he was paying for them.

"I'm in the kitchen," he heard her voice coming from down the hall. "I've got some breakfast." She moved fast. Her voice wasn't pinched mommy-voice either; the kind that offered food or comfort with the same cloying nurture that required a reassuring appreciation in return. Instead, her voice was confident and a little rough. Perhaps she had had a few too many cigarettes the night before, too.

Generally, these girls were as identical as their apartments. They were from Wisconsin or Michigan or Kansas. It didn't matter, they acted the same: fearful of men, happy with shopping and with sugary, alcoholic drinks. In Europe, it made a difference if a girl was from Krakow or Moscow or Prague, but all these Americans were from middling towns where they learned to speak with flat vowels and how to get into a good college, before they moved to Chicago with their business or law degrees and made lots of money.

"What did you call me?" the voice came bouncing down the hall.

"Potato," Alexi yelled back. He scanned the bedroom for envelopes or a magazine with an address label. She had a Martha Stewart Living on the nightstand, but it was a newsstand copy. "You know," he called out, "like honey or sweetheart." Names were overused anyway.

He walked down the hall to the combination kitchen, dining, and living room, with its floor-to-ceiling windows at the front. The windows overlooked the sidewalk, and across the street, the only remaining greystone two-flat left on the block. The kitchen could have been a set for a television show, with its stove positioned on an island between the cabinets and the rest of the room, and the countertop overlaid with a long slab of granite. She could have cooking demonstrations for her seated guests, if she wanted to. "Nice house," he said as he rounded the corner.

She was wrapped in a white terrycloth robe that hung loosely around her shoulders. Mandarin Hotel was stitched over the left breast.

"Good morning," she said. She was shorter than he remembered. He realized she'd been wearing very tall shoes. "You're all dressed already." Even though her voice had an undercurrent of aggression, everything she said was careful, like she strained her words through some filter of cheerfulness in the back of her throat. It reminded Alexi of the way refugees first talked when they made it to Chicago; everything they said was so considered. "I made breakfast." It was a flat statement. She was probably some sort of manager, he decided. She was used to people reacting to what she said, used to them reacting with some sort of physical movement or activity after she spoke.

"It looks very nice," Alexi said. He smiled. He had a careful, practiced smile to put people at ease. It was a smile that communicated, "I'm not dangerous." At least not dangerous in an "I'm going to kill you now and put you in the freezer" kind of way. There was often, when he was stuck in a place after sunrise, an awkward feeling of being with a stranger in the daylight, someone he'd already touched, wherever and however he wanted to the night before, but someone he didn't know. Because they had both made these agreements, about the night before, when it was still dark, and they had both been a little drunk at the time. But, being in the everyday kitchen, with eggs curdling on the stove and with that same coffeepot that had been sitting on the counter, unused and mocking for the past eight months, but was now being used and full of black liquid—it made everyone confused about where to put hands or how far away to stand from each other. It made everyone self-conscious.

Alexi had learned that, if possible, just a small bit of touch, on the back of the hand, two knees hitting each other under a table, or a hand placed on the neutral part of the back, and all the tension would dissipate. The long kitchen island made it difficult, because it put so much space between them, and Alexi couldn't casually reach over and make contact. It would look like lunging if he made a move.

Also, he knew that now that his sleeves were down, without the red flames and lounging pinup girls on his arms, she would feel even more unsafe. It took him some time to learn this one because it seemed it would be the other way. However, Alexi realized there were different kinds of safe. These girls would feel safe with a guy who was unacceptable, who they could never "date," because then they didn't have to care what happened. But the guy Alexi looked like now, with his pulled down sleeves, a little stubble just appearing, a smile of straight, white teeth, would look danger- ously like the guy the girl's sister had dated over Christmas or like some clerk from the law office next door. And here she would be thinking that she was now breaking every promise she'd made to herself in college about being independent and smart about this sort of thing, and here she was now making breakfast for some man on a Sunday morning like a suburban housewife. Alexi rolled up his sleeves to the elbow and the swirls and flashes of color blazed out against his creamy skin.

"I hope you like eggs," she said, dumping a curdled mess on a plate.

"They're great," he answered. "I don't really eat breakfast. Kind of disagrees with the beer." He patted his flat stomach.

"Oh," she said. Her shrug barely lifted the cotton robe. "That's fine." She pulled the plate away from him and picked up a fork, but she didn't take a bite and only poked at the eggs with the tines. "I'm not a great cook," she laughed. "Who has time." This was not a question but a statement.

"Yeah, I know." Alexi put his hands in his back pockets and rocked back a little on his heels. "Maybe I will have a few bites."

"Sure." And she pushed the plate over with the fork.

Alexi ate two bites. She had added paprika and too much salt. It was just how a café in Omsk had made them. "You are from Siberia?" he asked.

"My mother," she said. "A long time ago. I was born in Michigan." She nodded her head, using the tip of her chin for leverage, and then she took a long sip of coffee.

"Yeah, cool," he said. "I should go. Working every day." He smiled again.

She smiled back, and then Alexi remembered why he had approached her in the first place. Her smile was amazing, something more than what he usually saw in the Lincoln Park trixies. Everyone, he reminded himself, who falls in love always says the same thing: there was something different, something special that everyone else, everyone who looked just the same as that one, didn't have. Alexi wasn't worried about falling in love; he wasn't that cynical. But he wasn't too stupid to realize that some people did have something spectacular about them, inside them, and that sometimes it came out in these kinds of ways, in smiles, or their eyes, or the way they held a lit cigarette. He was glad when he saw it in someone, even if he didn't care to stick around long enough to figure out what it was. He firmly believed whatever it was would rub off on him, even if just a bit, for the little time they had spent together. He tried to explain this to his friends, but they only wanted to hear the details. Alexi never used names or identifying markers about what the girls looked like or where they lived. He thought he owed them enough respect to make them abstract.

Alexi put down his fork and stepped toward the door. He gave an awkward wave that he had practiced, and tried to be shy, but he couldn't help skipping down the front steps to the sidewalk. He never looked back because he knew they always were looking down.

Four months later, it was the end of summer and Alexi was back at the bar John Barleycorn. He didn't like to frequent a place too often. He didn't want to get a reputation with any of the regulars. However, he'd lost track of how long he had been absent because of a stomach flu he'd received from someone; he suspected it was from his boss. He even ended up in the hospital for a day after he fainted from the fever.

Even now, he should have still been in bed, if not all day, at least to get a good night's rest. But he'd needed the money, so he went to work, and then he wanted to relax afterwards. He'd lost several pounds, and his boss said he looked tense, but the low light of the bar made his sunken cheeks look good. The dark circles under his eyes and the strained, papery yellowness of his skin gave him an especially vulnerable look.

He ordered a draft beer along with a shot of Jack Daniels just as that girl from a few months back was getting the second bartender's attention. She stood just where the bar made a curve, and Alexi met her gaze. This sort of thing happened, of course, all the time to Alexi. Chicago was a small town. When a girl saw him, she would turn away; she always turned away. Alexi had thought a long time about why this was and decided it was not embarrassment. They, his conquests, just had some special place in their mind or their memories where they stored people like him, and after someone went into that room… well, it was an "enter only" type of place, no returns. So, Alexi and the girl would lock eyes a moment, there would be that slight ripple of recognition over her face before she registered that he was not meant to be there, and she would ignore him from then on. To Alexi, this was as close to absolution as he ever came.

Except this time she nodded. She worked her way around the bar, sliding her body between people to get past them. Her name came to him suddenly, as if something organic had fallen on top of his head from a tree. It was as if all of their names were floating about the room circulating on the currents of smoke and ceiling fan air, and hers landed on him just when he needed it.

"Hello, Clarissa," he said.

"Hello, Alexi," she answered.

He could not help notice how much sarcasm she put into his name. She said it in the same tone that his mother used when

Alexi snuck in at night. She, his mother, sitting at the kitchen table at three or four in the morning, the small lamp on the top of the refrigerator turned on as it always was because the light in the freezer had never worked. Alexi's mother sat at the table, her bare feet flat on the floor, shoulders square, her left hand gently fingering a drinking glass, half-empty or half-full, of whatever liquor she had around the house, and her right hand tending a cigarette or a cup of tea, or perhaps both. The image of his mother greeting him like this passed in front of Alexi's mind for only a moment before he dismissed it. The image was quickly followed by the thought, in the words and accent of his employer - "Men always marry their mothers"—so that when Clarissa stepped a bit closer, to allow someone to pass behind her, Alexi felt a tight pinch up and down his spine that he quickly shook off. The shaking looked like a chill.

"Are you cold?" she asked. "It's been cold."

"Yes, I've had a flu." He saw dark spots appear in her eyes. "Nothing serious. Just a cold. I feel fine now."

The dark spots disappeared. "Good enough for a drink," Clarissa said.

She raised her martini glass and Alexi was careful to hit it very lightly with his much thicker beer mug. He could not tell if what she said was a question or a statement. This confusion was one part of the Midwestern American dialect, along with the flat vowels and dropped contractions, that he never thought he'd master. He knew that if the speaker thought their question important, they'd ask it again. He took a gulp of beer and peered at Clarissa over the edge of his glass.

"I wondered where you went. I hadn't seen you in so long."

"I don't come here that much," he said. Alexi turned his body away from her so that he could slip away, but she managed to revolve around him, as if she were a moon. "It's far from my house."

"Oh, yeah," she looked back toward a group of woman Alexi noticed were the same she'd been with the first time they'd met, or perhaps they just looked the same. "I live around the corner. It's a little too much college frat atmosphere, but it's easy to get to."

"Yes." Realizing that he could offer no real reason for being there, Alexi took another sip of beer.

Clarissa looked over at her group of expectant friends. "Want to join us?" she asked and indicated with her head.

"No," he said. "No, I need to get going. I have to work again early. I should get some rest." He pointed to his eyes using the forefinger of the hand that held the beer.

"Just for a moment," she grabbed his forearm, just above his wrist, with her fingers. "I want them to meet you."

Later then, again, they were at her apartment. Clarissa's head was on Alexi's chest. He could feel her breath on his skin. Her breathing was very regular, very modulated. He was on his back, his right hand gently, but not absently, touching the edge of the bones that made up her face. His left hand was behind his head, his eyes open while she slept. He imagined them in a scene, at the end of a movie. The camera would show her hair tumbling over his naked chest. It would then pull back. The camera would float above them and keep pulling away, higher and higher. He expected that the scene would end when the camera hit the ceiling, but it did not; it continued to travel upward. He saw that the building had no roof, and the two of them, man and woman, were getting smaller and smaller in the frame. Then, the bed became only a shape in the square room, then he could make out the house on its rectangular lot, then it was only one of the many of the same on the block. Then Alexi tried to find himself again in the collection of buildings and houses and rooms, but he could not see where he was at all.

V

by Melanie Bell

You stopped us in front of the cathedral,
Windows tangerine and copper, translucent in the dark,
And said "Spontaneous," your word
Doled out every day like pennies at the corner store,
"Let's give spontaneous thanks for the beautiful things."
We stood there in front of glassy saints,
Five college kids,
And did.

You lived by theme songs—
Belting "Colors of the Wind" through
    an autumn-painted campus
To annoy us until we joined in,
"Lemon Tree" in 4 am wood-paneled rooms
Flickering with disco lights,
Limbs like starfish, bodies spiraling.
You lived alphabetically—
Valentine's birthday, viola, Vierka (your nickname
    for people that mattered),
Dead at 28 in Vienna.

You took everything for free—
Ribboned skirts and corduroy clothing swap jackets
Carried home in a Santa Claus sack,
Vegan soup kitchen dinners (your hands in suds to pay),
I thought it fearless
When you left early—never could stay
In one place long.
I didn't expect to see you again.

In Montreal we met in calf-deep snow,
In Fredericton biking a play from school to school,
Soon it was continents you pedaled over.
"To hell with reality!
I want to die in music, not in reason or in prose."
I thumb the book of quotes you wrote me
Before crossing the seven seas, simple as drinking water.

I would have e-mailed again sometime
To check: "How are you?"
Meaning "Are you still here?"
Expecting you to be.

If you could write back
I'd send you a second surprise party.
Collect old friends with potluck dishes,
Pizza, cream cake, red balloons
In that echoing wood-paneled room,
To sit and watch you laugh.

Alexis Rhone Fancher *White Flag*

L.A. poet/photographer **Alexis Rhone Fancher** is published in *Best American Poetry, Rattle, Poetry East, Hobart, Verse Daily, American Journal of Poetry, Plume, Diode, Wide Awake: Poets of Los Angeles*, and elsewhere. She's the author of five published poet collections, most recently, *Junkie Wife* (Moon Tide Press, 2018), and *The Dead Kid Poems* (KYSO Flash Press, 2019). *EROTIC: New & Selected*, publishes in 2020 from New York Quarterly. Her photographs are published worldwide, including *River Styx*, and the covers of *Pithead Chapel, Heyday,* and *Witness*. A multiple Pushcart Prize and Best of the Net nominee, Alexis is poetry editor of *Cultural Weekly*. AlexisRhoneFancher.com.

"Edward Hopper's painting, 'Morning Sun, 1952' fascinated me long before I ever thought to write about it. The alienation. The longing. Hopper's (always) extraordinary use of light. A friend had posted the painting on Facebook, and when I saw it, I commented: 'Nobody paints loneliness like Edward Hopper." Then I wrote 'White Flag.'"

Ali Abbas *The Book of Condolence*

Ali Abbas is the author of *Like Clockwork* a steampunk mystery published by Transmundane Press. His shorter fiction has been published by *Mad Scientist Journal*, Transmundane Press, and Death's Head Press. Ali blogs about photography, carpentry, and writing at www.AliAbbas.com and a full list of published works and free-to-read stories can be found on his author page AauthorAli-Abbas.weebly.com.

"Almost a quarter of a century ago, I went to a remembrance service for a friend. I found myself, a gauche and somewhat pretentious young man, standing in front of a creamy blank page, at a loss for what to write. Shelley's "Epipsychidion" provided an answer: "*Seraph of heaven too gentle to be human, veiling beneath that radiant form of woman*". The words, too melodramatic for our friendship, were all I had. That memory and finding a deep, destructive love worthy of the poem were at the heart of "The Book of Condolence". Other truths and memories are buried in it, rebar to fortify the poured concrete of imagination. For the record, I've never written a play nor known a film star. I do have an abiding admiration for the Greek poet George Seferis; his poem "Man" from *Mr Stratis Thalassinos Describes a Man* is also referenced in the story."

Alison Stone *Tenth Anniversary*

Alison Stone has published six full-length collections, *Caught in the Myth* (NYQ Books, 2019), *Dazzle* (Jacar Press, 2017), *Masterplan*, a book of collaborative poems with Eric Greinke (Presa Press, 2018), *Ordinary Magic*, (NYQ Books, 2016), *Dangerous Enough* (Presa Press 2014), and *They Sing at Midnight,* which won the 2003 Many Mountains Moving Poetry Award; as well as three chapbooks. A seventh collection, *Zombies at the Disco*, is forthcoming from Jacar Press in 2020. Her poems have appeared in *The Paris Review, Poetry, Ploughshares, Barrow Street, Poet Lore,* and many other journals and anthologies. She has been awarded Poetry's Frederick Bock Prize and New York Quarterly's Madeline Sadin Award. She was recently Writer in Residence at LitSpace St. Pete. She is also a painter and the creator of The Stone Tarot. A licensed psychotherapist, she has private practices in NYC and Nyack. www.stonepoetry.org www.stonetarot.com

"Watching my wedding video ten years later, I became aware of how clueless I was when I married about the actuality of living with someone and raising children with Them. The poem was a celebration of both the ritual (which, except for the priestess almost setting her sleeve on fire, was exactly what I'd wanted) and the reality that followed. It's also a celebration of my religion. I'm Pagan, which many people have fears and misconceptions about. I hope I conveyed some of the beauty of the ceremony, the spiritual grounding of the marriage, which has helped me through some of the challenging times."

Amanda Moore *Indication of Love*

Amanda Moore's poetry has appeared in journals and anthologies including *ZZYZVA, Cream City Review, Tahoma Literary Review, Best New Poets*, and *Mamas and Papas: On the Sublime and Heartbreaking Art of Parenting*, and she is the recipient of writing awards from The Writing Salon, Brush Creek Arts Foundation, and The Saltonstall Foundation for the Arts. Her essays have appeared or are forthcoming in *The Baltimore Review, Hippocampus Magazine*, and on the University of Arizona Poetry Center's blog, and she is a Contributing Poetry Editor at *Wom-*

en's Voices for Change. Currently a Board member for the Marin Poetry Center and 2019 Fellow at The Writers Grotto, Amanda is a high school teacher and lives by the beach in the Outer Sunset neighborhood of San Francisco with her husband and daughter. More at AmandaPMoore.com.

"Looking at the world through a child's eyes often offers clarity that the complicated business of adulthood obscures. When I first discovered my daughter's sloppy, round handwriting in the back of my favorite notebook, I was slightly annoyed that she had used a precious page to draft her answer to a homework assignment. As I read her description of the tiny painting on our mantle, however, I found a wisdom in her rendering that perfectly articulated, whether she realized it or not, a truth about motherhood I was just coming to understand. Though I was once her everything: her food, her comfort, her source of life, as she grows older, the best way to show my love is by removing myself from the foreground and into a more supportive role, "mostly behind." I am struck by how accurate, if deeply unfair, her simple observation of the painting has proven to be, and I'm ultimately grateful for her notebook transgression, as it regularly offers me a way of staying in the picture and indicating my love."

Anonymous *Daddy's Girl*

Anonymous works cross-genre in creative nonfiction, fantasy, experimental fiction, screenwriting, and just about everything else you can think of. Her creative nonfiction essay "Mermaids Singing" was initially published in *Rascal*, and *Rascal* has nominated the essay for the 2019 Pushcart Prize Anthology. *Perspectives* has nominated her short fiction story "Granny in the Forest" for their *2019 Best Small Fictions Anthology*. Anonymous' publishing credits include *DIN Southwest Literary Magazine*, Ashoka University's *Plot Number Two*, and others. She has many credits to her name as a journalist in the Corvallis *Advocate* and the Willamette *Collegian*. Anonymous has completed her MFA in Creative Writing and she tells stories to understand herself and the world. She shares them to teach others to love the world the way she does.

She wishes to let this piece speak for itself.

Beth Konkoski *A Drawn and Papered Heart*

Beth Konkoski is a writer and high school English teacher living in Northern Virginia with her husband and two children. Over the last twenty years, her work has been published in literary journals such as: *Story, Mid-American Review,* and *The Baltimore Review.* Her second chapbook of poetry, *Water Shedding*, was published in April 2019 by Finishing Line Press. She is a frequent reader in the Washington DC area and helps organize the Miller Reading Series, held each summer at Rock Creek Park.

"'A Drawn and Papered Heart' won first place in the F. Scott Fitzgerald Short Story Contest, sponsored by Montgomery County Community College and the F. Scott Fitzgerald Society. As part of the award, I got to read the story at their annual conference and give a little background on the piece. When I lived in San Diego, I did model for a life drawing class taught by a friend of mine, and the sense of attention and posing in the story comes from that experience. Everything else in the story is fiction. My favorite part of writing short stories is finding a frame to put around some experience or awareness I have about the world. It is great when a part of my reality becomes a story reality for characters I make up. I owe every story and poem I write to my daily journal. Recording impressions and events as they happen, then returning to the pages to recall experience is the way I get inspired to write."

Bill Stenson *Camping for the First Time*

Bill Stenson's latest novel, *Ordinary Strangers*, won the Hunt For The Great B.C. Novel Contest this year. He lives in the Cowichan Valley with his wife, the poet, Susan Stenson.

"Like most writers, I write about what interests me. Two years ago, on a road trip driving back from up north, I listened to a documentary radio program about the alternatives some are currently exploring in our ever-expanding world. What happens in 'Camping For The First Time' is a blend of these stories."

Carly Lynn Gates *The Writer's Wife*

Carly Lynn Gates teaches communication arts and advises the literary-arts magazine, newsmagazine, and yearbook at a public arts magnet high school in West Palm Beach, Florida. She holds an MFA in creative writing from The University of the South's School of Letters. Her essay "How Service Learning Cultivates Empathy and Social Responsibility" was published in the textbook *Creative Writing in the* Community in 2014. Her poetry has been published in *Flint Hills Review*, *Hawai'i Review*, and *So to Speak*, among others, and is forthcoming in the anthology *Pantoums for the 21st Century*. In 2015 she won first place for adult fiction in the Sinclair Writing and was an MFA scholar at the Sewanee Writers' Conference.

"Since my first reading of Galway Kinnell's *Book of Nightmares* as an undergrad, my mind kept returning to 'The Call Across the Valley of Not Knowing,' wondering how his first wife must have felt when she read this poem in which the narrator lies in bed with his hand on his wife's belly feeling the kicks of his unborn son while thinking about his true other half who he'd once met on an airplane, but subsequently lost. The narrator reveals his desire to suffer, wounded by the mismatch, for his art, to come to a greater realization of the self by embracing this failure—but what about his spouse? What of those who must suffer along with us? As a writer, I too know what it means to self-sabotage, to obsess over and romanticize, to hurt the people I love in my selfishness by both dwelling in sadness and exposing elements of my private life through my work. I'll never forget the words of my undergrad thesis chair when I brought this up to her all those years ago. She just looked at me and said, "When it comes to love, all bets are off with a poet.""

Claire Hawkins *Tina*

Claire Hawkins lives with too many sick and geriatric animals in too small a house in San Francisco.

"Though the 'Opioid Crisis' is currently the foremost drug concern, crystal meth (Tina) continues to ravage families.

Daniel Loring Keating *Canaries Built Our House of Shame*

Daniel Loring Keating grew up in post-Industrial New England, where he earned a BA in Creative Writing from Chester College of New England. He has an MFA in Creative Writing at the California College of the Arts, where he was the managing editor of *Eleven Eleven Journal*. His work has appeared in *LEVITATE Magazine*,

Chantwood Magazine, The Cerurove, Minute Magazine, Obra/Artifact, and *Petrichor Machine*.

"'Canaries Built Our House of Shame' started off as a much more abstract story about a funeral in which most of the attendees feel a deep moral ambivalence toward the deceased. That concept grew into a relatively specific story about the ways in which moral righteousness can interfere with concepts like love and acceptance. I'd like to think that the story's primary challenge is to show who/what makes a mockery of the idea of a funeral, or, on a grander scale, who/what makes a mockery of the notion of what it means to love someone who is gone and what it means to treat that grief in a 'proper' manner."

D. Dina Friedman *Bloodsister*

D. Dina Friedman has received two Pushcart Prize nominations and published in many literary journals including *Lilith, Negative Capability, The Sun, Common Ground Review, San Pedro River Review, Steam Ticket, New Plains Review, Blue Stem, Red Booth Review, Bloodroot, Anderbo,* and *Rhino*. Dina is also the author of two award-winning young adult novels, *Escaping Into the Night* (Simon and Schuster) and *Playing Dad's Song* (Farrar, Straus, Giroux) and one chapbook of poetry, *Wolf in the Suitcase* (Finishing Line Press). Dina moved with her husband to western Massachusetts 38 years ago because it was "a compromise between Brooklyn and the Ozarks." She currently lives in Hadley, next door to a farm with 500 cows. She has an MFA from Lesley University and teaches at the University of Massachusetts/Amherst. To learn more about Dina, visit her website at DDinaFriedman.com.

"To be truthful, I don't remember when or why I first began this poem. It grew and evolved over the years, as I played with easing it into a more formalized pattern of sound and meter. But, yes, I did have a so called "best friend" in elementary school whom I loved recklessly and who caused me much sadness and despair with her oscillation between acceptance and rejection. It's a common feeling in hopeless romance, I know, but I think the genesis is much deeper, and it always leaves me wondering what do we need to find in ourselves to get past the point where we think we need someone else's love to make us whole."

Evan L. Balkan *Another Country*

Evan L. Balkan is the author of six books of nonfiction, including *The Wrath of God: Lope de Aguirre; Revolutionary of the Americas* (Univ. of New Mexico Press) as well as many essays and short stories in an array of publications. His novel *Spitfire* was published in September, 2018, (Amphorae). His screenplay *Spitfire*, adapted from his novel of the same name, won the 2016 Baltimore Screenwriters Competition, a Saul Zaentz Innovation Fund Fellowship, a Rocaberti scholarship, and was a semifinalist in the Screencraft Family Friendly Screenwriting Competition as well as a finalist for an ISA fellowship; his screenplay *Children of Disobedience* won the 2017 Baltimore Screenwriting Competition. He is a co-writer for the television series, *Wayward Girls*. He coordinates the English Department at the Community College of Baltimore County, where he runs the creative writing program, and is an adjunct faculty member in Johns Hopkins University's graduate Teaching Writing program. He holds degrees in the humanities from Towson, George Mason, and Johns Hopkins universities. He has served as a guest lecturer at Yale, Johns Hopkins, Bryn Mawr, and many other institutions.

"I am interested in how men navigate relationships in a climate in which many of the old masculine tropes are, appropriately, being challenged and altered. There remains a tension between the thrust toward masculinity in its positive manifestations and the idea that *any* reflection or assertion of masculinity is inherently retrograde. I take no strong position here, but rather like to work in fiction with male characters who—subconsciously—struggle within those tensions."

Flo Golod *Maple Chaser*

Flo Golod lives in south Minneapolis with her husband Scott and cat Leslie. A retired non-profit consultant, mother, and grandmother, she's active in the Master Gardener Program. Her stories have appeared in two issues of *Talking Stick* (one received a second place award), the 2018 *Choices* anthology from Temptation Press, and the online journals, *Manifestations* and BoomerLit.com.

"After the 2016 election, I retreated from Facebook for a few months. Life in Trump times was (and is) absurd, depressing, and enraging. Rants and finger pointing made it worse. Someone posted a link to the Maple Match site and I started reading about Americans trying to wed their way into Canada. Heather and the narrator are not my children, but they could be."

Ivan Faute *This is How We Live Now That We are Free*

Ivan Faute has published stories in various journals and anthologies and his dramatic work has been produced in New York, London, Chicago, and elsewhere. His work has been nominated for a Pushcart Prize and named a finalist for the Calvino Prize and the ATHE Excellence in Playwriting Award. He teaches creative writing at Christopher Newport University in Virginia.

"Chicago is often called a city of neighborhoods; it is also a jumble of brick buildings, Midwestern earthiness, and waves of immigrants. This mix creates a dynamic, ever-shifting, and beautiful city of hardworking people, freezing winters, exuberant summers, and opportunities to fall in love with someone or something around every corner. This story is an intersection of all the problems and promise of Chicago, was inspired by her, and explores a small part of my love for her."

Isabelle Jia *Erased Boy*

Isabelle Jia is a Chinese American poet and undergraduate at Claremont McKenna College. Her work has appeared or is forthcoming in *Glass: A Journal of Poetry, Alexandria Quarterly, The Blueshift Journal, Rising Phoenix Review,* and many more. Jia has been recognized as a California Arts Scholar, by the Walt Whitman National Poetry Foundation, Hollins University, and the Alliance of Young Artists & Writers. She has studied poetry under author Jennifer Givhan, Kirk Glaser, and Hilary Darling. Currently, she works for The Speakeasy Project and *Bitter Melon Magazine*. For more on her work, please visit Isabellejia.weebly.com.

"I wrote 'erased boy' after remembering something my mother had said to me, years ago. She said something along the lines of, 'I wouldn't accept you if you were gay / it wouldn't matter / daughter / that's not acceptable / here.' I kept this memory in mind as I started to write that night. Prior to 'erased boy,' I can't recall a time I wrote a poem that embodies the voice of a different gender or sexual identity than my own. Taking on this new perspective wasn't too difficult because I still incorporated the themes I commonly use in my poetry: love, color, floral imagery, and juxtaposing words. The opening lines of the poem had been repeating in my head for a week or so before I put them down on paper. A few words such as 'wings' and 'dog' found from flipping through poetry collections. The rest is the result of a flood."

J. White *Different Ways to Say the Same Thing*

J. White reads avidly, writes feverishly, and edits professionally. He works as a technical editor for a telecommunications megacorporation in downtown Philadelphia, where he lives with his partner. His fiction and nonfiction works have been featured in publications like *WomanlyMag* and *MuslimGirl*, and in 2017 he received honorable mentions for Best New Writer and Best Short Fiction by *Glimmer Train Press*. He draws his inspiration from Lorrie Moore and Don DeLillo, and he considers Frank Herbert's *Dune* his personal bible.

"'Different Ways to Say the Same Thing' emerged in 2012 out of new love, imagined love, and an amalgamation of memories. I wrote this piece for a friend, at first, and also for myself, and also for my readers; I find it's always easier to write with someone specific in mind. I hope the piece resonates with you and makes you smile without wanting to."

Jenn Richter *Sisyphus in Love*

Jenn Richter has been published in *Blue Collar Review, Shakespeare's Monkey Revue*, and various anthologies. She has a BA in writing/literature from George Fox University and works as the early learning program administrator in McMinnville, Oregon, where she lives with her husband and family. In her spare time, she likes to read, write, and kayak.

"I wrote 'Sisyphus in Love' after standing by a friend while he went through several rounds of abuse and withdrawal from his partner—only to watch him take her back again and again. I wrote this poem when I realized that he has chosen this cycle as his destiny—and that nothing I can say or do will change that."

Kacie Berghoef *Siam*

Kacie Berghoef creates content, polishes essays, and writes stories. She is co-author of a nonfiction book, *The Modern En-*

neagram. Her work has also appeared in *WordWorks Magazine, ThoughtCo, Illumen Quarterly,* the *Transcendent,* and *Realm of Magic* anthologies, and more. Stay in touch at <u>kacieberghoef. com</u> and @kberghoef on Instagram and Twitter.

"I was inspired to write about Siam because I believe domestic rats are among the most misunderstood animals in the world. Having had several wonderful rats, and I've found them to be extremely clever, affectionate, playful, and hygienic creatures. As my true story shows, these small pets have the capacity to take up large spaces in our hearts."

Kate Hodges *Good Morning Beautiful*

Kate Hodges is an elementary and middle school teacher turned writer from Philadelphia. She has published several short stories and some poetry. She is currently working on a collection of short stories.

"I am very interested in the meaning behind silences, and in ambiguity. One of my friends was in a situation similar to the one presented here. Our friend group spent hours discussing the many possible meanings behind the maybe. We all had different interpretations. At the end of the story, there is a moment where Chris holds _____'s hand. It's such an interesting moment to me because he's offering himself to her, while at the same time telling her that she is wrong. There are so many ways to interpret wrong. It's such an unsettled space. I really enjoy reading stories and writing stories where there is that particular tension."

Kate Larsen *Monsters are Always Invited*

Kate Larsen is a lifelong resident of Colorado's San Luis Valley. She is happily married with a small herd of noisy children, a lot of horses, and two smelly dogs. Her work has been featured in *Garo* and *West Texas Literary Review.* She enjoys heavy metal concerts and the company of cows.

"I never choose a character, they simply find me—racketing around in my brain, pounding against my earlobes till their voices are clear, their demands, motives, felons, gracious works, are all come to fruition on the page. I've never created a story, only reiterated that which I was told."

Kelly Magee *The Origin*

Kelly Magee is the author of *Body Language*, winner of the Katherine Anne Porter Prize in Fiction, and *The Neighborhood*, as well as several collaborative collections. Her work has appeared in *Granta, Gulf Coast, Kenyon Review, Hobart, Crazyhorse*, and many others. She teaches at Western Washington University and can be found at KellyElizabethMagee.com. This story previously appeared in Elven Eleven, Issue 22, Sept. 2016.

"I have always been terrified by and fascinated with storms, especially tornadoes, and I love writing about them in odd ways: I've written stories about people who grow storms like vegetables, people who marry and procreate with storms, people who turn into storms... but this was my first story about a storm that inhabits a person. Once I landed on that idea, it seemed true to my experience of (some kinds of) people, but also allowed me to imagine the details of how a storm would look and feel inside a human body, which was really fun. This was the last story I wrote for a collection of fairy tales and retellings called *The Neighborhood*, many of which are about unconventional and troubled relationships."

Laura Lee Washburn *Before She Fixes Lunch: Aubade*

Laura Lee Washburn is a university professor, the director of creative writing at Pittsburg State University in Kansas, and the author of *This Good Warm Place: 10th Anniversary Expanded Edition* (March Street) and *Watching the Contortionists* (Palanquin Chapbook Prize). Her poetry has appeared in such journals as *New Verse News, Poet Lore, The Sun,* and *Valparaiso Review. Harbor Review*'s Washburn Micro-Chap prize is named in her honor. Born in Virginia Beach, Virginia, Washburn has also lived and worked in Arizona and Missouri. She is a founder and the co-president of the board of the charitable fund, Southeast Kansas Women Helping Women.

"Before She Fixes Lunch" is an aubade or "morning song" that describes, fairly accurately, I think, my husband's energy and my morning slowness at a certain time period of our marriage. This is a love poem from a city girl raised to stay up late and sleep late to her raised-on-a-farm up-and-at-'em husband.

Lawdenmarc Decamora *Little Things*

Lawdenmarc Decamora is a Best of the Net and Pushcart Prize-nominated writer. He holds an MFA in Creative Writing (Poetry) and is an MA candidate in Literary and Cultural Studies. His work, including short fiction, poetry, and criticism, has been widely published in 18 countries around the world, appearing in publications such as *Drunken Boat, Cordite Poetry Review, The Seattle Review, The Ilanot Review, SAND Journal, Columbia Journal* (honorable mention), *Yellow Medicine Review*, AAWW's *The Margins*, and elsewhere. He teaches literature and humanities at the University of Santo Tomas in the Philippines. He has works forthcoming at *The Common, North Dakota Quarterly, The Comstock Review, AJAR Press* (a bilingual journal in Vietnam), *Mingled Voices 4* of the International Proverse Poetry Prize 2019 Anthology (Proverse Hong Kong), and in the Scopus-indexed *Humanities Diliman: A Philippine Journal of Humanities*.

"'Little Things" talks about the everyday ideology of social life and its fundamental necessities to elevate personal expectations into a form of molecular truth pontificated by the intellectual joker. I like the idea of the intellectual joker lounging on our mental furnitures, observing the room of our often conscious comedy of further possibilities. Madness, lies, truth, and love are interpreted from the inside—the uncourted catastrophe turned spectacle—as they reflect the ideological state of the human condition from self-commodification to embracing religion. It is undoubtedly a refreshing experience writing this poem as my philosophical feeling for it oscillates between Slavoj Žižek's stepping out of ideology through the intellectual joker, and John Carpenter's untold truth in *They Live*."

Lisa Dordal *Sixth Grade*

Lisa Dordal teaches in the English Department at Vanderbilt University and is the author of *Mosaic of the Dark*, which was a finalist for the 2019 Audre Lorde Award for Lesbian Poetry. She is a Pushcart Prize nominee and the recipient of an Academy of American Poets University Prize, the Robert Watson Poetry Prize, and the Betty Gabehart Poetry Prize. Her poetry has appeared in *Best New Poets, Ninth Letter, CALYX, The Greensboro Review, Vinyl Poetry*, and *Nasty Women Poets: An Unapologetic Anthology of Subversive Verse*. Her website is lisadordal.com.

"Ten years ago, I re-connected with a friend of mine from grammar school who I hadn't talked to in over twenty years. When I found out he was gay, I knew I had to write this poem. He and I were the only two people in our larger group of friends who were 'married off' in grammar school—and the only two people in that group who (as far as I know) now identify as gay or lesbian. After re-connecting with Bruce, I started to wonder if he and I had been drawn to each other because, deep down, each of us knew we were gay. Or if the ritual of being married off was some deeply subconscious attempt on the part of our classmates to "correct" us. Or perhaps it was all a coincidence. Who knows? In any case, I've always been fascinated by the ritual we engaged in and the way we so deliberately mimicked adult behavior. One of my friends even made a toaster for us out of a shoebox. Complete with buttered toast made from construction paper. Three days later, Bruce and I got divorced. In the settlement, I got the toaster."

Lisa López Smith *V*

Originally from British Columbia, Canada, **Lisa López Smith** lives and writes from her farm in Mexico. When not wrangling kids or rescue dogs or goats, you can probably find her riding her bike. Recent publications of poems and essays can be found in: *TJ Eckleburg Review, Sky Island Journal, Tilde, Esthetic Apostle, SAND, Mothers Always Write, Lacuna Magazine*, and *Coal Hill Review*.

"I had never seen all the old film reels from when I was a kid until recently when my mom had them all put on a disc. My dad usually did the filming so he rarely showed up in them, but his voice got recorded as he was talking and filming me climbing playground equipment in the park. His voice was so familiar even though it had been more than twenty-five years since he had died."

Lorna Wood *Second Honeymoon*

Lorna Wood is a violinist and writer in Auburn, Alabama, with a PhD in English from Yale. She co-won third prize in the 2019 *Online Writing Tips* Short Fiction Competition and was a finalist in the 2017 *Jerry Jazz Musician* Short Fiction Contest. In addition to *Jerry Jazz Musician*, her literary fiction has appeared in *Wild Violet, Blue Monday Review*, and on Kindle. She has also published genre fiction, creative nonfiction, poetry, and scholarly essays, and she is Senior Editor for *Gemini Magazine.*

"Traveling with my husband in the Netherlands a few years ago, I imagined how the art, the food, the fancy hotels, the romantic scenery, might be experienced by a couple who were trying to force romance to blossom again. The Hague, with its rain, lawyers, and masterpieces, seemed a promising setting for a tale of troubled middle-aged love. Through my protagonist's reactions to the powerful paintings in the Mauritshuis, I explored the ways art may illuminate what is hidden or confusing in all our lives."

Marian Armstrong Rogers *The Astonishment of it All*

Marian Armstrong Rogers studied at Pace University and worked for the mental health department in Westchester County, New York, for many years. Her work has appeared in *The Journal News; The Sun* magazine; *Writer's Journal; Bagel Tuesdays,* an anthology; and *Astonishments: Stories as True as memory,* a book that won third place in the Wordwrite 2016 contest for self-published memoirs. Now retired, she can be found with canary-pad and pen in hand, or at her computer, working on a new collection of stories whenever she is not enjoying the company of her daughters and grandchildren who often visit her at her home in Mt. Kisco, New York.

"In spite of being relieved of the exhausting care of a husband who suffered from Alzheimer's disease, I missed Sam intensely when he died. Writing gave him back to me for a time and triggered memories of joy, some of which are included in 'The Astonishment of it All,' such as the beginning of our romance when sitting on that old bench in White Plains, and the magical Thanksgiving we shared so many years later. I'd wondered if I could continue to love Sam at all as he changed and changed again. Instead my love for him grew stronger, deeper, his need somehow bringing out the best in me. I only realized that when writing about us. It was an unexpected gift."

MeeRee Orlandini *What She Told Me Was This*

MeeRee Orlandini is a poet and fiction writer based in South Philadelphia. She recently graduated from the University of the Arts with a B.A. in creative writing. Her work takes on the curiosity and quietude of a morning cup of Joe. She is a first grade assistant teacher at Germantown Friends School.

"'What She Told Me Was This" is, at its bones, a found poem. Nearly all of these lines were things said to me by one person—a smart and funny person but also an incredibly honest one. The title of this publication is *What We Talk About When We Talk About It*. For me, the 'It' is always (Raymond Carver's) love, humanity, what we come to mean to each other. Sometimes when we talk about it, we talk around it. Sometimes we talk about everything but it: definition through negation. "If I were to describe you, I would just describe all the things that aren't you." I wanted to write a poem that blurted out the thing, that both confronted and evaded, that searched so earnestly for a solution."

Mel Carlson *The Strike*

Mel Carlson worked at *Poetry Magazine* while he attended Northwestern on the GI bill. Throughout the 1950s and early 1960s he wrote drama and docudrama for public broadcasting and the CBC in Canada. Subsequently he taught film writing and aesthetics in the Film Department at San Francisco State before retiring in 1988. His semi-autobiographical story, "Walking on Water", was published in Tin House, volume 26.

"This story draws from my childhood in the mining district of Southern Missouri where I lived within walking distance of my grandparents' home. Superficially, they were opposites, he the son of Swedish immigrants, and an implacable Socialist, she the descendent of 1665 Dutch settlers, and the president of a local, all-female-run bank. Photographs depict them—as I recall—always leaning toward each other, as if drawing strength from their union."

Editor's note: Mel Carlson passed away in early November 2019 at the age of 96. He will be sorely missed.

Melanie Bell *V*

Melanie Bell holds an MA in Creative Writing from Concordia University and has written for various publications including *Autostraddle, Cicada, The Fiddlehead, Every Day Fiction*, and *CV2*. She's the co-author of a nonfiction book, *The Modern Enneagram* (Althea Press, 2017). You can visit her website at InspireEnvisioning.com.

"'Viera" was a friend who died young. She was one of the most enthusiastic people I knew, traveling the world and seeking out new experiences. I wrote this poem to honor her adventurous life."

Pamela Balluck *Tight*

Pamela Balluck was born in New York and raised in California and Montana. Her fiction has been awarded publication prizes from among others, *Western Humanities Review* and *Green Mountains Review,* and her work has also appeared in such journals as *Southeast Review* and *PANK*. Her nonfiction has most recently appeared on the *Prairie Schooner* blog and an essay winning the *Southeast Review* prize is listed as "Notable" in *Best American Essays 2015*. She teaches writing at the University of Utah in Salt Lake City.

"An earlier draft of 'Tight' was published online by *Night Train* as Firebox Fiction in 2010. It is the germ of a novel-in-progress called *Once Removed* involving multiple generations of a family that originally landed on Tiburon Peninsula with the now defunct railroads in the late 1800s and have since then watched the ferries and the city across San Francisco Bay. As an adult woman fiction writer, I have found only mildly interesting the somewhat common scenarios of men successfully attracting girlfriends and wives a couple or a few decades younger, not to mention the slightly more curious men with women as young as their own daughters—what more piques my interest is not the phenomena of 'cougars,' women pursuing much younger men, but those of young men acting on attractions to decade(s)-older women, especially when it's genuinely about love and/or lust rather than love of her money or her lifestyle, and how older women consider such pursuits. In 'Tight,' I coupled this curiosity with the numerous stories I've heard—across generations—about forbidden romances (brief to deep) between cousins: first cousins, second cousins, first and second cousins once removed, and cousins completely unrelated by blood. What I'm beginning to explore in 'Tight' is whether, and if so how, loves like these might be managed in a tight-knit family intending to remain that way."

Rebecca Pilling *Obed:A Short Play*

Rebecca Pilling would prefer to spend her time baking a new pie recipe, stitching a new tongue-in-cheek cross-stitch pattern, or curled up on her porch with a good book and a large, hot coffee, but something inside compels her to write. She enjoys creating everyday characters with a supernatural twist, and writing little snippets of their lives. Her odd little stories, often speculative, often optimistic, often about cats, have been featured by HauikUniverse (as Bex), and Silver Birch Press. She lives in New England with her husband and their two cats, Sunny and Shadow.

"My parents got the first family pet a few years before I was born—a ginger tom called Chris. When he was tragically hit by a car, we waited an appropriate mourning time, then found a feisty calico kitten to bring home—so the cycle began. It's no wonder three of my four siblings continued the tradition as adults. 'Obed' was inspired by my sister's cat, a beautiful tabby called Finn. One night, I was watching television, Finn was curled up on a rocking chair, his head pulled back, his ears turned slightly, and he was giving me the stink eye every time I laughed at a joke, as if some-how he understood what was going on but thought I was an idiot for being entertained. The idea amused me, tickled me more than the show did, the idea that cats might understand sitcoms, but they just don't care for them. So 'Obed' was created."

Richard Weems *Theory*

Richard Weems the author of three short fiction collections: *Anything He Wants* (finalist for the Eric Hoffer Book Prize), *Stark Raving Blue*, and *From Now On, You're Back*. Recent appear-ances include *North American Review*, *3Elements Review*, *Flash Fiction Magazine*, and *Black Works*. He lives and teaches in New Jersey.

"'Theory took its inspiration from a friend who was a rather per-sistent bachelor and seemed to enjoy the gamesmanship that came with the act of dating, a practice I have long abhorred. From there, developing the story became an exercise in studying the different ways someone could be alone while in a romantic rela-tionship. I would eventually come to show this story to my friend. He of course saw nothing of himself in the narrator, which was probably a good thing.

Sage *The Alchemyst*

Sage is an MFA candidate and Teaching Fellow at St. Mary's College in California. Their work appears in *Empty Mirror, North American Review, Penn Review, The Rumpus,* and elsewhere.

"'The Alchemyst" was written while watching the deer on my campus come right up to the cars in the parking lot. Back home they're more skittish, not used to people in what was once their world. I've been thinking a lot of what it means to enter love fully and without fear, and of course the old metaphor of a deer in the headlights is an apt way to describe me when it comes to anything regarding romantic affection. There is also the matter of queer love—of never knowing quite where you stand with friends who you want to be more than friends. I'll let that speak for itself, for and to queer readers. A queer deer in fear. That's me. That's all of us, the lonely who eat the loneliness. Then something mundane collides with something else mundane, and love is born from the collision. You could say that's how a poem is born. That is how this one was born."

Sarah Russell *If I Had Three Lives*

Sarah Russell's poetry and fiction have been published in the *Kentucky Review, Red River Review, Misfit Magazine, Rusty Truck, Third Wednesday,* and many other journals and anthologies. She is a Pushcart Prize nominee and her poetry collection, *I lost summer somewhere* was published in April 2019 by Kelsay Books. She blogs at SarahRussellPoetry.net.

"I was in a writing slump, so I emailed Ryan Stone, my writing buddy in Australia, and asked him to send me a great prompt. He emailed back that one of his favorite groups was The Whitlams, and they had a line in their song "Melbourne" that he loved—"If I had three lives, I'd marry her in two." I thought about it for only a minute or two, and the poem "If I Had Three Lives," started writing itself. Only one problem: I didn't have a last line. I refined and thought about the poem over a week or two, and I finally realized that the poem was a love letter to my husband—that though I was wonderfully happy in the two lives we shared, if I had that "ideal" single life again, I would still long for the kind of relationship we have shared for thirty years. That's when the last line came to me, and I knew the poem was complete."

Sean Finucane Toner *A Graveside Nuptial*

Sean met his wife, Robin—also a writer—in an MFA program, where they were both writing fiction. After graduation, Sean turned to creative nonfiction, capturing his journey as a blind and brittle diabetic, and his great love for life, art, and family. "A Graveside Nuptial" originally appeared in Hippocampus, then Best of Hippocampus, and then Selected Memories: Five Years of Hippocampus Magazine. Robin is grateful to Darkhouse Books for including this essay in this edition. [Editor's note: Robin, we are grateful to have the opportunity!]

Sean Finucane Toner's literary essays have been published in Best of Hippocampus, Best of Philadelphia Stories, Brevity, The MacGuffin, The Monarch Review, Ardor Magazine, Apiary, Opium, Perigee, and other literary magazines. His creative nonfiction has found a home at a Literary Death Match, and he has won 11 prizes at the Philadelphia Writers Conference, including a First Prize by Popular Vote. Sean lost his sight to diabetes when he was 29 years old. He died in 2018, at age 52.

Sharon Charde *Another Fire*

Sharon Charde, a retired psychotherapist and a writing teacher since 1992, has won numerous poetry awards, the latest being 2018 finalist in the Blue Light Press chapbook contest for *Unhinged,* published in 2019, Sixty Four Best Poets of 2018 by *The Halcyone*, and semi-finalist in the 2019 Grid contest for full-length collections for *The Glass Is Already Broken.* She has been published over eighty times in journals and anthologies of poetry and prose, including *Calyx, Mudfish, The Paterson Review, Ping Pong, Rattle, Poet Lore, Upstreet,* and *The Comstock Review,* and has had seven Pushcart nominations. She has also edited and published *I Am Not A Juvenile Delinquent,* containing the work of the adjudicated teenaged females she has volunteered with since 1999 at a residential treatment center in Litchfield CT. She has three first prize-winning chapbooks, *Bad Girl At The Altar Rail, Four Trees Down From Ponte Sisto,* and *Incendiary* as well as a full-length collection, *Branch In His Hand,* published by Backwaters Press in November 2008, which was adapted as a radio play by the BBC, broadcast in 2012. *After Blue,* for which she won honorable mention in Finishing Line Press's 2013 chapbook contest, was published in September 2014. She has been awarded fellowships to the Vermont Studio Center, Virginia Center For The

Creative Arts, The MacDowell Colony, and The Corporation Of Yaddo.

"I met Tessa many years ago at a poetry workshop, and serendipitously re-met her at a recent writing residency. We immediately slid into a relationship that felt as though it had existed for lifetimes, spending hours talking over meals, taking walks, and catching up on life histories. Since I'd last seen her, she'd become a fire-eater and snake-charmer, worked in a carnival sideshow for a time, and had written a book about her experience doing that, concurrent with her mother's dying, "The Electric Woman." I was thoroughly entranced, and wanted to hear every detail of how she'd come to learn such skills. The poem came from this chunk of sharing time with her. As any good poet knows, when you sit down to begin a poem, you never know what the poem is going to tell you and how it will end. I certainly didn't expect this ending, but despite the fact that we both know our respective mother-in-law and daughter-in-law love us, the emotional truth of the poem says otherwise, at least for the life of the poem."

Shelley Valdez *Last Words from a Pillar of Salt*

Shelley Valdez is a queer Filipino-American writer, artist, editor, and performer from California's Bay Area. She worked as the poetry editor of the Santa Clara Review for several years. Her work has won multiple prizes, and has been published by poets.org, The Best Emerging Poets of California, Quiet Lightning, and elsewhere. Mostly, she wants to tell good stories, give good love, and make good art.

"'Last Words from a Pillar of Salt' was inspired both by the biblical story of Lot's Wife, and by the Mitski song, 'Last Words of a Shooting Star.' It also came, in part, from the intersection between faith, family, and queer identity in my life—and all the unfinished reconciliation that comes with it. Lot's Wife found me somewhere in the middle of that chaos, in the way she wrestled with love and loss and a divinity she did not understand. She also brings up the notion of necessary disobedience, which feels especially relevant today. She was not given a name, or a voice, but she did get to make a choice—one that belonged only to her, regardless of the consequences. I like to think that she doesn't regret it. I like to think she would have something to say."

Susannah Carlson *In the Haunted Toyshop Late One Spring*

Susannah's poetry, essays, and short stories have appeared in numerous literary journals over three decades, including *Sequoia, The SFSU Review, Narrative, Reed, and Sixfold.* She has won numerous awards for her work, including a national essay contest when she was twelve that resulted in a three-day "safari" in Los Angeles with Cleveland Amory, and lunch poolside at Joan Rivers' house. As managing editor of the Darkhouse Books Riff Series, this is the third anthology she has conceived and edited. She lives in the San Francisco Bay Area with her partner, her son, a Craigslist mutt, and Kyle, the one-eyed chiweenie.

"When my son was five years old, we made an agreement. If he would calmly let me get him ready for school every morning for two weeks, I would give him the Barbie he so desperately wanted. After two weeks of blissfully easy mornings, my son and I made the long trek from our home in the Santa Cruz Mountains to the Toys-R-Us in Sunnyvale, which was as famous for its ghosts as it was for its toys. There, he quickly found the Barbie of his dreams, a ballerina, complete with pink tutu, something I would have found repulsive as a child."

Susan Cummins Miller *One Night and a Quarter of Tomorrow*

Tucson writer/geologist, **Susan Cummins Miller**, a research affiliate of the University of Arizona's Southwest Institute for Research on Women, compiled and edited *A Sweet, Separate Intimacy: Women Writers of the American Frontier, 1800-1922* and pens the *Frankie MacFarlane, Geologist,* mysteries. Her award-winning poems, short stories, and essays have appeared in numerous journals and anthologies, including *What Wildness Is This: Women Write about the Southwest, And All Our Yesterdays, SandScript, Sandcutters, OASIS Journal, and Roundup! Great Stories of the West from Today's Leading Western Writers.*

"Observing the flowering cycle of saguaros in the Tucson Mountains on the anniversary of her mother's death brought back memories of family stories and inspired "One Night and a Quarter of Tomorrow.""

Thomas Kearnes *Hurry*

Thomas Kearnes graduated from the University of Texas at Austin with an MA in film writing. His fiction has appeared in *Gulf Coast, Berkeley Fiction Review, Timber, Hobart, Gertrude, A'cappella Zoo, Split Lip Magazine, Cutthroat, Litro, PANK, BULL: Men's Fiction, Gulf Stream Magazine, Wraparound South, Night Train, 3:AM Magazine, Word Riot, Storyglossia, Driftwood Press, Adroit Journal, The Matador Review, Pseudopod, Underbelly Magazine, Black Dandy, the Best Gay Stories series, Mary: A Journal of New Writing, wigleaf, SmokeLong Quarterly, Pidgeonholes, Sundog Lit, The Citron Review*, and elsewhere. He is a three-time Pushcart Prize nominee. Originally from East Texas, he now lives near Houston and works as an English tutor at a local community college. His debut collection of short fiction, *Texas Crude* is now available at Lethe Press, Amazon, and Barnes & Noble.

"The worst part about becoming a writer is that you can never un-see the man behind the curtain, madly manipulating the levers. Better to just enjoy the story and assume all the headaches and insecurities that surface during the act of creation have been resolved and forgotten. I do remember this story surprisingly rife with continuity issues I'd naïvely assumed were reserved for novelists. I remember my anxiety over whether I could write a "happy" ending without selling out the darkness that has become a cornerstone of my literary career. Happy stories aren't a natural fit unless you, the author, are a happy person—and happy people rarely devote their entire lives to telling make-believe. Perhaps the only subversive element at play here was my decision to make an entire Boy Scout troop my en masse antagonist. If you enjoy "Hurry," feel free to Google my name and visit my older works."

Timothy O'Leary *Hillbilly Love Story*

Timothy O'Leary's short story collection, *Dick Cheney Shot Me in the Face – And Other Tales of Men in Pain* (Unsolicited Press), was released last year. His work has been honored with the Aestas Short Story Award, multiple Pushcart Prize nominations, and has been a finalist for the Mississippi Review Prize, the Mark Twain Award, The Lascaux Prize, and many others. He graduated from the University of Montana, and received his MFA from Pacific University. More information can be found at TimothyOleary.com.

"I live in a rural area and spend a lot of time tramping through the woods, which makes my fascination and fear of snakes a bit problematic. I tend to keep a keen eye out for anything slithering around me, and sometimes even envision peculiar places a snake might wander. I always open the mailbox slowly and stand back in case there are unwanted visitors. 'Hillbilly Love Story' was born out of this irrational phobia. Snakes and romantic obsession seemed to make a good pair."

Winter Ross *She Who Hears the Cries of the World*

Winter Ross is a visual artist, writer, and street medic. She is the author of an illustrated chapbook of visionary prose: *4 Warnings: Shamanic Journeys.* Her short story, "Orienting Heaven", received first place awards from the New Mexico Press Women's Association and the National Federation of Press Women. Her work can be seen at CeremonialVisions.com._A version of this memoir was published in the literary magazine, *Pilgrimage: Story, Place, Spirit, Witness.* Volume 31, Issue 1, Crestone, Colorado, 2006

"'She Who Hears the Cries of the World" is a memoir of an incident that occurred on the way to a Buddhist retreat. It gives some insight into how deeply rescuers are affected by those they seek to help. There is a saying among emergency medics: 'It is an honor to be with a person on the worst day of their lives.' Over the years, the rural highways and the sacred places of Colorado and New Mexico have often provided the author with opportunities to repeat those words. She always carries a trauma kit and a sage bundle in the trunk of the car."

Woody Woodger *In My Movie, Everybody Dies: An Open Letter to My Uncle*

Woody Woodger lives in Lenox, Massachusetts. Her first chapbook, *"postcards from glasshouse drive"* (Finishing Line Press) has been nominated for the 2018 Massachusetts Book Awards and her work has appeared, or is forthcoming, from *DIAGRAM, Drunk Monkeys, RFD, Exposition Review, peculiar, Prairie Margins, Rock and Sling,* and *Mass Poetry Festival,* among others. Her poetry has been nominated for Best of the Net. In addition, she has a regular column with COUNTERCLOCK Literary Magazine.

"I had written enough "fuck you" poems. Kent had died a little over a year ago and left the family suspended in water the way any death leaves a family, and I had done the righteous anger shtick until every lyric I could wring out of the grief felt vacuous and re-cycled. His body was stuffed with enough of my sophomoric kin-dling, like bible pages stuffed into the cushions to pad out the couch. You get it. I was as tired with myself as I was with him. It's always that way—grief mercifully tires you out. Outrage burns fast and reckless. And, eventually, it becomes apparent that the only person you're hurting with your indignation is yourself. They are dead. They can't hear you. So, like my therapist won't stop saying, the only path where YOU survive is forgiveness. That's where this poem was born from—the morning-stretches of forgiveness and rehabilitation."

Sanctuary

A Collection of Poetry and Prose
Edited by Susannah Carlson & Peter Bradbury

Descansos
Words from the Wayside
Susannah Carlson, Editor

A Murder
of
Crows

Edited by Sandra Murphy

About This Book

The typeface in this book is 11.5 Garamond and Helvetica. The title font is Black Chancery. It was laid out using Adobe InDesign software and converted to PDF for uploading to the printing facility.

About Darkhouse Books

Darkhouse Books is dedicated to publishing literary, mystery, science-fiction, and horror.

Darkhouse Books is located in Niles, California, an inadvertently
preserved, 120 year old, one-sided railtown, forty miles from San Francisco. Further information may be obtained by visiting our website at www.darkhousebooks.com.